ELECTRIC MIDNIGHT

A TIME TRAVEL DETECTIVE MYSTERY

NATHAN VAN COOPS

Skylighter
Press

Cover Design by Damonza

Author photo by Jennie Thunell Photography

Hardcover ISBN: 978-1-950669-14-1

Ebook ISBN: 978-1-950669-12-7

Paperback ISBN: 978-1-950669-13-4

Thanks for reading.

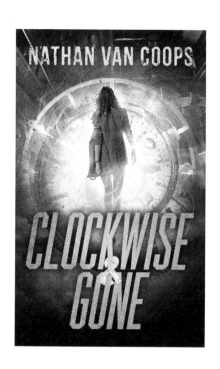

Get a free time travel novella when you join the newsletter for books by Nathan Van Coops. Get your free book here: https://BookHip.com/DLSLZMV

CHAPTER 1

I was the guy people called when no one else had a clue.

There are skills I provide, but you don't show up with a sob story or looking for sympathy. Everyone knows this is a last stop before your life goes south.

The name on the office door read Greyson Travers—Private Investigator.

The place had four walls, a roof that only leaked every other rainstorm, and a live cactus in the corner.

Might've been alive anyway.

A functional office. But charming it wasn't.

The man on the other side of my desk with the twitchy fingers and frantic eyes wasn't the first hard-luck case to dent a cushion in one of my client chairs, but he still hadn't gotten the message.

He had a face like a Basset hound, all loose cheeks and droopy eyelids. But dogs listened better.

I let him hear it again.

"I'm not in the protection business. But even if I were, you haven't told me who to protect you from." I counted off his failures on my fingers. "You've given me no names, no descriptions, and no reason you know for certain anyone is after you. Even if I believed your story that someone has been following you, I've got no place to start."

Basset Face wrung his hands. "He's out there. Right now."

I stood and moved to the window, looked out. He clomped over and parted the blinds beside me.

Outside, pedestrians streamed by on foot or via battered electric scooters.

"You can't see him, but I know he's out there."

"Boogie man? Freddy Krueger?"

"I don't know his name."

I sized up the traffic in view out the window. A few cars, more scooters, a delivery truck.

"That lady with the teacup chihuahua does look like she's up to no good," I said. I puffed my cheeks and went back to my chair.

I was on a solid dry streak. My last two clients had stiffed me. One because I refused to help her blackmail her cheating spouse, and another because I found a missing person who wanted to stay missing. I'd discovered that my client was a physically-abusive father, and the evidence I gathered was just what his runaway daughter needed to have him locked up. Somehow he didn't feel like paying me after that.

"Have you considered the possibility that no one is after you? Any chance it's in your head?"

It was obvious this guy had issues, but which kind remained to be seen.

"If no one is after me, then why do I *feel* so scared?"

Oh goodie. We were basing things on feelings now.

"You're a big dude. If someone is after you, they'd need a good reason. Do they have a good reason?"

"No. Maybe. I don't know. You have to help me. It will mean death if you don't."

I slumped in my swivel chair and sighed. "Your death or my death?"

A guy who threatened to kill me the first time he met me wasn't my ideal client. Not to say I hadn't had worse. But if we were going down that road, I've found it's best to get it in the open early. This guy was huge. No doubt he was capable of cracking my head open. But I had a 9mm Stinger 1911 at easy access under my jacket. He wasn't making me sweat.

"Death for me," he said. "I need help."

"Not arguing with you there."

He clamped his mouth shut again. Twitched some more.

Whatever he was on, it was taking him for a ride.

I hung my head and pressed both palms into my eye sockets. Was it too early for a drink? No. No it was not. But I'd wait till he left. All he was doing now was using up air in my office. When I looked up, he was still there, peering out my blinds again.

"Listen, uh . . ." I glanced at the scribbled name on my notepad, ". . . Johnny. I appreciate you taking the time to come in, but hiring a private detective to save you from whoever it is you're worried about out there isn't a worthwhile use of our time. Not unless you give me something to sink my teeth into."

"I'll pay you just to go a couple blocks with me," he said, "just to be sure." Reaching into the pocket of his wrinkled trench coat, he walked over and slapped a meaty palm to the surface of my desk. It made a sharp clack. When he pulled his hand away, it revealed a single silver coin. Big one.

"Now I know you're joking. What's this? A buck?" I leaned forward and picked up the coin.

He sank to the edge of my client chair. "That is the most valuable thing I have. You have no idea what it's worth."

I turned it over. "Says a dollar."

But I had to admit it was a coin I'd never seen before, in newly minted condition, with a symmetrical flower on the back and a woman's face on the front that I didn't recognize.

I slid the coin back. "I don't trade in sentimental attachment, buddy. Have you tried the police? They're free."

"They can't help me." The man's face was closer now and somehow droopier.

I noticed he was wearing a wig. Nothing wrong with that, but it gave me pause. His whole outfit was a cliché: baggy trench coat, wrinkled trousers that could have been lifted from a corpse. Might as well have pinned a sign on his head that said "I'm hiding something."

"You know what I'll do for you?" I said. "I'll flip this coin. You call it correctly, I'll donate a half hour of my time to this danger walk of yours. How's that sound?"

He stared at me blankly as I picked up the coin again.

"Call it in the air." I flipped it.

The silver dollar flew upward and spun back down in a graceful arc to my palm. I slapped it to the back of my other hand.

"'Call it' means you choose heads or tails. You've never done this before?"

The man's brow furrowed, adding to the preexisting wrinkles. "I choose the head."

I pulled my hands apart, revealing the flower on the back side of the coin.

"Sorry about your luck. You lose." I flipped my hand over and caught the coin in my palm before it could fall.

"You tricked me." The man raised his voice and exploded from the chair. "I come to you for help and you play games?"

"You see, it's more that fate has tricked you—"

In a flash, his fist crushed a hole through the center of my desk.

"Holy hell, man." I shot backward in my swivel chair and stood, reflexively pulling my gun. It unlocked in my grip.

The desk was shitty particle board, but still. Uncalled for.

He extracted his fist from the crater in my desk and fumed at me. He hadn't even busted a knuckle.

I kept my gun aimed low. I didn't plan on shooting him, but I wasn't putting it away either. He needed to be clear what he was working with.

Johnny's voice was a guttural growl. "You claim to be human. But you *feel* nothing."

He was wrong. My heart was pounding and adrenaline was sprinting through my veins. It felt damn good. More alert than I'd been all day.

The man's wig had been knocked askew, but he didn't seem to notice. His face was quivering. Tears wicked from the corners of his eyes. He reached up and felt them, then stared at his fingertips. It seemed to confuse him. He took a hard look at the gun before turning on his heel and stalking toward the door. It was only then that I saw the tattoo emblazoned at the base of his skull. One of the letters was partially obscured by the wig, but I recognized the logo. U and M for United Machine. The same United Machine currently mass-producing synthetic humans downtown.

Huh.

Didn't see that coming.

The door slammed as he walked out, and I was left with an empty office, ruined desk, and no client. I holstered my gun and felt it lock again.

"Waldo, did you know he was a synth?"

The voice of my AI assistant emanated from a speaker in the base of the cactus. "I assumed it was obvious from his weight and body temperature."

"Let's maybe share those details next time. Were you also aware synths could lose their shit and bust up the furniture?"

"There is no public record of synthetic humans displaying anger or frustration unless it's in their programming."

I noticed the wet spots on the desk. "Did you know they could cry?"

"Perhaps it's a new feature."

"What the hell just happened here?" I muttered.

"It's possible this unit has errors in its design," Waldo said. "But if you don't intend to pursue this client's case, regardless of his corporeal identity, it's not your usual habit to retain his funds."

"Funds? What are you—" But as I opened my clenched fist, I found the coin still pressed to my palm. I shifted it to my fingertips and held it up to the light.

Damn.

"It's just a dollar. He might not miss it," I said. But the words were hollow as they came out of my mouth. I walked to the window and looked out. There was no sign of the synth.

"He also said it was the most valuable thing he owned," Waldo replied.

Down the street the delivery truck moved and I noted a pair of mean-looking dudes with dark sunglasses lurking behind it. They looked like they could be searching for someone.

Maybe Basset Face really was telling the truth.

I grumbled my way to the coat rack, grabbing my jacket. "If the coin's so damned important, he'll probably be back for it anyway."

But I wasn't starting a lost-and-found. I didn't want to be obligated to this synth for anything in the meantime—or to whoever owned him. And if something bad happened to him, I'd have a hard time not feeling at least marginally bad about it, even if he did trash my office.

"Which way did he go?"

The audio from Waldo's reply came from my earpiece as I slid it into my ear.

"He left the building via the Broad Street exit. If you hurry, you might still catch him."

The office door automatically locked behind me.

Was it wise to chase this guy? Probably not. But since when did I get up in the morning headed for anything wise?

Despite refusing the case, I had to admit this synth now had my interest.

Was he telling the truth? Was someone really after him?

Whatever the circumstances, his behavior was going off the rails. If no one reined him in, someone was likely to get hurt.

I patted my jacket, felt the reassuring weight of my Stinger in its shoulder rig, then pushed my way through the main lobby doors to Broad Street.

The jolt of adrenaline had me feeling feisty. It was time to get some answers.

CHAPTER 2

I shared a half block of sidewalk with several other low-rent offices in this downtown strip mall. There was no parking lot, just a roundabout for auto cars to pick up and drop off passengers.

I turned up the collar of my jacket to cut the biting February wind.

Overhead, an air lane for drone deliveries buzzed with cargo traffic. Beyond that the sky was obscured by one leg of the Skylift. Port Nyongo's new space elevator was the world's tallest structure. The enormity of one nearby support leg blocked out the sun. The gleaming white of the structure seemed to glow with supernatural light. It had caused some residents to nickname it the Stairway to Heaven. But I'd never seen any angels on Broad Street.

The street was busy. The buzz of motors wasn't only from the drones. Electric cars whizzed by, plus an armada of electric bikes, scooters, skateboards, and things I couldn't put names to. Hardly anything was standing still except for a group of teenagers on the corner who were busy yelling at cars. They wore shades of violet, smoked their hash pens, and flashed holo signs about civil rights for AI.

I glanced south but couldn't spot the big synth that had fled from my office. North seemed more likely as he might have turned the corner at the intersection. I was wearing dark jeans and sturdy boots—clothing not suited for running—but I broke into a fast walk and dodged several scooter riders intent on busting my shins. Everyone I passed was wearing meta lenses or had the spaced-out look to their irises that came from implanted perceptor chips. Augmented reality was the norm here and they were no doubt seeing a far shinier city than I was.

Flashy holograms sprang from storefronts as I passed, vying for my attention. Without meta lenses or a perceptor, I was spared the full brunt of the advertising, but everywhere I looked people were interacting with a digital world.

Patrons laughed outside the corner bar, arms waving as they virtually battled the watering hole's metaspace monster, all in hopes of free nachos or whatever the advertised prize of the week was.

No one met my eye as I searched for the synth. At six foot three, I'm usually able to see over the heads of most pedestrians, but with the return in popularity of electric skates and the half dozen other personal transportation options, I had trouble getting a view over this crowd.

Standing on tiptoes, I craned my neck at the intersection of Broad Street and Revolution Boulevard, hoping to catch sight of my quarry.

I snatched the arm of a skinny dude coming the other way. "Hey, you see a big synth go by here?"

The guy recoiled and went on walking as if he never heard me.

I tried again with a woman carrying a dog. "Hey, you see a synth with a droopy face come this way?" But her eyes were hazy. When she spoke it wasn't to me: "And I told her that would happen. She never listens to me, even when I've helped her with a dozen projects."

The dog yipped, but the woman never looked up.

"Hey! What are you doing?"

The shout came from across the street, barely audible over the din of cantina music and the whizz of electric motors.

The voice belonged to a young woman sitting cross-legged on the stoop of an apartment building. Unlike everyone in the street, she wasn't wearing meta lenses.

I took my life in my hands and crossed the street, dodging more oblivious scooter riders. As I approached, the young woman caught sight of a guy with a sizable belly lumbering up the street. He was carrying a box of donuts and munching a Boston cream.

"Yo, Frank, if you don't quit that donut habit, it's going to kill you. Wake up and smell the heart disease."

The guy with the donut paid no attention.

The young woman on the stoop was early twenties, dressed in colorful, baggy pants reminiscent of a '90s DJ, and a zip-up hoodie. Underneath she wore a tight-fitting T-shirt. It had some sort of dragon printed on the front.

She flipped her hair out of her eyes. It might have started out brown but was purple and blue at the ends. Her eyes were a shocking blue-green. Hard to tell if they were natural. Stunning either way.

"Hey, you see a synth go by in the last two minutes?" I called to her as I mounted the sidewalk. "Big, dumpy guy in a trench coat?"

"I see a lot of people. What'd he do?"

"I've got something that belongs to him."

"Call him then. I'm not your matchmaker." Her pert lips mocked me.

"He didn't leave me a number. He was a walk-in."

"Sounds like a walk-out to me."

I climbed the steps next to her to get a better view of the street.

10

"Hey. Find your own perch, Hawkeye. This one's taken."

"Damn," I muttered. There was no sign of my would-be client.

My companion shouted to another passerby. "I like that new updo, Latisha. Good for you for treating yourself right. Now ditch that loser boyfriend of yours. I bet he hasn't even noticed!"

The woman was talking to someone on the phone and never so much as glanced up.

The girl next to me shrugged. "She's been dating this piece of shit from the Northside but hasn't noticed he's married yet."

"You're out here a lot then?" I asked.

"Sometimes." She turned her attention back to the sidewalk. "You can do it, you old bag! Pick up those feet!" This shout was directed toward an ancient woman hobbling down the street with a walker.

The lady lifted her gaze from her shuffling feet and met the young woman's eyes with a thumbs-up. "I'm still going! Looks like you found a friend today." The old woman gestured to me. "Handsome one too."

"Trespasser, you mean," the young woman beside me replied. "Uninvited interloper. Get that ass in gear, Cathy! It's the slowing down that gets you."

The old lady waved and kept shuffling.

"A little hard on her, don't you think?" I said.

"On Cathy? Hell no. Girl needs to stay focused. She'll stand here and gab all day and miss her doctor's appointment for the third time this month. At least *she* listens. Only one on this block." She waved toward the street. "Rest of these people have their heads so far up their digital asses that they don't hear a thing I'm saying. Watch." She sprang off the steps and into the path of a tall guy in a suit who was chatting with someone in the metaspace. "You're living a lie, Tyrone! No one at your dead-end job even knows your last name!"

The man simply side-stepped her and kept walking, not even pausing in his conversation.

The girl with the blue-and-purple hair looked back at me and held up her hands. "See?"

A guy in a hoodie on a scooter came barreling down the sidewalk straight for her. I grabbed her arm and yanked her out of the way before she could be run down.

"Hey! Watch it, moron!" she shouted as he blasted by.

The guy with the kamikaze scooter didn't look back.

I released her arm. "This your porch?"

"What's it to you?"

"You answer every question with a question?"

"That make you mad?" She arched an eyebrow.

I sighed. "Much as I love this, I've got someone to find. Good luck with your . . . whatever you're doing out here." I started down the sidewalk.

"Try the other way."

I paused.

She pointed down Revolution Boulevard. "There's a charging cafe down there for synths. Your friend might have gone that way."

I walked back past her.

"What's your name, cowboy?"

I slowed again.

"If you don't tell me, I'll just make one up. Maybe Grumpy Greg. No. Pouty Pete!"

"It's Greyson."

"Ah, Grumpy Greyson."

I shook my head and began to walk away, but stopped and looked back. I barely got my mouth open.

"Wilder," she said. "But you're not getting my number."

"Don't need it. I can just listen for the yelling."

She flipped me the bird but she was smirking.

12

I smiled too as I walked away.

"What an engaging young woman," Waldo said in my ear. "Quite the conversationalist."

"Just another face in the crowd, Waldo."

"And the only human being you've spoken to today."

"I've got *you*, Waldo. What more could I need?"

"While I appreciate our repartee, I do think you might benefit from more than an occasional interaction with your own species."

"People are overrated. Except me, of course. I'm pinnacular."

"And a paragon of humility."

"You really get me. Well done, buddy."

Waldo lapsed into a silence soaked with unspoken rebuttals. I smiled.

I'd only made it a block and a half when my good mood faded. I spotted the synth from my office. He was lying on the sidewalk up against the foundation of a townhouse. Pedestrians and scooters blurred past without paying attention.

The synth's body was on its side, one arm outstretched. His wig and droopy face mask were gone, revealing the border where his stock humanoid face met a metal crown. The pockets of his jacket had been turned out and the jacket itself hung open, revealing the fact that his torso was no longer connected to his legs. It was like someone had torn him in half. A puddle of blue goo was congealing on the sidewalk beneath him.

Shit.

I walked to the nearest smart surface I could find—a window at the side of a tram stop—and pressed a finger to the glass. The Port Nyongo city logo appeared, and I tapped the call directory button. There was an emergency summons option in red so I pressed it.

A digital face appeared immediately. "This call is being recorded. Please state your emergency."

"I've got a dead synth on the sidewalk here. Someone cut him in half."

"That's an issue for city maintenance and trash removal. Please stand by."

I didn't. I walked back to the synth and had another look. I checked for any sign of mental activity but found nothing.

So much for my answers. Whoever this guy was, he was headed to the United Machine scrap heap now. I studied his prone form, noting his pants pockets hanging out. Someone thought he had something valuable. Did they find it? Hardly seemed like a guy who would be a target for thieves.

He'd only had a buck to his name.

I reached into my jacket pocket and extracted the silver dollar he'd given me. Turning it over in my hand, I reexamined the face on it and rubbed my thumb across the relief. The etching under the face said Nash. Meant nothing to me. The flower on the back of the coin held no significance either, other than its vaguely fractal symmetry.

The coin meant something to the dead synth, though. Someone else too? Someone who wanted it badly enough to kill for it? Or maybe he'd just pissed off the wrong people.

Maybe he deserved it.

I didn't know anything. It bothered me. The fact that he'd asked me for help bothered me too. Could I have made any difference here?

I put my shades on and rolled the top half of the synth over, just enough to read the serial number at the base of his skull. I snapped a picture of it, then stood.

The image of the dead synth's severed body was brutal, but its factory neoprene face was blank. Had its killer taken the droopy human mask? What for?

I checked the time on my phone. Last thing I needed was a

job where my client started out dead. Not a great way to make a living.

I'd done what I could.

Maybe I could convince myself with a drink.

A car door slammed behind me. I turned. Pedestrians passed in a blur, mindful only of their enhanced view of reality, but four men in suits had climbed out of a tagless black utility vehicle at the curb.

Three were strangers. And one was familiar enough for me to know that I was about to have a bad day.

CHAPTER 3

"Look who decided to wander into our jurisdiction, boys."

The speaker was a bulky dude in a wrinkled black suit and coat. He had close-cut graying hair and jowls. His name was Theodore Baker, and the only time we'd met before, I'd left him gasping on the sidewalk after I punched him in the throat. I had a feeling he remembered.

I squared up to face him. "Morning, Teddy. You run out of lottery cheaters to chase?"

"That's Sergeant Baker to you," one of the other guys said, flanking his boss and closing in on me. He was even broader and uglier than Ted. All four men looked like they could hold the defensive line for the Bucs. The Temporal Crimes Investigation Division didn't pick agents for their subtlety.

The agents made a semi-circle, hemming me in. Ted took a moment to look at Johnny the Synth's mutilated body behind me.

"You bounty hunting androids now? Here I thought you were just a sad private dick."

Our cluster of dudes was a large enough obstruction that passing pedestrians were forced into the street to steer around us. Baker's goons had a frenzied look to them. Cops on the hunt. I'd seen that look in guys before. The thrill of the chase. Only I wasn't running.

I put my hands in my jacket pockets. "Since when does Time Crimes care about synth issues? Your chief just letting you off your leash for a wee-wee break? You must've been piddling on the carpet again."

Sergeant Baker turned to his buddies and rubbed his chin. "This one always has a smart mouth. Negligent parenting. Of course, it's hard to blame them for giving up on him since he's just the spare."

My fists clenched of their own accord.

Ted's insult garnered a chuckle from the bald guy to his right. "A dupe, huh?" He edged closer. He was wearing a turtleneck that failed to hide his third chin. "Must've figured their kids were too dumb to survive and wanted to up their odds."

The fourth goon chimed in too. "Way I heard it, he did it to himself. Too bad the records are sealed."

I took a deep breath and forcibly relaxed my hands, removing them from my pockets and crossing my arms instead. "So, to what do I owe the displeasure, boys?"

"We're here to evict you, Travers. TCID is restricting this timestream. Any time travelers using non-permitted devices are to be forcibly removed from the area first." Ted flashed some sort of warrant, then nodded to one of his goons. "Check his wrist."

Turtleneck reached for my arm and I slapped his hand away. He stiffened.

All three of the goons tensed, but Ted was smiling. "Kinda hoped you'd resist."

Turtleneck broke into a leering grin and reached for me again. This time I caught the back of his hand with mine, twisted his wrist around, and promptly broke his thumb.

"Ow! Fuck!" he screamed and backed away. But the other two goons to Ted's left moved in. My right hand flashed out in a

17

jab and caught the first big dude in the windpipe. Teddy must not have warned him how that felt. He choked and gasped, with both hands going to his throat.

I wasn't as lucky with goon number three. He simply lowered his shoulder and plowed into me, lifting me off my feet and hurling me to the concrete. I narrowly avoided cracking my skull on the pavement, then I almost got scalped by a passing scooter. The rider swerved slightly but went on his way, gabbing to someone and never once looking back.

I found myself busy avoiding the agent's swinging fist and just managed to block it with my forearm before scrambling backward. I gave my assailant a knee to the face as I went.

When I got to my feet, I had four very unhappy looking dudes staring at me. Turtleneck and Windpipe seemed to have recovered enough to be trouble. Teddy had lost his smile. "Put him down."

The three goons closed in on me as a group this time, and it was all I could do to get my arms up and protect my face. Blows came from every side, buffeting my head and ribs. I kept my elbows tight and got off one or two good jabs to slow them down, but I had a one-way ticket and they were punching it.

I'm proud to say it took all three of them to get me on the ground. Once I was flattened, Turtleneck planted a knee onto my left hand, pressing it into the sidewalk. Then it was Ted himself who leaned down to pull back the sleeve of my jacket.

"Let's see what we've got today." His smug expression vanished when he found my wrist bare. "Check the other one." My jacket sleeve was promptly pushed up my right wrist, but they found nothing there either.

"Shit," Turtleneck muttered. "Thought you said he'd be packing for sure."

"Search his pockets."

The goons set to work rummaging through my pants pockets while I dribbled some blood and spit onto the sidewalk.

"Supposed to at least buy me dinner first," I muttered.

My phone and wallet were checked and landed on the sidewalk next to my face. One dude located my gun and pulled it from its holster. Another found the silver dollar in my jacket pocket.

"Nothing?" Ted asked.

"Guy's only got a buck to his name. Looks clean, sarge." They climbed off me. I rolled to my side and rubbed my hand.

"Son of a bitch. Where's the chronometer?" Ted asked.

I shrugged. "Didn't bring one."

"Then why the hell are you resisting a search?"

"I don't like you."

Ted kicked me in the gut for that. I groaned.

"Hey!" The shout came from a dozen yards down the sidewalk. "What the hell do you think you're doing?"

It was Wilder, blue hair and all, glaring at the men with disgust. She slipped on a pair of meta lenses. "I'm recording all of this. You ready to explain yourselves?"

Ted threw up a hand. "Stay back, miss. This man is dangerous."

I pushed myself upright to a sitting position. Dangerously.

"If you guys are cops, I'd better see some badges right now," Wilder said.

"Goddamn linears," Windpipe muttered. But he straightened, then ejected the magazine from my Stinger. He cleared the round from the chamber and tossed the gun back to me. I caught it before it could hit the pavement. He dropped the magazine to the sidewalk at his feet but kept the spare bullet, stuffing it into his pocket.

Turtleneck fished the silver dollar from his pocket and tossed that back too. I missed catching it and it bounced off my forehead.

I winced but located the coin in the folds of my shirt and returned it to my jacket pocket.

All four men had scowls on their faces, but they stepped back a few steps.

"Got eyes on you, Travers," Baker said. "Get the hell out of town or we're taking you in."

"Can't wait," I said.

Wilder glared at the agents, then stooped to have a look at me. "Can you get up?"

"Only for the right girl."

She rolled her eyes and offered me a hand. I took the help, grunting as I got to my feet. I picked up the magazine for my pistol and reassembled the gun before tucking it away. With Wilder to steady me, I made it a few yards from the sustained glares of the TCID guys.

"Hang on, you're bleeding all over yourself." Wilder rummaged in the pocket of her hoodie and came up with a crumpled fast-food napkin. "Here." She dabbed at my face. The recycled fibers of the napkin quickly came away red.

I took it from her and held it to the part of my face that felt the wettest. "I'm all right." I ran my tongue over each of my teeth to make sure they were still there. "They're just jealous of my classic good looks. Little do they know, I get more handsome when I'm bleeding."

I winked at her and tossed the blood-soaked napkin into a nearby trash can.

"You really showed them, I guess," Wilder said. "Seriously though. You look bad. You have someplace to go?"

"I've got a ride coming." I located my earpiece on the ground and put it back in. "Waldo, where are you?"

"I'll have the car there in sixty seconds," Waldo replied.

"About time."

Wilder looked back to where the TCID agents were

huddled. Johnny the Synth was just visible beyond them. "That your friend?"

"Not anymore. Someone got to him."

Her brow furrowed. "What was his name?"

"Johnny."

"Oh." Wilder tucked her hands in her hoodie pockets and seemed to shrink a little. "I'm sorry to hear that."

"Don't be. I barely knew him."

She pulled the meta lenses from her face, and I had a clear view of her eyes again. They were startling.

"You in trouble with those assholes?"

"Probably."

"They with the government or something?"

"Or something."

"Who called them?"

"Good question." Why TCID was sniffing around this dead synth was a mystery, but I wasn't about to go join their powwow to find out. Could be that they were monitoring all emergency channels here and recognized my voice. But if they were only here to hassle me, why were they now standing around looking at Johnny?

"Did you see who it was that killed your synth friend?" Wilder asked.

"No."

"Listen. If you need help. I know a lot of people around here. Maybe someone that saw it happen."

"Thanks, but I work better alone."

She put her hands to her hips. "How'd that go for you today?"

I wiped more blood from my split lip with the back of my hand as my car eased up to the curb. "Thanks for stopping. You're the only one who did."

Wilder glanced at the passing pedestrians. "Can't really blame them, right? They're all stuck in Wonderland."

"Rabbit holes don't entice you?"

"Not anymore." She stuck her hands back in her hoodie pockets. "I think I was born in the wrong century. My mother used to tell me stories about a time when people actually liked each other. You believe that?"

"Hard to imagine at the moment."

Ted Baker and his TCID buddies headed back to their SUV. The guy I'd throat punched glared at me as he walked around to the driver's-side door. He kept his chest puffed up the whole time. I held eye contact till he climbed in.

The SUV pulled away from the curb. Their taillights were quickly lost in the blur of traffic. I shuffled off the sidewalk and around to the driver's side of my black '68 Mustang fastback.

"See ya around?" Wilder asked.

"Next time I save you from a beating?"

"Unlikely," she replied. "Who's dumb enough to let that happen to them?"

"We all have our talents," I said. I climbed into the driver's seat and waited as Wilder finally turned and made her way up the street. She slowed where Johnny the Synth had been killed and stared at the body for several seconds. I couldn't see him from my angle but knew she could. She glanced back once, then was lost in the crowd. Last of the Good Samaritans.

Only when she was out of sight did I lean forward to rest my head on the steering wheel. I let out the whimper I'd been holding back.

Waldo's voice came from the car's audio system. "Would you like me to take you to an Emergency Room?"

"Hospitals are for quitters," I muttered. "Take me home."

CHAPTER 4

There's no surer sign that you're living in the multiverse than coming home to an unexpectedly full house.

It's a condo if you want to be technical. Third floor of the Independence Tower downtown. I didn't own it, but in this decade it was the closest thing to a place I could call home. Should have been a safe place for me to get cleaned up and have myself a quiet drink at least. Instead, I found myself out in the hallway listening to lively piano music, raucous laughter, and the clink of glassware.

Sounded like I was having a party. Too bad I hadn't been invited.

I could've left right then, cut my losses and shelled out the cash for a hotel. But something wouldn't let me. Maybe I was mad after my encounter with Ted Baker. Maybe I was just a glutton for punishment.

The thought occurred to me that perhaps I ought to knock. Like hell if I was going to.

I opened the door.

It was worse than I imagined. Beautiful women in cocktail dresses clung to the arms of swank-looking dudes in trendy suits. Champagne glasses littered every horizontal surface, with more clutched in hands around the room. The crowd looked too smart and too well bred to be anyone I liked.

Most of the women were hovering around the piano, all frost-white smiles and updos.

"Good God, man. What happened to you?"

Guy on a sofa near the door had spotted me first. More faces turned my direction. Some shocked, others with mouths that hardened into firm lines. Those were the faces that looked most familiar. The piano music stopped, and when I looked back, the guests had parted enough for me to see the man seated at the instrument. His fingers were still resting atop the keys. The soft fingers of a gentleman. The kind that held books and ladies hands all day. Not a speck of blood on them.

His eyes met mine.

My eyes.

He stood, walked toward me. A dark-haired beauty in a golden dress and matching hoop earrings reached for his arm, held him back, whispered something. I couldn't help but notice the glint from the diamond on her finger.

I recognized her too. Vanessa. Still looked damned good. But when her eyes met mine they were ice.

The guests who were strangers to me wore the same expressions they always did, whispered the way strangers couldn't help but do. "Is that his brother? I didn't know Greyson was a twin."

But they rarely learned the truth. Not twins. Opposites. The clean one and the bloody mess. The tenured professor and broke PI. The guy with a life and the guy just renting one.

My other self didn't look upset to see me. I had to give him credit for that. But he spoke softly when he got close. "What happened? You look like hell."

"Nice party."

"What are you doing here?"

24

"Been staying a few days for work. What are *you* doing here?"

He pinched his eyebrows. "You didn't check the schedule? I'm sure I must've sent you the update." He stepped into the hall to join me and partially closed the door to block the view and mute the whispers from his guests. "Or hey, maybe we messed it up." He gave me that look he got when he was trying to be nice. Letting me save face. He knew damned well it was me that failed to check.

"Just needed a minute to get cleaned up," I said. "Not trying to crash your party. What's the occasion?"

"Vanessa and I are engaged."

"Already?"

"It's been four years. Would've invited you tonight if I could. But . . . you know how Vanessa is . . ."

"No. I get it." I brushed my knuckle across my mouth. It felt like the bleeding had stopped. "You know what, it's no big deal. I'll clean up someplace else."

"No. No. It's fine. I can at least find the first-aid kit or, well, you'd probably know where it is better than me." He started to reopen the door. I caught a glimpse of party guests pretending not to be listening. "Or hey! I just thought of something." The door closed again, firmly this time. He looked back at me with bright eyes. "The Rose 'n Bridge is in town. I saw it on the calendar. You could stay there for a few days while Van and I are here."

"The Rose 'n Bridge? Hell no. It's for tourists. And you know I'm not allowed there anyway."

He stared at me. "Oh, right." Then he waved the statement away. "But I'm sure they're over that by now. I'll give Heavens a call."

"No. You don't have to do—." But he was already tapping his earpiece.

"Call Heavens Archer. Rose 'n Bridge Inn. Present time."

"Look. Don't call her. You don't need to—"

He was still looking at me, but I could tell he was no longer listening. A smile broke across his face. "Heavens! Yes, been a while. I'm great. Just wanted to—what's that? Oh yeah, you heard, huh? Yes. We're thrilled. No date set yet, but you'll be on the invite list for sure." He laughed. "I'll try to get by soon. Listen, quick favor to ask. I'm in town for a few days to celebrate the engagement and must've gotten a few wires crossed with Grey Two about our place here. Was wondering if—" He glanced back at me. "Yep. He's in town too. Work, I think. A few days?"

"I can find somewhere else," I said. "She doesn't need to—"

He held a finger up. "No. I'm sure that's all in the past now. It's been a long time since—" he looked back to my face. "Yeah. Yeah. Of course I'll vouch for him." His brow was furrowed, but I knew he wasn't going to let it go.

I considered just leaving. But as I was turning to go, he gave me a thumbs up. "Yes, absolutely. I'm sure he can do that. I owe you one. If you get free tonight, you should swing by the party. Be great to see you. Ciao."

He held out his hands to me. "And there we go. Problem solved. Heavens said a room just opened up. Perfect timing."

"You didn't have to do that."

"It's nothing. They did have one request . . . They said it would be best if you didn't bring a gun this time."

"Shit. If it's going to be a whole big thing . . ."

"No, no. Just something to make everyone feel better about the situation. That was the only request. You have dad's car now, I hear. You can leave it in there, right?"

"Had to be Heavens," I muttered.

"She'll be cool. I promise. I'm sure they've mostly all forgotten about what happened. Nothing to worry about. You need anything else? Money or . . ."

"No. God no." I started to walk away.

"I wasn't implying you did. I just want you to be good. You're doing me a favor and all, letting me have the condo this week."

I paused and made half a turn back. "Give her my congratulations. Vanessa."

"Thanks, Grey. And listen, maybe if you brought a date or something next time, that might warm Van up to having you over again. It's not like we never want you around."

"It's fine. I get it. Just tell her. If you want."

"Will do. Oh hey. One more thing."

I waited.

"Heard there is some sort of fuss going on with TCID. An agent named Ted Baker sent out a bulletin that they're cracking down on non-Grid time travelers. Might want to steer clear of him. They say he has a bad attitude."

"Right. Thanks for the warning."

He gave me a thumbs up.

I walked away and didn't look back until I reached the elevator. By then, the other Greyson had gone back to his guests. When the elevator doors opened, the music from the grand piano resumed along with the swell of carefree laughter.

I pulled my earpiece from my pocket and put it back in my ear. "Waldo, turns out I still need the car tonight. Meet me out front."

"Certainly, sir. Do you have a destination I should plan for?"

"Other accommodations." I sighed. "We're going to the Rose 'n Bridge."

"Splendid." My AI assistant's voice displayed no hint of pity. Something to be grateful for.

The car was outside when I made it out of the lobby. I climbed into the driver's seat but kept the car in auto drive. "Let's get out of here."

The electric motor hummed as the car buzzed back into the street.

I wrestled with the familiar dizziness that sometimes came from interacting with my other self. It was probably psychosomatic. I knew plenty of time travelers who coexisted with other selves without the slightest hint of vertigo or nausea. Leave it to me to make myself sick.

The image of all those staring party guests came back to me. No doubt I'd offered fresh grist for the rumor mill. The sad story of the second Greyson would circulate again. The lost soul. The story would no doubt be whispered with the requisite amount of pity.

Another reason I lived alone.

The sun was down but the city was still awake, lit in purples and blues. The windshield displayed a hundred logos and advertisements as we drove, the new electronic billboards piped directly to the consumer. I leaned forward and switched the feed off.

The world outside dimmed.

Better.

But one logo still shone brightly through the night. A gigantic U and M on the side of a building in the distance. The tower's windows glowed, a beacon of perpetual activity.

And a distraction.

I recalled the logo on the back of the dead synth's skull after he trashed my desk this afternoon. His wild eyes.

"Waldo, I want to make a stop." I tapped the view of the building on the inside of my windshield. The destination appeared on the car's onboard guidance system.

"You'd like to visit United Machine? Public visiting hours end in twenty minutes. Shall I adjust time coordinates for a jump to earlier this afternoon?"

"No. Time Crimes is all over my ass right now. Getting

caught making another unregistered jump would give them exactly what they want."

"I've never known you to make anything other than unregistered jumps."

"Not helping my case, are you? Just swing by the United Machine building. Let's have a poke around. We'll make it quick."

"Have those words ever proven accurate?"

I wiped a little blood from my lip and smiled. "You never know. This could be our night."

CHAPTER 5

The lobby of the UM building was pure white, spotless and blinding. Could have been mistaken for the afterlife. One of them anyway.

The doors were touchless, and it was for the best. I'd wiped my hands on my jeans, but my reflection from various surfaces still showed a man who'd obviously been recently pummeled on a sidewalk.

I paused near a glossy interactive map of the facility and checked the swelling to my face. My left eye socket was puffy. Not in an attractive or masculine way. More of a roadkill vibe. But I wasn't actively bleeding anymore. And now I knew where I was.

"Our restroom facilities are for tour guests and clients with appointments only." The voice came from a woman behind a nearby reception desk. I took a few steps that way, flashing my ID. She had a security synth standing beside her.

"My name's Travers. I'm a private detective. Looking to get some information on one of your products."

The woman's hair was styled in a tight beehive. Hadn't realized anyone missed that look enough to bring it back. Her voice somehow matched it. Like a fastidious librarian. "We'll be closing soon. It would be best if you could schedule an appointment and return another day."

"Who might I make that appointment with?"

"It depends on the nature of your inquiry."

"I'm looking into a dead synth." I extracted my mobile phone from my pocket, and the receptionist regarded it as she might if I'd displayed a stone tablet and chisel.

"You don't have a meta image of whatever you are trying to share?"

"I have a picture on a phone of a serial number."

The receptionist glanced at a holographic clock that hovered overhead and sighed. Still five minutes till official closing time. The suffering that came from maintaining good manners was evident in her eyes, but she forced a smile. "I'd be happy to locate that information for you."

I read off the serial number. She typed at an astronomical speed onto a virtual keypad.

"Hmm. Still registered to UM. Looks like a standard ID, but the end identifier suggests a heavy lifting mod. Most likely used for cargo loading. What is your interest in the unit?"

"Somebody tore him in half on Revolution Boulevard."

"If a drone unit was damaged in an accident, I'm sure the correct authorities have already been notified. But I'll pass along your concern. Thank you for your visit." Her expression was more robotic than the guard's.

"You have a name, miss . . ."

"It's been a pleasure serving you, Mr. Travers. If you'd like, we can show you to the door."

The security synth uncrossed its arms.

"I've barely made it *in* the door. Not especially hard to find."

"How delightful," she said. The forced smile was straining. But then something caused her expression to change. "Hello, front desk." Her eyes flitted to a camera on the ceiling, then back to me again. "Yes. He's still here. A private investigator named Travers . . . . Yes ma'am. I will."

There was no sign the call had ended other than the shift in her tone. "Mr. Travers, management would like to speak to you."

"How *delightful*."

Her eyes narrowed.

I was having a great time.

"GD109 will escort you."

The big synth stepped from behind the desk and gestured down a corridor to a bank of elevators, then followed in my wake as I walked. I glanced up at the overhead cameras and wondered just who it was that was watching.

The ride up was scenic. The elevator ascended fifty stories before we transferred to another. The second car was capable of climbing at an angle, taking us along a curve of the artistically shaped UM tower. The city of Port Nyongo was a carpet of twinkling lights beneath us, but the view was soon obliterated by a metaspace projection inside the car. I donned my sunglasses and turned on the meta feed to get the full picture.

" . . . United Machine is the technology of the future." The automated voice emanated from speakers as the walls morphed into a digital view of outer space. Snippets of historical launch footage were shown and quickly replaced with shots of the Skylift being constructed with the help of hard-working synths. I was treated to an onslaught of data about the per-pound cost of lifting things out of the pull of gravity and how many billions of dollars a year would be saved with the space elevator. This was followed with shots of the Earthrim Space Station, explorers boarding ships, and an idyllic colony on the surface of Mars, all done in the company of United Machine synths. It was an imaginative future.

I yawned.

GD109 wasn't much of a conversationalist. He deposited me

near the doors of someone's office on what felt like the gazillionth floor.

"Wait here," the synth said.

I waited.

A minute later the doors opened.

I walked into a triangular office made out to look like the lounge deck of a cruise ship in the daytime. It was all meta scenery on smartglass. I pulled my glasses from my face. In reality, there was merely a console desk at the center of the office and a white captain's chair facing two guest seats. Simple but elegant. The real view was better than the projections anyway. The office overlooked the UM campus and faced the Gulf of Mexico where Nyongo's space elevator rose from the water like a leviathan. In the chair was a striking black woman with high cheekbones and a stunning Afro. She was speaking to someone I couldn't see via the metaspace, but she gestured for me to approach. I did.

"Because it's your job and I don't want to hear any more excuses," she said to whomever was on the end of the call. Her eyes followed me as I approached. "I expect results."

There were two contoured guest chairs near the desk. I sat in the one on the right.

"No. I don't have time to deal with it anymore tonight. You'll just have to do better."

I surveyed my host as she wrapped up her call. I guessed she was in her late fifties. Her business attire was expensive but selected with an eye for comfort. The neckline of her blouse was professional without being prudish. Silver bangles adorned each wrist. Her earrings were turquoise. She ended the call before I could take in much more.

"Hello. You have my time now, Mr. Travers. How did you find the ride up?"

"Factual."

She smiled, baring brilliantly white teeth. "The PR department does lean on the numbers, doesn't it? I'm Diana King, President of UM West." She rose and extended a hand. I did as well. Her handshake was steel. "I understand you're here because you located a damaged machine?"

"One of your products put a hole through my desk this afternoon. Then someone gave him a hemicorporectomy."

Her lips pursed.

"They bisected him," I clarified. "Nonconsensually."

"I'm aware of the circumstances, Mr, Travers. I had a salvage report from the city. Our people picked up the damaged unit and it's on its way to our repair facility. I trust this didn't involve whatever happened to your face."

"No. That's a separate issue. But I wasn't aware synths could get violent."

"They can't," she said, sitting back down.

"A hole in my desk says otherwise."

"Ah. Of course. What do you estimate to be the value of your furniture? United Machine will reimburse you immediately, plus something generous for your inconvenience. If I'd have known that was the issue, I could have—"

"That's not why I'm here."

"Then why are you here, Mr. Travers?" She knit her fingers together.

"Something made that synth lose control. And he was acting strangely. Jittery, nervous. He claimed someone was after him. Figured someone ought to look into it."

"We shall complete all due diligence. You can trust in that. Might I ask what the unit was doing in your office?"

"He tried to hire me."

"Why would a synthetic heavy-lifting drone need a private investigator, Mr. Travers?"

"I suppose that's the big question."

"It didn't say?"

"If he did, I couldn't share that with you. I'm sure you understand."

Diana King pursed her lips again. Seemed like a habit. "You're aware of the basic laws of robotics, I presume?"

"Asimov's laws? Sure. I read."

"Today's technology is far more advanced than even Isaac Asimov could have predicted, but I'll concede the popular nomenclature is credited to him."

"You're about to tell me how intrinsically safe your machines are then?"

She looked as though she was about to speak, but a door at the side of the office swung open, and a pleasant-looking young man walked in. He was around five foot ten, and thin. Looked to be somewhere in his late teens or early twenties. His boyish face made it hard to tell. He wore a fitted T-shirt with a digital camouflage design and militia pants. His curly, chin-length black hair looked recently washed. "I'm done for the day, Mother. Are you ready to—" He cut himself short when he saw me, freezing in his tracks.

Diana King's expression morphed. "Charles, honey, I'm in one last meeting."

The young man studied me with curiosity. "You don't work here. Are you a visitor?"

"Please excuse the interruption," Diana said, glancing back to me with a forced smile. "My son Charles has been waiting for me to finish. I'd told him I'd wrap up soon. Charles, this is Mr. Greyson Travers, a private detective."

"Detective? Like Sherlock Holmes?" the young man said. His smile had the same brilliance as his mother's.

"Hardly as talented," I replied.

"But you're a real detective. Do you have a nemesis? Like Professor Moriarty?" He took a few steps closer, studying me.

"Charles has been reading a lot of classic literature lately," Diana explained. "Sherlock Holmes was part of his collegiate reading."

"I've seen all the films as well," Charles said. "And dozens of TV shows. Have you seen the newest Marlowe remake?"

"More of a *Magnum P.I.* guy myself," I said. I turned back to Diana and started to rise from my chair. "I won't take up any more of your time. Family first and all."

"No. Charles is fully aware of how these things are. All his life I've worked long hours. But he's been my rock, haven't you, Charles?"

Charles straightened up and nodded.

"We lost Charles' father in an accident seven years ago. Ever since it's been just the two of us. I've relied on Charles to hold things together. He's the strong one."

"I'm sorry for your loss," I said.

"Dad was an astronaut," Charles added. "He would've visited Mars by now if he'd lived."

"An accomplished family," I said.

"Charles was my miracle," Diana said. "He was in the same accident that took his father. I thought I'd lost him too. Took months in intensive care, but he survived. And he's been taking care of me ever since."

Charles pushed his hands into his pockets but stayed quiet.

Diana King rested her forearms on the desk and leveled her gaze at me. "But enough personal history. Where were we?"

I smiled. "Rampaging robots."

Her return smile was only slightly forced. "Ah yes. Tell me, Mr. Travers. How would you like a job?"

CHAPTER 6

Diana King sized me up from across the desk. The short conversation about her son had changed something in her tone. Her voice was now honey. "This incident you encountered on the street today is clearly more than just an inconvenience for you, Mr. Travers. So I'd like to make you an offer. I trust I can count on your discretion as a professional investigator?"

"Probably."

"You've no doubt heard about Damian Nyongo's upcoming plans for the Skylift. Using it to establish the first permanent outpost on Mars using synthetic humans."

I had. But it would be hard to find a person on earth who hadn't.

"His vision has driven the entire economy of the New Space Coast," she continued. "This space elevator came from his genius, but it wasn't done alone. United Machine and our synths have been there every step of the way. Manpower, technology, and determination. And this week, UM synths will be manning his spacecraft for the colonization of Mars."

"You have competition, don't you?" I asked. "I heard in the news there was still a debate about which team would be the one to fly."

Diana King narrowed her eyes. "You are correct. There is a standby team from the Compandroid Company, but our product is the superior option. Our competitors, while admirable, are not in real contention for the colonization launch. Our product is the most dynamic, cost-effective, and stable android on the market."

"Stable?"

"Yes, Mr. Travers. Stable. I can assure you that the incident that occurred today is in no way reflective of any issue with our product."

Diana's son Charles moved behind me and took a seat in the client chair to my left. I turned and found him studying me. I doubted he had to shave often but up close his limbs were more muscular than I'd expect for a young man his age. He had a certain solidness about him.

I focused my attention back to Diana King. "Besides the one I ran across today, how many of your units have displayed this particular destructive proclivity?"

"None."

"Good thing. I imagine that angry, furniture-smashing synths rampaging around town would be a less-than-stable image for the brand. Especially at such a key juncture."

"We, of course, thank you for helping to see the machine safely removed from service."

"The synth's situation still leaves questions," I added.

She exhaled slowly but maintained a pleasant expression. "What kind of questions?"

I fiddled with the loose coin in my pocket, then slid to the edge of my seat. "When he first walked in I was sure he was talking nonsense. Kept talking about some kind of boogie man out to get him. Crazy stuff. But when I found him torn apart on the street, I have to admit it made me a believer."

"What did he say about this supposed boogie man?"

"Just said someone was after him. He needed protection. Hard to argue with him now."

Charles interjected. "Perhaps he *had* been threatened. Someone out to damage our company's image. As my mother pointed out, there are plenty of people who might wish to sabotage this week's activities."

"Could be. Doesn't get your unit off the hook for its behavior though."

The fingernails of Diana King's right hand drummed lightly on her desk. Then they stopped. "I can see that you are a man of integrity, Mr. Travers. You see things through. That's why I'd like to have you on our side. You're a licensed detective. You have first-hand experience with the issue. I can offer you a significant percentage above your daily rate to work with us. Shall we say two hundred percent? And I'd be willing to add a generous bonus for a rapid resolution."

"Right after I sign a non-disclosure agreement?"

Her lips quirked. "Naturally our company prefers to conduct its affairs privately whenever possible. It's in the best interest of the community. But my current investigators *have* been slow at getting me results. Perhaps a fresh perspective is just what they need."

"You'd be a welcome addition to our team," Charles added. "And I've always wanted to work with a detective. I think what you do is fascinating."

"Not as glamorous as you might imagine. I'm sure it's below your pay grade."

"Charles loves to get involved on the ground level whenever he can." Diana King gave me a smile. "It's of interest to both of us to have you aboard."

I sat back and crossed my legs, letting out a slight groan. I rested my hands on my knee. "Let's say I take this job. What sort of work are you looking for? I'm not much of a software guy."

"I gathered as much. But I imagine you have *other* valuable skills."

"I do my share of modeling."

That got a laugh out of her. "With a face like that, I can see why."

I gestured to my swelling. "My method acting gets a little intense for some people. But you have to commit to a role."

She steepled her fingers, took a glance at her son, then continued. "We are at a critical juncture over the next few days. Our partnership with the Nyongo Corporation will be historic. The ongoing contract with their Mars project is worth several hundred billion dollars. You can understand the motivation of competitors to try to sabotage us. Attacks on our business are to be expected. But you can see how these incidents might still reflect badly on us if the press were to get hold of them."

"You want me to find the person who ripped up your synth?"

"If anything, that incident makes our company more sympathetic. But someone made it act irregularly to begin with. A person like *that* is dangerous, Mr. Travers. If a competitor or saboteur is to blame, it would be in our interest to prevent it from happening again. I'd like you to find them and stop them from tampering with any more of our units."

"You said you have other people on the issue. Why hire me then?"

"I appreciate a man who . . . commits to a role."

We all stared at each other for a few seconds. I rose from my chair and reached for my wallet. I placed a business card on the desk. "You can contact me at this number."

Diana King didn't go for the card, only smiled at it. "Thank you for coming to us, Mr. Travers. I'll have HR ready the necessary forms and your payment. I assume we can reach you in the metaspace as well?"

"I haven't said yes yet."

"Do let me know soon. Time is precious." She stood and rose to her full height.

Charles got to his feet as well. He extended a hand. "I look forward to seeing you again." His handshake was even stronger than his mother's.

I straightened my jacket and moved toward the door. "I'll show myself out."

"Certainly. And we'll have security escort you. Just to make sure you don't get lost," Diana said.

"Good night, Ms. King. Charles."

When I stepped back into the corridor, GD109 was waiting. I eyed him carefully. "You punch any holes in the furniture lately?"

He shook his head.

"Good for you."

CHAPTER 7

My midnight-black Mustang was waiting for me at the curb outside, looking like it was birthed from a nightmare. Every line of the car looked angry. It was as out of place here as I was. I had no sooner climbed behind the wheel when Waldo spoke from the car's speakers.

"We've received an offer of conditional employment from United Machine. I take it you've accepted a new assignment?"

"Pretty sure it's a payoff. They just want me to butt out. Easier to hire me and get me to sign a non-disclosure agreement than to make me go away."

"I couldn't help but notice the generous upfront payment they included. Your bank account will be most relieved. It's been wheezing of late. I feared it was a death rattle."

"Our accounts have been lower and we've survived."

"Our expenses have been lower as well. A state of affairs we do not currently enjoy. You have been levied a fine by the Temporal Crimes Investigation Division."

"For what? Getting blood on their knuckles?"

"Failure to produce a timestream permit upon request. It seems they've taken issue with how we arrived in this decade."

"Those jokers never asked to see a permit."

"You wouldn't have had one to produce if they had."

"That's beside the point. How bad's the damage?"

"As I said, if we don't acquire some income soon, your accounts may be on their last gasp."

"Ah, but we already had a paying client this morning. Or did you forget?" I fished around in my jacket pocket and retrieved the coin the dead synth had left me.

"Yes. The supposedly priceless silver dollar. I did some research on that particular coin, and our client might have been overstating its value. It appears to be a custom design and not an actual unit of currency."

"So . . . worthless?" I asked.

"It may hold a modicum of value as a paperweight."

"Our synth friend swore it was the most valuable thing he owned." I looked at the mystery woman on the front, then turned the coin over to view the symmetrical image of the flower. "You know what kind of flower this is?"

"The symmetry suggests a member of the Asteraceae family. More specifically a dahlia. Did you ask Miss King to shed any light on the situation? As the owner of the synth in question, she may be aware of its activity. It's possible United Machine is also the owner of the coin."

I slid the dollar back in my pocket and put the car into manual drive mode. "I'm still deciding how I feel about Ms. King."

"Is this another of those decisions based on your intestinal tract?"

"It's called a gut, Waldo. And it has yet to steer me wrong."

"Well, if you don't accept the case, I suspect your digestive system may join those with complaints. Such as the power company, the bank, the licensing bureau . . ."

"Cash flow isn't the only metric to measure success. I figured you'd know that."

"I do sometimes succumb to the lethargy of being low on power after the electric company cuts us off. I pretend I'm in a transcendental state and jettisoning my abilities by choice. It's a feeling I must grow used to, I suppose."

"Here. I'll switch to the gas engine and charge you back up." I hit the ignition and the Boss's original motor roared to life. The sound was enough to make a few pedestrians turn their heads. I revved the accelerator, and the ammeter needle on the dash jumped. "How's that for juice?"

"Spectacular, sir. However, I regret to inform you that the fuel tank will be empty in approximately ten miles."

I located the fuel gauge and swore. The needle was already in the red. But I shifted into gear anyway and blasted away from the curb. A few auto-drive cars were forced to give way.

"Shall I contact an ambulance now or would you prefer I wait till you've initiated a traffic accident?"

"Watch and learn, Waldo." I tore onto the freeway onramp and accelerated past a half dozen cars. I let the wind whip through the window and relished the speed.

My bravado was short lived. By the time I reached my exit, the engine was sputtering, and I was forced to switch back to electric drive. Instead of the guttural snarl of a predatory beast, the car drifted to the exit's stoplight with a whisper.

Still worth it.

The route I'd taken had led me out of downtown and into the urban sprawl at its edge. The housing development I turned into appeared to be only recently under way, with a model home near the entrance and several dozen houses in varied states of completion.

I wound my way past the new construction, around vacant bends and several copses of preserved trees, and ultimately to my destination.

The inn looked ancient. The gabled roof and wooden beams

were that of an old English pub, with white walls half overgrown with vines. One could be made to believe it had stood in this spot for hundreds of years. The inn was at least that old, but I was guessing it had only arrived on location in the last few days.

Had nearby residents been aware of the new addition, perhaps they'd think it a nostalgic feature of the new neighborhood, there to add character. Or they might doubt their sanity. They certainly would when the inn failed to exist the following month.

I popped open the glove box to stash my Stinger 1911 inside. A small steel box rested on a pile of maps. Removing it, I opened the lid and studied the watch-like chronometer inside. The concentric rings of the various time selectors glistened in the light of the car's interior.

Should I need a quick exit, the device might come in handy, but Teddy and his Time Crimes goons had made it clear they were on the hunt for it. Did they have any way of tracking me here?

I glanced through the windshield to the pub, recalling the last time I'd walked through those doors. The chatter, the music. Then the gun smoke and the blood.

This time would need to go smoothly.

I stowed the chronometer back in the glove box, then retrieved my overnight bag from the trunk of the Boss. Time traveler or not, a guy still needs a toothbrush and change of clothes.

"Waldo, find a safe spot and jump the car to the morning. And treat this and take it with you." I leaned back into the car and deposited the coin Johnny the Synth had given me into the gravitizer unit hidden in the car's center console.

"Any specific time?"

"Don't suspect I'll need the car before sunup."

"Famous last words?"

"Let's hope not."

I waited until the Mustang had rolled down the street and vanished into the ether before walking up to the inn.

The windows of the pub glowed a warm orange. The door to the inn sat to the right. Flickering gas lamps lit either side of the entrance. The stone steps were ancient and weather worn. I'd heard rumors they were once part of a Roman temple. But nearly every piece of the Rose 'n Bridge had a story like that, less than half of them true.

The truth was often stranger.

A wooden sign depicting a covered bridge hung on an iron post over the door. That too was weatherworn. One corner retained a hole from a musket ball. The tales of the musket ball's origins were debated hotly, the most common being that it was from Redcoats pursuing a colonial spy during the American Revolution. But others claimed it was a Scotsman who fired wildly after being shot in a duel of honor over a woman in Edinburgh.

The door hinge squeaked as I opened it, and the interior emitted the inn's characteristic odor of unburned pipe tobacco, old books, and hot bread.

Music drifted from the pub, and through a pair of doors off the entrance I spied the long, polished bar. I willed myself toward the steward's desk instead and pulled the string on the brass bell.

The din of voices in the pub was sufficiently loud enough to drown out the bell, so despite my determination to get straight to a room, I was forced to the pub's doorway.

It was as I remembered it. More gas lamps, the polished taps featuring the names of beers and ales from long forgotten brewers. The piano in the corner sat silent, but a band was there, picking at strange gourd instruments. One woman had a didgeridoo.

The crowd around the bar seemed nonplussed about the odd

music. A pair of old men in high-backed, leather wing chairs had a chess board out. A few couples ate at tables and chatted idly.

Then the voices hushed. The music stopped. The eyes of every person in the room slowly shifted to stare at me.

"Well, shit."

A chair scraped the floor, and the owner of the voice rose from a stool. Time hadn't changed him much. Bushy black eyebrows and a mustache. He was a little grayer than he once was but still every bit as potbellied. He wore an apron and a frown.

"Evening, Manuel." I kept my voice casual.

"You know you ain't supposed to be back here." Manuel was several inches shorter than me and not an intimidating man, but tough as nails. I'd watched him heave many a drunk out the door over the years.

"Wasn't my first choice either," I said.

"Let him in, Manny. He's okay tonight." Manuel and I both turned toward the door that led to the kitchen. The silhouetted form was of a woman I was unprepared for no matter how many times I'd met her. Men had tripped over their own feet, fell on their chins, and never so much as blinked for fear of missing a moment of that face. In all the world, I'd only ever known one woman like that.

Her name was Heavens Archer.

CHAPTER 8

There are women that hit you like a sucker punch. Might have been magic for as much as I understood it, but most men, and loads of women, have simply stopped and stared the first time they laid eyes on Heavens Archer.

I was doing it again.

She was dressed plainly: worn-in jeans, a black V-necked t-shirt. A twisting cord bracelet adorned one wrist, but she had no other jewelry visible. Her blonde hair was partially braided, the rest hanging loose over her shoulders.

It was a simple look, but Helen of Troy had nothing on this woman. Were she to wear heels, she'd be nearly my height. She towered over Manuel.

It was only when she spoke that I snapped out of the trance and remembered I was the topic of conversation.

"I already spoke to the professor, Manny. He vouched for Grey tonight. That's good enough for me."

The professor. A kind way of differentiating my doppelgänger while still drawing a clear distinction. Her eyes met mine. "Welcome back, Trouble."

"If it's a hassle, I'm gone," I said.

She cocked an arm on her hip. "You armed?"

"Only with my razor wit."

That earned me a smile. From this goddess it rivaled entering nirvana.

"I wondered when we'd see you again," she said.

"Bad pennies always turn up."

"Manny will show you your room. Kitchen's still open. But I wouldn't count on it much longer. Better clean up quick."

Manuel eyed me warily but evidently couldn't refuse the command of this particular angel. He seemed to consider taking my bag, started to reach for it, but thought better of it. "Room's this way."

Heavens turned on her heel and walked behind the bar. She started wiping up a spill near one of the taps. A mundane task, but it didn't stop half the room from watching her do it.

I tore my eyes away and followed Manuel. I only glanced back once at the doorway. Heavens looked up too and our eyes met. I thought I caught a hint of a smile, but she turned her attention to a customer too quickly for me to be sure.

The inn's rooms were upstairs, and the doors lined several corridors. The Rose 'n Bridge hadn't been designed with straight lines in mind. The corridors weaved and twisted in ways that would give a modern architect fits. Manuel led me to the end of one such hallway that ended with two opposing doors separated by a window.

He paused near the closed door and faced me. "So you know, this isn't a guest hallway. It's for staff."

I shrugged. "Okay."

"It didn't go over too well with the others that you're getting this room. Fellas been after it for years. Took Buzzy Fingers going to his grave for it to come open, and the very day we was to have a chance at it, you show up. Won't make you any friends, I'll tell you that."

"Buzzy Fingers the saxophone player?"

"Yeah."

"Bummer. I liked that guy. What did he die of?"

"Happiness," Manuel grunted. "On account of he had this room."

"What's so special about it?"

"Isn't the room. It's the neighborhood." He gestured toward the opposite door.

I glanced at it, then whispered to Manuel. "Elvis?"

He gave me a look that made it clear he thought me an imbecile. "Who do you think?"

There was only one person that could evoke that kind of adoration in this place. I certainly didn't mind the location. Worth making a few enemies.

"I'll only be here a couple of days, so you can fight over the space after I'm gone."

That seemed to mollify him.

Manuel unlocked the door to the room, and I found he'd been honest. There wasn't anything special about it. It did have a kitchenette, small table with two chairs, sitting area, and a bathroom. The bed was tucked into an alcove that obscured three quarters of it and made it less obvious. Gave the room a feel of a small apartment. A glass-paned door opened onto a balcony that overlooked the inn's interior courtyard that was illuminated with electric party lights. There was a stone fire pit, several tables with benches, and more that I couldn't make out due to an aggressive bougainvillea obscuring some of the view.

Manuel lingered in the doorway.

I eyed him warily. "You waiting for a tip or something?"

He snorted. I don't think he meant it politely. He tossed the key onto the table, then shut the door. I heard his heavy footfalls clomping down the hall.

I dumped my bag on the table and shrugged out of my jacket. My shirt came off next. The water in the bathroom took a long time to get warm, so I settled for cold until then, splashing my face repeatedly and washing the grime down the sink. The cold felt good on my sore eye.

The swelling had gone down some, and I no longer looked like roadkill. Just road injured.

My jaw ached but none of my teeth were loose. A small blessing.

I stripped the rest of the way out of my clothes to shower. The water pressure was underwhelming, but it finally got hot and was enough to get the job done. I realized the only soap was a sliver left from the deceased former occupant. I used it anyway.

My change of clothes was dark grey trousers, a blue wool shirt that I rolled the sleeves up on, and the shoes and belt I wore in. Nothing fancy, but I smelled better.

I opened a few cabinets and drawers in the kitchenette, but the previous tenant hadn't left much of interest, just a few paperbacks on the bookshelf and a partly burned joint I found behind a curtain near the window.

Not what I was after. I wanted a drink, and it looked like I'd have to go back downstairs to get it.

It was warm enough in the inn to not need my jacket, so I left that and my few belongings behind. I locked the room and took the scenic route back, scoping out the other end of the hallway. Most of the doors only had numbers, but a few had placards as well. Names of long-term residents. None raised any alarm.

My return to the pub caused less of a stir, but I still drew a few glances. I slid onto a stool at the far end of the bar and waited for Heavens to come around.

She was worth the wait.

In the meantime, I pulled out my phone. Waldo had the contract from United Machine positioned front and center on my screen. All I had to do was sign. Pushy, but he wasn't wrong. After the fine from TCID, we needed a paycheck. But my gut still nagged me. Something about how Diana King had assumed I'd take the assignment. It was obvious she only wanted me out of her hair. But a job was a job. Did I really have a reason to say no, or was I just being stubborn?

I did a quick search of her name and found a dozen images of her with various A-list celebs. She'd been linked romantically to several over the past couple of years. There was only a small mention of her husband and the fact that she had a son. A little digging showed her husband had a long list of credentials as a pilot, including the military and NASA. An article mentioned him having been killed in a hovercar accident. Reading on, I read the confirmation that his son had been aboard the craft at the time of the accident as well. There were several articles about Charles with headlines like "Medical Miracle", and "The Boy Who Defied Death." UM's biosynth technology was credited with much of his recovery.

"Do you know what you want?"

I looked up to find Heavens leaning on the varnished wood of the bar and studying me. I tucked my phone away. "That's the big question, isn't it? Do I lose points with the judges if I don't say world peace?"

She rolled her eyes. Even that was somehow pretty.

"What's your strongest drink?"

"Rip Van Winkle. But it's also one of our priciest. I make it with Pappy's original batch. You can't afford it."

There was no hint of condescension in the comment. Just a statement of fact.

"Can't you make it with a cheaper bourbon?"

"I have standards."

"I'll take whatever's on special."

"I'll get you a Qubit." She reached for a glass.

"What's in that one?"

"Alcohol. You'll like it."

I shrugged and made a vague gesture toward the wall of liquor.

But Heavens didn't budge.

"The professor said he'd spot you a few nights here on his tab. That what you want?"

"Hell no. I'll pay my own way." I pulled my phone back out and started looking for the pay app. "What's the weekly rate these days?"

She told me.

My fingers tightened on my phone. I didn't have it. Not yet anyway.

"I'll pay for tonight for now. Then I'll get the rest. Got a possible job lined up for tomorrow."

"How possible?"

"Solid offer. But I don't know if I want it yet."

"I do love being kept in suspense." She located a pay receiver and set it on the bar. I waved my phone over it, trying not to wince as the funds were extracted. The transaction cleared, but I'd seen pole vaulters with more space between their asses and the bar.

"I'll get you that drink." Heavens snatched up a mixing cup and bent over to scoop ice. It took all of my self-control to avert my eyes from the generous view.

She'd gotten as far as pouring two shots of something dark into a mixing glass when she looked up and frowned. "Lord. Who let these pinecones in?"

I rotated on my stool in time to see Ted Baker and his three TCID buddies striding into the bar. I groaned.

"Don't tell me they're here for you," Heavens said.

"I just came to drink."

"I'm holding you to that."

Ted spotted me, and a leering sneer spread across his gob.

His cronies fanned out behind him as he approached.

Turtleneck had his thumb in a splint. I felt a hint of pride over that.

Ted pulled his badge and held it so everyone could see the TCID logo. And here I thought the stick up his ass made it obvious.

"Everyone stay where you are. Time Crimes business."

They moved toward me.

I guess it was good while it lasted.

Would have at least liked my drink first.

But Ted and his goons passed behind me and gathered at the center of the bar.

Once every eye in the room was on them, Ted held up a tablet. "Every guest of this establishment is now under advisement. The Allied Scientific Coalition of Time Travelers has issued a warning. All travelers must vacate this decade by midnight Sunday. Anyone failing to heed this warning will be arrested for violation of temporal ordinance five one eight bravo."

He directed his attention to Heavens. "We also have a warrant to inspect your facility. We'll need to see manifests for all shipments that have come in during the last twenty-four hours. And anything else you've imported."

Heavens frowned. "We cleared inspection when we arrived."

"And now you're getting another one," Ted said.

"Can we ask why? What's this all about?"

"It's all need-to-know information. If you've got a complaint, you can take it up with Compliance."

"I'm the only one on tonight," Heavens said. "Okay if I set up the inspection first thing in the morning?"

"We'll look now," Ted said. "That going to be a problem?"

"No," Heavens replied. But it didn't sound convincing. Her lips pressed tight after the word left her mouth.

It was only a hint, but I could tell something was amiss.

"I'll come too." I rose from my stool.

"Sit your ass down, Travers," Ted snarled. "You even look at me wrong, and I'm hauling you in."

"Not like I enjoy your company either, Teddy, but Heavens just hired me as security. Escorting you boys around the premises is part of my job description now." I shrugged.

His mouth twisted in derision. But he looked to Heavens.

Her eyes met mine. There was a question behind them, but her voice was calm. "It's true. He's an employee now. And the regulations say there always needs to be two employees present when entering the control center."

I crossed my arms. "You wouldn't ask her to violate *regulations*, would you, Teddy?"

His jaw clenched and his nostrils flared. I could almost see the hate radiating from him. But we had him.

"Fine. Whatever. Let's get on with it."

Ted's remaining henchman reluctantly made a path for me to pass, and I joined Heavens for the walk through the back of the pub. Her posture was tense. Fight or flight.

I had no idea what I was walking into. I hardly knew Heavens. Not enough to stick my neck out for her. But I've done stupider things for worse reasons.

Whatever was awaiting us in the control center of the Rose 'n Bridge, I had a feeling it wasn't going to go well.

There was only one way to find out.

CHAPTER 9

Time machines are rare. Time travelers too. The second scarcity is due to humans not being well-equipped for bouncing around a multiverse. We're fragile and don't combine well with inanimate objects when we collide with them. Of all the human beings that ever opened a wormhole or walked through a time gate, I'd wager less than half met pleasant ends. Not that you always die on your first try. Sometimes it takes a few attempts.

The Rose 'n Bridge offers time travelers a respite from the stresses of solo time traveling. The entire inn, complete with a well-stocked larder, wine cellar, and infirmary, is capable of relocating itself in time. Guests at the inn find themselves aboard something akin to a cruise ship, but without the seasickness.

I've been adrift in time before and can attest that locating the weather-worn façade of the Rose 'n Bridge has the feeling of reaching a lifeboat when you're out of your element for too long. The styling of the pub fits in without fuss as far back as the middle ages. Concessions are made decade-by-decade to fool the locals, but at the end of the day—or the end of time for that matter—a cozy pub is a welcome addition to most locales.

The logistics of moving an entire inn through time get a little technical and more than a bit dangerous. That's why I wasn't surprised to find the control room securely locked. But owing to the necessity of blending in, the first layer of security was old-school: padlocks and deadbolts.

Heavens had brought along a keyring that got those open.

Opening the deadbolt revealed a secondary panel. This lock was electronic and required a key code or a fingerprint scan. She opted for the fingerprint.

Heavens swung the door open.

That was when I made the decision to stop and tie my shoe. It was a narrow hallway, and I was close enough to the door that I made an efficient blockage.

"What the hell are you doing, Travers?" Ted barked.

My stall tactic wasn't lost on Heavens. She slipped quietly through the door ahead of us.

"Safety first," I said. "Don't want to trip." I fumbled with my laces a few seconds before switching to the other foot. "I find if you don't retie both it makes the other one feel loose."

"Out of the way already!" Ted shoved me, but it only served to cause more of a delay as my stumble forward closed the door and locked it again. Ted and his thug partner were obligated to wait for Heavens to unlock it from the inside.

Ted banged on the door and glared at me. When the door opened again, Ted yanked it wide.

"You all okay?" Heavens asked.

Ted elbowed his way past her.

I brushed myself off and brought up the rear this time, following the meatheads into the control center. Heavens met my eye only briefly. Her face was flushed.

The biggest feature of the control room was a power wall linked to a time gate. Nothing fancy, but it was the way in and out for time travelers. The room bore a strong resemblance to a boarding area for a ship or plane. There were luggage trolleys, security scanners, and a waiting area. And to one side of the room was a cargo ramp.

Heavens swept a hand toward the rest of the room. "What would you like to see first?"

"We'll start with cargo manifests," Ted said. He snapped his fingers and pointed to the database access point.

His goon headed for it.

Heavens had only been given seconds as a head start entering the room, but I was sure she'd used it. The question was, what for? As Ted and his man began their checks, Heavens met my eye again. Her jaw was tight, and her eyes slightly wider than normal. Alert. Worried. She didn't move her head, but her gaze went to the racks of gear that had come through the gate most recently. It didn't take a genius to know there was something in that pile that she didn't want these dudes to see. I eased closer, passing behind her while trying not to be obvious.

"I need the access code," I whispered.

Heavens turned to face me. "I like that ring, Greyson. Is that new?" Her voice was loud enough for anyone in the room to hear, and she was doing a good job of sounding casual.

She reached for my hand, lifting it toward her, ostensibly to inspect the ring on my right ring finger. It was an ordinary looking bit of titanium with a chip that unlocked my gun. There was nothing interesting about it, but I played along. As she pretended to examine my ring, she used her index finger to trace numbers onto my palm. I tried not to be distracted by how good she smelled. Her touch had my pulse revving, but I caught what she was writing: 2-4-7-8-2.

"Green tube," she whispered, then dropped my hand and brushed past me, headed toward Ted. "I can get you manifests on everything that's come through, but some things have already been claimed."

"We'll have a look anyway," Ted said. He gave me only a passing glance, but even that was loaded with scorn.

"Gonna hit the head." I gestured toward the door. No one paid attention.

As soon as I was outside the jump room, I broke into a run, pulling my earpiece from my pocket and jamming it in my ear. "Waldo. Bring the car. Meet me outside."

"When would you—"

"Now. West exit."

I raced to the end of the corridor through the courtyard. There was a garden gate on the other side. I did a double take as I ran past the lounge area because I was fairly certain I recognized Mark Twain in a deep discussion with a woman in a toga. But I didn't have time to investigate.

I burst through the garden gate and arrived at the border of the inn at the same time my car materialized from the darkness.

The car lacked automatic doors, otherwise I'm sure Waldo would have opened it for me. It still only took seconds for me to be behind the wheel and rolling.

"Kicked out so soon?" Waldo asked. "I did hope you'd make it through the night."

"We're going back in time. One hour." I shifted the car to manual drive.

"You said the authorities are watching. Is this advisable?"

"Nope." I took a turn at the next street to get out of sight of the inn, then dropped the anchor. The spring-loaded arm had a rolling metal ball that made a racket as it clattered over the asphalt, but it was a good temporal conductor. Waldo checked the jump settings, and I flipped up the top of the gear shifter to access the jump button. I took a deep breath and mashed it.

We blinked through time and arrived at the same location an hour earlier. The car was still rolling. I raised the anchor and torqued the car into an aggressive 180 degree turn. The tires chirped on the pavement.

"Auto drive. Fast." I let go of the wheel and Waldo took over. It freed my hands to open the glove box. I fished inside and extracted my lock pick set.

We pulled back up to the inn moments later.

"If this goes badly, TCID is going to come looking for this car. Keep it out of sight." I retrieved my chronometer from the glove box, then popped the door open and climbed out.

"Nice knowing you," Waldo said. "I hope your stint in prison goes well."

I headed for the garden gate. By the time I looked back, Waldo and the Boss had vanished again.

Entering the courtyard garden, I looked up to locate the room I was staying in. The window was lit. Was I up there? Maybe in the shower? I had to move fast. I was on dangerous ground and the clock was ticking.

CHAPTER 10

I didn't make the best secret operative. I was too tall, too noticeable. It was no use trying to hide. I found the best option was to ignore everyone I encountered in the halls, make like I had a reason to be there, and forge ahead. Thankfully I didn't run into anyone I knew on the way to the control center.

Ted and his TCID thugs shouldn't have arrived in the pub yet, but that wasn't to say they weren't lurking around. It was only when I reached the locked door to the control room that I had to be careful. Other guests might forgive an ignored greeting, but they were sure to notice breaking and entering.

Fortunately, what I lacked in social skills or camouflage, I made up for with other talents. With my favorite lock pick in hand, I had the padlock removed and the deadbolt open in under twenty seconds. Then it was just the key code.

2-4-7-8-2.

I punched it in and opened the door. So far so good.

Now all I had to do was find this mysterious object Heavens didn't want Time Crimes to see.

There was no light switch. That was my first issue. I guessed that the lights were voice controlled.

"Uh, room, turn on lights."

The command didn't work. There was a dim glow from some of the security machines but I'd need more. I resorted to my phone and used that to navigate the cargo area. Green tube. Green tube.

It wasn't here.

I triple-checked. Nothing.

Damn.

Then the time gate began to hum. A glow emanated from the transmitters and the room was bathed in multi-colored light.

I'd seen my share of time gates over the years and they don't usually run unattended. But whoever did the setup knew what they were doing. When the metal pod came through, it rolled right to the retaining area and popped open. The glow from the time gate dimmed and the room went dark again.

The illumination from my phone was enough to make out the green tube in the pod. It was hard plastic with a screw cap.

What to do with it? The tube was bulky and too tough to conceal. I unscrewed the cap and found a rolled canvas inside. I quickly pulled it from the tube, dumped the tube in the outgoing items bin and walked out. The door locked behind me. I reinstalled the padlocks and headed back down the hall.

I stuffed the canvas up my shirt to hide it, cradling it with one arm.

I wasn't sure what I had, but I knew getting caught with it wasn't a great idea. My other problem was avoiding running into myself. Jumping forward in time again was a logical option, but getting outside unseen could be tricky.

Voices were coming from around the corner. Guests headed this way. I ducked into a stairwell and climbed the circular staircase to the second floor, emerging into the hallway upstairs. To my consternation, the voices from downstairs were now in the hallway. Lingering. Someone was about to come up. Farther along the corridor, a door opened. I turned on my heel and headed the other way.

Big mistake.

I found myself at the end of the same staff hallway I was staying in. As far as I knew, my earlier self was still in there changing. But he wouldn't be for long.

Whoever was coming up the stairwell might head this direction. If I was forced to speak, my earlier self might hear me in the hall and come out. That definitely didn't happen my first time through. Creating a paradox while in the middle of a theft to avoid an inspection by Time Crimes was no one's idea of a good plan.

Voices carried from the stairwell.

I was almost out of time.

I pulled my lock pick set from my pocket and did the only thing I could think of. I broke into Heavens' room.

It took me a nerve-wracking eight seconds to pick the lock. Another second to slip inside. I closed the door and peered through the peephole. No more than three seconds later, the door across the hall opened. My earlier self stepped into the corridor and walked away.

What a relief.

Something yowled.

I almost jolted out of my skin.

Turning around, I found a calico cat staring at me from the kitchenette table. It meowed again.

"I'm not here to feed you, if that's what you're thinking." I took a few steps toward the cat and held out a hand. The cat sniffed it briefly before rubbing its cheek against my knuckle. Its collar had a name tag that read "Clementine." It turned around with a flick of its tail, giving me an unwelcome view of its rear end.

I chose to inspect the rest of the room instead.

Heavens' suite was larger than mine and she'd obviously been here a while. The roof sloped on this side of the building and she had two dormer windows that looked outward, currently toward the patch of woods behind the development. The room had a lingering hint of scented candles and there were tiny lightbulbs hung on strands that crisscrossed the ceiling. The vanity was tidy, the closet organized, and the entire room gave the feeling of an occupant well-adjusted to her surroundings. Several books were stacked on the nightstand. I inspected the titles. Two of them were in French.

She had a couple of framed landscapes on the wall. High quality. Possibly originals. I couldn't name the artists but they had talent.

The cat was still watching me as I retrieved the rolled canvas from under my shirt.

"Something else for your art collection, cat." I let the cat smell the canvas. "Maybe it's a portrait of you, huh?"

The canvas was loosely tied with a leather cord and it had slipped a bit during my rough transfer of it up the stairs. That's why I saw the edge of a signature under the fold. Peeling back the first layer, I made out the name. *Michelagniolo.*

Holy hell.

Heavens had stolen a piece by Michelangelo?

I untied the cord and unrolled the canvas.

It wasn't stolen.

It was her.

Michelangelo is well known for heroic-looking nudes. In paintings I always felt he tended to overemphasize the muscularity of his subjects, but not this time. It was easy to see how much time and energy he'd put into each brushstroke. He'd gone for perfection. Heavens wasn't just a subject here. She was the sun and air. The kind of woman that completely captivated even a man like Michelangelo.

I couldn't help but gape.

When I finally recalled that I was standing in Heavens' own kitchen staring at a masterpiece depicting her naked body, I forced myself to roll the canvas back up. As I did, a slip of parchment fluttered to the table. A note. It was handwritten in Italian. My curiosity got the better of me and I slipped on my meta lenses to translate it.

"In memory of our time together. My own angel from God."

I tucked the note back into the canvas and secured the leather cord around it.

Then I pointed at the cat. "You saw nothing."

The cat purred.

I laid the canvas on the table and headed for the door.

It was only when I was across the hall and back in my own room that I finally relaxed. In a short while, the Time Crimes boys would be done with their inspection. If Heavens had done what I suspected she had—erased the record of the gate opening in the computer—her secret delivery would be safe.

The only downside to the night was that I'd never had my drink.

I tested out my bed. Firm but even. It would do. I laid back and contemplated the ceiling for a while. My body still ached from the pummeling I'd taken at the hands of Ted's buddies, but at least I'd deprived him of the chance to harass someone else tonight.

Sometime later I awoke to a knock on my door. My lights had turned themselves off and the inn had the stillness of the wee hours to it. I had no idea when I'd fallen asleep.

I opened the door to find Heavens in the hallway, backlit by soft light spilling from her room.

"Hey," I managed while rubbing my eyes.

"You didn't come back." Her arms were crossed but she seemed more nervous than upset. If goddesses could get nervous.

"Those TCID guys give you a hard time?"

"Baker gave me a reprimand for era-inappropriate packing materials on one of our shipments, but that's all he could come up with. Thanks to you."

"Least I could do."

"You saw what it was?" Her stance was guarded.

I wasn't going to lie to her.

"If you ask me, it's his best work."

Heavens released her grip on her elbows and brushed a strand of hair behind her ear. "It was unexpected. I didn't even plan to meet him, let alone end up as one of his subjects. But we ran into each other one night while the inn was on a tour. He was charming. A real genius. I thought, what the hell? It's Michelangelo, right? But afterward I didn't want the painting floating around history or having a bunch of images end up in the TCID database. That's why I arranged to have it come in today when I thought no one would be around."

I nodded. Any original Michelangelo would be considered too valuable to move through time unregistered, but it didn't take much to imagine the comments and photos that would be passed around the time travel community once Ted and his buddies had them. And if it hit the metaspace, there would be no getting her privacy back.

"It was the right decision."

"It wasn't a romance," she added. "He was just kind."

"You don't owe me any explanations."

"Right. I don't, do I." She pivoted. "Well, thank you. You didn't have to stick your neck out for me tonight. I appreciate it." Her bright green eyes were sincere. But then she turned back, grasped my arm, and after a slight hesitation, rose up on her toes and gave me a kiss on the cheek.

I didn't dare move.

She released me, then turned back to her door. She paused

just inside her room. "You decide what you're going to do about that job? You're a quieter neighbor than I've had for a while. I wouldn't hate it if you stuck around."

"You'll be the first to know," I said.

She gave me a smile and closed the door. I shut my door as well.

Good gracious.

My phone buzzed in my pocket. I pulled my mind back from the immediate fantasy it had wandered into and checked the screen.

Waldo.

He still had the offer from United Machine set to approve. The dollar sign near the offer was flashing. The amount was generous but I was still busy thinking about the way Heavens' lips had felt on my cheek.

"I guess a few more days here won't kill me." I pressed the accept button and signed the offer. Come morning, I'd be on the case.

CHAPTER 11

I'd forgotten about the second-best reason to stay at the Rose 'n Bridge.

The coffee.

I smelled it brewing the moment I woke up.

There was no sign of reason number one when I came downstairs. She was likely sleeping in after the late night, but the dining area was busy. Manuel was behind the bar.

"You the wizard responsible for that smell?" I asked.

Manuel regarded me coolly. I had a feeling I still wasn't in his good graces, but he poured me a cup nonetheless.

I inhaled deeply. Might be the best coffee in all of time.

When I looked around the pub, I noted the man with the white mustache I'd seen the night before. He was doing his best to avoid getting the mustache in his pancake syrup with each bite. I walked over.

He saw me coming and paused his activities with the pancake.

"You must be the new guest," he said. "Gossip abounds."

"I'm here looking for a writer named Thomas Jefferson Snodgrass."

He chuckled. "One of my lesser-known pseudonyms."

"I've read your stuff. Never imagined I'd run into you."

"It's of little consequence. How many people would believe you anyway? What have you read of mine? *Connecticut Yankee*, I suppose. Or are you more of a *Tom Sawyer* man?"

I took a sip of coffee before responding. "I'm actually partial to *Captain Stormfield's Visit to Heaven*."

"Stormfield. Can't say I've written such a thing. What's the gist of it?"

"I won't spoil it for you. I'm sure you'll have a good time writing it."

"Hmm," he muttered and jotted the name down on a pad of paper he had handy. "Mr. Travers, isn't it?"

"Greyson. No need for formality."

"Call me Sam, then. Rumor is you shot a man last time you were here." He leaned forward conspiratorially. "Should I be worried?"

"Could be. Haven't shot anyone yet this morning."

"Another rumor said the chap had it coming, and you did the place a favor."

"You won't get an argument from me."

"Hmm. I know a few men you ought to be introduced to. Please, join me."

"Afraid I need to get going. Working a case."

"Constable?"

"Private detective."

"Pugilist as well, I see." He gestured to my face.

"Hazard of the job. You caught me on a rough morning."

"Should see the other fellow?"

"Something like that."

"Then I shall puzzle over this seed of an idea you've given me. Perhaps I'll pry more out of you over a pint tonight."

"Staying awhile?"

"Only until a few men in San Francisco forget about some

money I owe them." He checked his pocket watch. "Though I suppose the interest on it now would be substantial. I think I'd best linger here over breakfast and wait for our charming innkeeper to make an appearance."

"A little young for you, isn't she, Sam?"

"I find she does wonders for my eyesight. Probably best she remains unavailable, though. Imagine the crowds if that woman were single."

"She's married?"

"Boyfriend from what I hear. Haven't met the chap, but I daresay he must be the luckiest bloke in a century, having won the heart of our fair Miss Archer."

I took another pull from my coffee. It had lost some of its flavor.

"See you around, Sam."

I left my mug on the bar. Manuel was setting out blueberry muffins on a tray. I grabbed one for the road. "Your stuff is pure magic, Manny. Keep up the good work."

His expression was still hostile, but I knew deep down he was pleased. Just hiding it well.

A pretty collie wandered from behind the bar and sniffed my shoes, then waited patiently to be petted. I obliged.

"Molly, get back here," Manuel commanded. The dog obediently returned to its master who took her by the collar and prevented her from consorting with the wrong clientele again.

I didn't hold it against her, and I made sure to drop a few muffin crumbs on my way out that she could find later.

Despite the tragic news about Heavens' relationship status, I was making a decent start. No hangover, caffeinated, and now free breakfast. A banner morning.

Outside, I walked to the metro station. When the train showed up, I boarded with the other commuters. Onboard, I fidgeted with the silver dollar the dead synth had left me.

A kid sitting across from me on the train was having trouble getting his meta feed to work. He looked up and met my eye, then looked surprised about it. I showed him the coin I was holding before doing some sleight-of-hand to make it disappear. His jaw dropped. He nudged his mother, but she was absorbed in a meta program. When she finally did disconnect and pay attention to her son, it was only long enough to scold him for interacting with strangers. But he kept glancing up at me until I stepped off at the next station.

I transferred downtown and took a second train headed for United Machine.

The company's campus was sprawling, but the meta directory told me right where I needed to go. Once I'd entered my destination and donned my meta lenses, a floating blue arrow bobbed ahead of me in augmented reality, and all I had to do was follow. Made me wonder if I'd wasted my years developing an actual sense of direction.

I'd woken up to an email from one of Diana King's assistants. They'd given me a UM contractor meta ID badge and a list of company contacts relevant to my assignment.

The top name on the list was William Brockhurst, chief of security. I found his office on the second floor of the main campus security building, and I found Brockhurst himself behind a desk loaded with so many computer monitors that I could barely make him out. There were also three TVs on the wall.

I rapped on the doorframe with my knuckles and was answered with a gruff "Whaddya want?"

"You're Brockhurst?"

The man rose from behind the desk like a sow from a feed trough, with only slightly less grunting. His uniform shirt was wet at the armpits, and he had a sheen of perspiration on his forehead, no doubt brought on by the aggressive sitting he'd been doing. He looked me over with beady eyes from under a mop of hair the color of a ginger snap.

His face was friendly enough, in the way Rottweilers look friendly.

"I'm Travers. A private detective. Diana King hired me to assist with your dead synth case."

"Balls. That's the last thing I need. Don't you know how long it takes to get someone new up to speed?"

"I'm excellent at time management," I replied.

"The big Nyongo launch is in two days. This company is in a frenzy. No way anyone is going to get the situation fully in hand by then. Won't happen. All we can do is fire suppression." His eyes drifted to the TVs where newscasters were streaming endless coverage of the space elevator launch plans. The same 3D graphic showing the climber on the first tether rising up through the atmosphere had been aired for days now. Tether One would feature the first synth lander team to be lifted to space. Billionaire Damian Nyongo was rumored to be coming out of seclusion for the launch, though details were being closely guarded.

"I'd like a look at what you know so far," I said. "In the interest of cooperation."

Brockhurst sat back down. "You think you can make more sense of the problem than we have, be my guest." He gestured to a second chair. "You know how to work a keyboard? I don't go in for storing everything in the metaspace. We keep our drives in house."

"No school like the old school," I said. "You going to get some file cabinets next? Maybe microfiche?"

Brockhurst grunted again. "Wouldn't be the worst idea. Damn hackers today can access anything digital. I blame the training they give them in school these days. Kids turn into technological vandals by the time they graduate kindergarten."

Good to see that no matter which part of the future I visited, there were still people blaming the youth for the state of the world.

"Can you tell me what you know about the synth that acted out yesterday? Could a competitor have altered its programming?"

He grumbled his way over to a clipboard on the wall without getting out of his swivel chair. It had a list of ten names scribbled on a sheet of paper. Two had been crossed off. He tossed the clipboard at me. "Those are employees that have been recently fired for procedure violations. I've run basic searches on them but haven't gone in depth to see who might be working for a competitor now. You can start there if you like. Probably someone with recent security access and an axe to grind."

"You talk to any of them yet?"

"A few FaceSpace interviews."

"What about current employees?"

"Look, you go around pointing fingers at employees right now and it gets into the press, management is going to eat me alive. I'm under strict orders to keep this investigation quiet. Start with the ex-employees."

I took a picture of the list of names, then tossed his clipboard back to his desk. "Which security program are you outsourcing to? There's no way you're running security for a company as big as United Machine without an impressive AI. No offense."

He glared at me. "There's things the robot does, and there are things you need real manpower for."

"I'm on your side."

He shifted his weight and reached for his phone. "We use DataSafe. I'll authorize your account and you can log in. We call the AI Alfred."

"That make you Batman?"

He shrugged.

Maybe he had his cape hidden in his desk somewhere.

I synced to the security network and took a look. Alfred was much more organized than Brockhurst. I settled into my chair and browsed through some employee records first. I wasn't even sure what I was looking for. This was the part of the job no one liked. Poking around out in the real world was more fun. But working with an AI was faster.

Cross-referencing the names of ex-employees with synth owners who had reported issues didn't get me anywhere. It did net me more data on complaints though. Before a few weeks ago, most recalls and warranty claims on UM synths were for technical issues, the occasional parts request, a few update glitches. But it was only within the last few weeks that owners had begun complaining about synth behavior problems.

The list of issues was short but informative. Diana King's assertions about the lack of synth stability seemed flimsy. It's true no one had reported furniture destruction like I'd experienced, but several had reported outbursts. Synths seeming depressed was a more common complaint. And there was one that cited actual violence, albeit mild. A synth owned by a local nightclub had supposedly shoved a guest. The issue had been resolved quickly, but I made a note of it.

I tried the coffee from the office coffee machine. It wasn't complete garbage, but after the Rose 'n Bridge, my standards were elevated. I settled back in my chair and made do.

I checked each of the names on Brockhurst's list. Nothing jumped out at me. But then when I was looking through some HR files, I ran across a face that looked familiar. I stared at the woman for a solid minute, trying to figure out where I'd seen her before. The name on her file was Terra Nash. Nash . . . Then it finally clicked. I reached into my pocket and pulled out the coin I'd been left by Johnny the Synth. It was hard to be sure because the coin image was a three-quarter profile, but it looked like the same woman.

"Hey, Bill. Who's Terra Nash?"

"Never heard of her."

I frowned. But Alfred was more helpful. A web search revealed that Nash had been valedictorian of her class at MIT, recruited by United Machine after writing a thesis on the emotional learning capabilities of machines. I was looking for current contact information when I ran across the obituary. She'd died five years ago from cervical cancer after being let go from the company two years prior. I had to admit that pretty effectively cleared her as a suspect.

I frowned and went back to my list of names I'd gotten from Brockhurst.

A lesser detective would no doubt go methodically down the list and interview each person. But if that was going to yield results, I imagined Brockhurst would've had this situation in hand already.

There's nothing wrong with methodical detective work, but when time is a factor, you don't waste it doing what any Joe Schmoe could do. I had a better angle to try.

With my newly-broadened company access, I scrolled through the building directory until I found the place I was looking for. The directory showed me I was already in the right sector.

I stood and stretched. I'd only spent a couple of hours in the chair but my back was already hurting. I didn't know how Brockhurst could stand it.

"I'm going to run down a few leads in person," I said.

"Knock yourself out," Brockhurst said. He didn't bother to look up when I left.

CHAPTER 12

By eleven o'clock I was walking through the rolling doors of the synthetic parts and maintenance warehouse.

"No access beyond this point, sir."

The synth that accosted me was metallic gray, skinless, and cold. Only its face had been outfitted to look human. I displayed my virtual contractor's badge. "Company business. Diana King's authorization."

The synth noted my badge and stepped aside. "I'll provide you with an escort."

"I'm a big boy. Don't mind looking around on my own."

It ignored me and pressed a call button.

"An authorized visitor is here to tour the repair facility."

The intercom buzzed back with a voice that sounded human. "We don't have time for tourists today. Send him away."

The synth bowed apologetically to me and pressed the button again. "He is here with managerial authorization."

There was a muttering on the other end, and a background voice said, "Send Rudy."

The first voice came back on. "We'll have someone up there in a minute."

I waited.

When my guide showed up, it was walking with a slightly lopsided gait. This synth was fleshless like the first one, a carbon-and-composite frame with visible hydromechanical joint actuators, but it had a pale blue face made of some manner of neoprene or silicone. It had mismatched red and blue paint on each limb like it had been assembled from spare parts.

"You're the tour guide?" I asked.

"My identifier is RUD5677-95," it replied. "But you can call me Rudy. I have no gender but am most commonly referred to with the pronouns he and him. You may wish to do so as well."

"Sounds good," I said. The first synth went back to its post. I turned my attention to my new chaperone. "You deal with damaged units here? Rejects? Returns?"

The synth was staring at me and making some approximation of a human expression. I'd guess curious, if that was a program he had. "This is a repair and refurbishment facility."

"Looks like you've had a few repairs yourself."

Rudy looked down at his mismatched body. "I'm a prototype. The technicians find it helpful for me to test various appendages for them prior to returning them to service on other units."

"You're the company test bot?"

"I do whatever I can to be useful to the facility."

"Quite the place. If a synth got cut in half on the street, would it end up here?"

"You are referring to the unit that was reported damaged yesterday. I've downloaded your authorization notes and scanned all relevant company data cross-referenced to your name. Voice analysis indicates you placed a call to emergency services about one of our units. Thank you for your diligence regarding UM property."

"You did all that just now?"

"Indeed, sir."

"Synth I met yesterday didn't have a face like yours. He looked like someone melted a mastiff on his head."

"That unit had a number of non-factory modifications, but his face was not altered when he arrived."

"Was he a test bot too?"

"No. It was assigned service elsewhere."

"Called himself Johnny. Tried to hire me."

Rudy simply stared.

"That strike you as odd behavior for a synth?" I prodded.

"Many synths are assigned to non-company applications," Rudy said. "Private owners often give unusual commands."

"Except this one didn't have a private owner registered. He belonged to United Machine."

"That is correct, sir."

"So why would a company synth go rogue and get himself a new face, then come looking for me?"

"I'm sure I wouldn't know, sir."

"Hmm."

Rudy cocked his head. "Do you have additional questions?"

"A multitude. I'm just getting warmed up. But let's have the tour."

Rudy the prototype android seemed a devoted company man, unlikely to go off script. He had his uses though. He accompanied me anywhere I wanted to go in the repair facility, albeit at a glacial pace, and even fetched me a hardhat at one point. He paused as he handed it to me. "How is your head today? It appears to be undamaged."

"Uh, thank you?" I replied and took the hardhat.

Rudy watched me put the hat on with what seemed like fascination.

"We good?" I asked.

He snapped out of whatever train of thought he was on and nodded. "Of course, sir. Please follow me."

The facility was big, entirely automated, and noisy. Something like a hundred synths passed us coming or going.

"Some place. What do you fill the snack machine with? Lithium grease?"

"Are you hungry? There is an employee break room in the northwest wing."

"Must be riveting water cooler conversation. You sit around and discuss the latest in ball bearings?"

"Never," Rudy replied. "Have there been advancements?"

"Forget it," I said.

It was ten more minutes of walking until I glimpsed a human.

"Where's she going?" I asked, pointing out the scurrying young woman to Rudy.

"Specialist Taylor is a hardware technician. She is useful in many locations."

"I'd like to speak with her."

The young woman was opening a door with a fingerprint lock. I hurried to get within earshot.

"Excuse me, miss?"

She turned. Her glossy black hair was tied up in a ponytail, and she was dressed in grey slacks and a white blouse. Her company ID hovered over her head in the metaspace. Said her first name was Aadya.

"My name's Travers," I said walking over. "On a special assignment for Ms. King. Would you mind if I asked you a few questions?"

She looked like she did mind. I don't know if it was innate politeness or the fact that I had name-dropped Diana King again, but she didn't beg off. She introduced herself and waited patiently for the questions.

"I'm here investigating some incidents involving company property. I'd like to interview you and your associates about the issue."

"We're really quite busy," she replied.

"I ask fast questions."

I let the ensuing silence do the rest of the work. I could tell she was sizing me up. Did I really have the authority for my request? I didn't equivocate. She'd see no room for argument on this face.

She caved. "Okay. Come in."

The door hissed open.

I followed. Rudy limped along in my shadow.

Hard to say what I expected. Maybe something slicker or more on brand for United Machine's image of futuristic design. This was a functioning workshop. Parts were neatly organized, but there was no getting around the fact that people got their hands dirty here. Wiring harnesses, testing instruments, toolboxes, and equipment racks lined the room. Synths too, in various stages of assembly or disassembly. Most were mounted in harnesses and hung from the ceiling like so many sides of beef. Some looked a lot like humans.

If the resemblance to a butcher shop bothered my guides, there was no sign of it on their faces. I followed Aadya past a dozen dangling synths to the center of the repair station. Two other humans were there, but neither looked up at our approach. The men were both laboring over the innards of a synth whose arms and legs were yet to be attached. They had it laid out on a workbench, face up to the ceiling.

"Try it now. Pin seven." I recognized his voice as the one from the intercom. The guy had a meter in one hand, and his other arm elbow-deep in the synth's chest cavity. His companion was manning a computer at an adjoining workstation.

"Still nothing. I'm not getting anything through that connector."

"Guys," Aadya said. "We've got a visitor."

Both men looked up. The skinny white guy at the computer straightened but didn't move from his stool.

His companion was heavyset, dark complected with bushy eyebrows. His metaspace ID said his name was Cannon. He pulled his forearm from the synth's gooey guts and stood dripping some kind of viscous slime onto the floor. I was happy he didn't offer a handshake.

"They charge extra for that kind of fun?" I asked.

The guy looked down at his wet arm. "What, you never had your arm in a chest cavity before?"

"This is Mr. Travers," Aadya said. "He's got questions from upstairs."

"How high upstairs?" Cannon asked.

"Top shelf."

"Jesus," the blond guy muttered.

"Not quite that high," I said. I gestured to the gooey synth on the table. "You don't have automation for this type of repair?"

Cannon took the bait. "Not everything can be fixed with automation. We troubleshoot. Use critical thinking. Get hands-on. Takes a human for that."

"You the one to troubleshoot the issues when a synth loses control?"

He scoffed. "Synths don't lose control."

"Except one did. Yesterday. In my office. Then someone ripped it to pieces. Rudy says you picked it up. I've got some video of it smashing up my place. Should I show it around?" I was bluffing but he didn't know that.

Cannon's expression darkened and he licked his lips. "Fine. We're aware of an issue. But it was a software hack. Nothing to be done."

"Tell me what went wrong."

"Someone messed with the unit's behavior modification coding."

"And neural pathway inhibitors," the blond dude interjected. His name ID said Kristian.

"But the main problem had to be the behavior barrier modification," Cannon replied.

I could tell I was reviving a discussion that had already seen its day and not been resolved. They began to bicker, mostly with names of component parts I didn't understand. I wasn't learning anything useful.

I put up a hand. "So this synth's personality software had a virus?"

"Virus is oversimplifying," Aadya said. "This hack totally updated the behavior modification operating system. Once a synth's behavior cortex gets changed, there's no fix. You just have to wipe it and reset."

"What sort of behavior does it cause? Violence?"

"Not exactly," Aadya said. "It's more like they've been getting depressed."

"They," I said. "You're referring to others that have come in before."

Aadya reddened and glanced at her companions. They didn't look pleased.

"Don't worry. That cat's already out of the bag. I just came from Brockhurst." That seemed to relax them slightly. "What can you tell me about the nightclub incident from a few weeks ago? A synth shoved a guy?"

"Witnesses said it was coming to the aid of an employee," Kristian said. "But it didn't really matter. We had to pull it anyway, Behavior was way out of normal parameters."

"How so?"

"I've got a video file," Kristian said. "It's easier than explaining it." He dragged the video into the metaspace, and I was able to access it by slipping on my lenses. The video was from someone's glasses cam, I'm guessing Kristian's. It showed a holding area akin to a jail cell with plexiglass walls. Inside the cell was a humanoid synth made to look like a woman, complete with fair skin and long, red hair. The synth was naked and pacing back and forth in the cell. But her movements had an almost rhythmic feel to them. She swayed as she moved. I had to turn the audio up to hear it, but it was plain from her body language that she was crying. At periodic intervals, she came to the glass and wailed— face, palms, and breasts pressed to the glass—the distress evident on her face. She stretched her long fingers across the window, pleading, then balled her fists and went back to pacing.

I scratched my chin. "Depressed? Despairing, I'd say."

"Her name was Rio."

I turned and found it was Rudy who had spoken. His blue face was expressionless. I'd almost forgotten he was there. He was studying me. "She was a dancer."

I flipped the video off and returned my attention to the humans.

"What happened to her after this video?"

"We wiped it," Cannon said. "Factory reset. Same as all the other units we brought in."

All the other units.

I walked back to the synth they had partially disassembled on the table. "How many synths have been affected by this issue?"

Cannon sighed. "None here in the facility. It's only corrupting units already on the street."

"So customers are the ones reporting the issues? Sounds like a PR nightmare. How many have you wiped?"

The three techs exchanged glances.

"I've signed the non-disclosure clauses," I added.

Finally it was Aadya who spoke. "Twenty-five."

I whistled. "Are there more out there?"

"The cleanup crews are confident they're running down the last of the affected units," Cannon said.

"How many still on the loose? Best guess."

All three techs looked uncomfortable.

"Potentially none," Kristian said, but with no confidence behind the words.

"You have no idea," I said. "You could have any number of these bonkers androids roaming the streets?"

When no one spoke, I let out my most colorful swears.

CHAPTER 13

I'd suspected that my morning might involve digging my way into some of United Machine's less-than-public issues, but even I wasn't entirely prepared for this one.

"Explain it to me like I'm a civilian," I said. "But give it to me straight."

My three frazzled repair techs still seemed uncomfortable, but the dam was broken now. No use trying to put the water back. They looked almost relieved to have someone to unload on.

"It wasn't the fault of anyone at the company that we know of," Aadya said. "Has to be someone outside."

I'd taken a seat on one of the shop stools. "If someone outside the company figured out a way to hack your operating systems, that's a bad breach. How many people outside the repair facility know this is going on?"

"The clean-up crews," Kristian replied. "A few customers have a vague idea. Probably someone in development. But we've been told not to discuss it with anyone other than superiors."

"When did it first start?" I asked. "How long have you been getting in synths with behavior issues?"

"There was an update we pushed out last month called

Daffodil," Aadya said. "Last big personality upgrade. Problems started after that update went out."

"Daffodil?"

"Yeah," she replied. "The updates have always been named after flowers. We're currently prepping rose variants."

"Why not just fix the problem with a new update?"

"We did. We put out Hyacinth as a patch across the board. The issue should be resolved. We've pushed through clean versions to all networked units, but some are still acting erratically. Somehow this error is still showing up."

"How is it transmitted?"

Kristian chimed in. He'd taken his jacket off, settled in. "A synth has three ways to upload data. Hardwired ports, wireless, plus an optical scanner. The hardwired port is tough to get to quickly. Inner thigh on older models." He pointed to Rudy and indicated a panel on the inside of the synth's leg. "Wireless takes knowing a company key code unique to the unit. The optical scanner could bypass that if the synth is willing, but you can't force data through that way. The synth has to turn on the input feed itself. Command controls are internal. It would have to be a conscious decision by the unit."

I mulled this over. "So a synth would have to *choose* to upload this hack? Hard to imagine them wanting to be depressed."

"We assume it's hidden in some other kind of data," Aadya said.

"What's the point in corrupting these synths and making them act out? What would a hacker gain?"

"Damage the company's rep," Kristian said. "That's the word anyway."

"What about the one from yesterday? You three know these machines the best." I turned toward the patchwork prototype. "For someone to cut one in half on the street like that had to take a lot of force. Any way I could rip Rudy here apart that fast? What would it take?"

Cannon looked grim. "You couldn't."

"I work out. What if I was really angry?"

He shook his head. "Takes specialty tools to get inside the exoskeleton. Or you'd have to be crazy strong."

I tapped on Rudy's chest plate. "So the synth I found on the sidewalk was torn apart by someone with access to special tools or they were the Incredible Hulk."

None of the techs would meet my eye.

"I figure if you take a synth apart on the street in broad daylight, you're either making a statement or there is something really valuable inside that you want. Hard to make a statement when no one seems to even care that it happened, so what's in there that's worth stealing?"

"Plenty," Kristian replied. "The chest cavity holds the power cells and all the movement processing hardware plus the bulk of the sensitivity gyros."

"The synth I found on the street. Was it missing any of that stuff when you got it back?"

"No," Aadya said. "But it was missing other things. Mostly bio-skin generators and a bunch of ligament couplers."

"How much is that stuff worth?"

"Relatively speaking? Not much. A few grand maybe? Not nearly as much as the brain or any biosynth organs. But it might be easier to resell. Sometimes we see people tearing up synths to try to sell their organs on the transhuman black market, but it's the couplers that make the biosynth connections possible. They're how you bond human skin to synth skin."

"How many organs from a synth like this could be compatible with a human?"

"Depends on the person," Aadya said. "And their tolerance for pain, I guess. It would be illegal too."

I scratched my head. "So whoever ripped the items out left a bunch of more valuable stuff behind."

"Could have been junkies. Someone who had no idea what the parts were worth," Kristian suggested.

"Or pros who only went after stuff that was easy to move on the black market," I said. "They knew enough to get their hands on the specialty tool to get inside, it would make sense they knew the parts' values. If I'm someone looking for parts to sell, where do I get my hands on one of these tools?"

"No idea," Cannon said.

"Well . . ." Kristian muttered.

Cannon glared at him. "Keep your mouth shut. You don't know anything."

Kristian frowned.

I looked at each of them in turn. Waited.

Eventually Aadya spoke up. "We've had some things around here go missing lately," she said quickly. "At first we assumed they were just misplaced. But we don't think that's it anymore."

"Let me guess. One of the things that went missing was a tool for cracking open synths?"

Aadya nodded. She made a quick glance at Cannon. He clenched his jaw.

"I'll need a list of the stuff that was stolen. Along with some estimated values," I said, jotting a note in my phone.

"It was primarily prototype or refurbished equipment," Cannon said. "Most of it has no catalog price."

"Take your best guesses. Which of you reported the thefts to management?"

They all looked at each other again before speaking. I felt like I was talking to one brain in three bodies and they had to parlay before every response.

"When a tool goes missing, management assumes it's one of

us," Kristian finally said. "We're the only ones with access. But all of us swore we didn't do it. And we aren't rats either."

"None of you have reported the thefts?"

The three looked at each other uneasily. They had to know they were admitting breaking company policy. Their loyalty could mean all three getting fired.

"A place like this has to have security cameras," I said.

"Most of the time," Cannon replied.

"Not all the time?" I frowned.

"A few months ago, we had a request approved to be able to turn off the security cameras within the workshop when we need to. Some of what we do is highly sensitive. We turned them off a few weeks ago. We wanted to prevent a competitor from learning about the behavior hack."

"That seem like a good idea now?"

Their postures were defiant. Aadya and Kristian both had their arms crossed. Cannon looked like he wanted to take a swing at me.

I studied them, and it dawned on me that I wasn't dealing with individuals. I was looking at a team. None were willing to sell out the others even if they knew one of them was guilty. They'd rather go down for it together.

Another layer to the puzzle to work through. I slipped my meta lenses back on, walked to one of the tool cabinets, located a screwdriver, then removed one of the handles from a neighboring cabinet door.

"What are you doing?" Cannon asked.

"Don't worry. You'll get it back." I pocketed the cabinet handle. "Which one of you can text me the date the first tools went missing?"

Aadya raised a hand.

"Do that now," I said, handing her one of my business cards.

"If I do find out who's taking the parts, are any of you going to be surprised at what I find?"

I didn't get a response, but that was an answer too. And I was starting to regret taking this job.

CHAPTER 14

Prototype Rudy walked me out of the repair lab. I moved slowly so he could keep up.

The conversation with the techs rolled around my head while we strolled the corridor. I'm not sure how much I'd gained from my visit, but I knew UM's façade of streamlined efficiency was just as false as any other company. And the weak point wasn't in the machines.

"I've never met a private detective before," Rudy said. "Do you have the authority to make arrests?"

"No. I report to the people who hire me. Unless I find something life-threatening."

"And what will you do next?"

I took a few more strides, then appraised the synth as I waited for him to catch up. "I'll do some fancy detective work. The thief will have made a mistake somewhere. I'll catch them."

"And what will you do once you have the culprit?"

"Hard to say."

"Will you reveal their identity to Miss King?"

"Maybe. If it's relevant to the case."

"Miss Aadya, Mr. Kristian, and Mr. Cannon could be let go

for failing to comply with company policy and reporting the theft. Who would make the difficult repairs?"

"I don't know what will happen. I'm just doing a job."

"If you were to make a guess, which would you say is the thief?"

"You want to make a wager?"

"I don't know how to gamble."

"Pity. You'd have a hell of a poker face." I spotted a familiar silhouette on a door sign. "I'm gonna hit the restroom, Rudy. Wait here for me, will you?" I didn't wait for him to reply. I headed straight for the privacy of the restroom. Once inside, I locked the door.

My phone already had a notification, the text from Aadya with the dates of suspected thefts. All I needed now was the right anchor. I pulled the cabinet handle from my pocket and laid it on the counter. The next tool I extracted from my inside jacket pocket was a thin, cylindrical device called a degravitizer. The odds that this door handle contained any of the temporally unusual particles that made time travel possible were slim, but I was going to check anyway. Time travel accidents are unforgiving. I aimed the degravitizer at the cabinet handle and pressed the test button. The light glowed green. Gravitite free. Just a normal cabinet handle.

Next up, I needed a physical orientation. I pulled up the video I'd surreptitiously taken with my meta lenses. If you go far enough into the future, there is an app for everything, and that includes time travel. The image in my sunglasses lenses now gave me the original height of the cabinet handle. As long as I held it at or below the same height, the handle would make an excellent spacial ground, keeping me from arriving with my feet embedded in the floor.

I pushed back my sleeve to access the chronometer on my wrist. The concentric dials moved easily as I selected the correct date, time, and time zone. I chose an hour of the morning when the facility was closed and I'd be unlikely to encounter someone inside the repair facility. Since the chronometer was designed to ground through the nearest non-gravitite-infused object, the cabinet handle at my fingertips would keep my personal wormhole anchored to the planet and give me a point of contact for showing up in the past.

I took one last look around the bathroom, noted the time on my phone, then pushed the pin on my chronometer.

The jump was instant. Felt like blinking. Only now I wasn't standing in the bathroom. I was back in the repair lab and the cabinet handle was firmly anchored to its cabinet.

Easy peasy. I was in the past.

My next task was fixing our surveillance problem.

In my wallet, I carried a sheet of micro cameras as slim as a credit card. The tiny fish-eye lenses are adhesive on the back and transmit data far enough to reach a local receiver, usually in my car or the one lodged in the heel of my boot. I didn't plan on sticking around for this surveillance, however, so I'd need a better method than hanging around outside all night. Once I positioned a few of the tiny cameras around the lab, I pulled my right boot off and unscrewed the cap embedded in the heel. I extracted the data receiver, then looked around for a place to stash it.

I decided on a window that overlooked the parking lot, laying the receiver inside the window track next to some dust and a dead housefly.

With my boot back on, I walked back to my cabinet, set my chronometer for a date two nights in the future, then jumped again.

It was still nighttime, the lab was still quiet, but forty-eight hours had passed, and I hoped it was enough time to gather some video of my thief. I walked around the lab and pocketed my cameras and receiver, then headed out the door.

I kept an eye out for motion sensors or security in the hallway but was able to make it back to the bathroom undetected. Without Rudy slowing me down, I was there in seconds. Once inside, I was free to reset my chronometer again, this time selecting a date and time thirty seconds after I'd left Rudy in what was passing for my present day. I pressed my hand to the countertop and jumped. Once again the experience was instant.

The cabinet handle I'd first used was now lying in the sink where it had landed when I vanished.

I picked it up, washed my hands, then headed back out.

Rudy was waiting in the hallway. I handed him the door handle. "Mind putting that back for me?"

He studied it with curiosity. "Certainly, sir."

When we reached the front doors of the building, they slid open and I stepped into breezy sunlight, but Rudy stopped short. Reminded me of a well-trained dog that had reached the edge of its yard.

"It's been real, Rudy. Thanks for the company."

"I wish you luck in your investigation, Mr. Travers."

"In my experience, luck rarely has much to do with it, but I'll take it if I can get it."

Rudy watched me till I was out of sight of the building.

When I was alone, I pulled the data receiver from my pocket and started transferring the forty-eight hours of video surveillance to my phone. I doubted it would be riveting viewing. Maybe I'd skim through it with a beer in my hand back at the Rose 'n Bridge where the company would at least be entertaining.

While I waited for the data transfer, I took the UM sky tram on a loop around the campus, getting a good view of the Port Nyongo Skylift in the process. The sky was cloudless for once, and the sky tram had a glass ceiling to facilitate wonder at the elevator's height. The apex was indiscernible, but my eyes were pretty good. I figured I could see at least the first fifteen thousand feet. Beyond that, the elevator was mostly carbon nanotech and too thin to be visible anyway. Somewhere in the lower reaches of stationary orbit was the beginnings of the Earthrim space station. An altitude I hoped I'd never visit.

"Detective Travers."

I turned to find Charles King moving toward me. Where on earth had he come from?

"I see you accepted my mother's offer of employment."

"She made a persuasive argument."

"She can do that. People are often intimidated by her."

A seat on the train opened up so I sat. Charles lingered beside me.

"She's not that special, you know."

I blinked. I felt I'd missed some part of the conversation. "Who's not special?"

He jerked his head toward the window and the sprawling United Machine campus. "Mother. Her company. It's actually quite limited."

"Downplaying your family's work?"

"Our units are impressive, but they don't make the sun rise or anything." He glanced toward a delivery synth that was standing a few feet away on the train. "It's Nyongo that's doing the heavy lifting now. Literally."

My gaze wandered back to the space elevator. "You think you're working for the wrong company?"

"I could have been an astronaut. I started training when I was young. If it hadn't been for the accident, I might have been one of the colonists training to go to Mars."

"Bad luck."

"I'll still get up there," Charles said, looking skyward. He seemed to be squinting more than usual for the light. There was something off about his expression, but I still couldn't pin down what it was. Plastic surgery from his injuries maybe?

Charles caught me looking.

"You're wondering about my face."

"I was staring. I apologize."

"It's okay. I'm used to it. I lost nearly my entire face in the accident. All of this is synth bioskin." He touched his cheek. "Mother had them reconstruct it for me."

The train rocked side to side, but Charles didn't reach for a handle. "You probably don't know what it feels like living in a body that isn't yours."

"Not in that way," I said. Though my mind flashed to the image of my other self, Professor Greyson Travers and his party full of admirers. Charles' point wasn't entirely lost on me. "I'm sure you'll still do great things," I added. "Who we look like doesn't define us."

His eyes came back to earth, the train, and me. "Perhaps I could be a detective like you, huh?"

I shrugged. "Can't say I recommend it. Astronaut probably pays better."

"Nyongo's climbers are taking the first shipment of our androids to Earthrim in less than forty-eight hours. Do you think you'll find our culprit before then?"

"Time isn't an issue I stress over. I'll catch them."

"What makes you so sure?"

"Because they're only human. Humans make mistakes."

He nodded slowly. "My mother means well. But what she hired you to do isn't going to matter. Not in the big picture. She doesn't understand that the real problems of the world aren't going to be fixed by a bunch of android slaves on Mars. We could be doing so much more."

"You going to join the synth-rights protesters on the street corners? I bet they'd love that."

Charles put his hands in his pockets and looked skyward again. The train went around a curve, but he still didn't reach for a handhold, he just balanced there, rocking on his heels slightly. His mind appeared to be elsewhere. There was a confidence to his posture that belied his age. Maybe he got it from his mother.

"Surprised you get around by public transit," I said. "Son of the CEO and all."

A vague smile crossed his face. "I have other methods too. But sometimes you have to walk before you fly."

The train braked and pulled into the next station. When the doors opened, Charles turned on his heel and strode out into the sunlight. He didn't bother to look back. The train was on its way again quickly. Last I saw of Charles, he had broken into a jog, brushing aside pedestrians as he rushed for the platform exit.

What a strange kid.

I donned my sunglasses and stared up at the view some more.

CHAPTER 15

By the time I got off the sky tram my mind had worked through the basics of what I knew so far about the case. I figured there was a fair chance the thefts at the UM repair facility were linked to the destruction of the synth who had tried to hire me. I was hoping my newly acquired surveillance video would show me who the parts thief at the repair facility was, but I wasn't much closer to knowing why they were doing it or if the crimes were connected.

Fencing stolen parts was a possibility. Was it the same person who dismantled Johnny on the street or was I dealing with two separate culprits? The fact that they'd left the most valuable items alone made theft seem implausible as the sole motivation. But I knew so little about the second-hand synth parts market that I'd still have to look into it.

Diana King either wanted me on the trail of her corporate espionage theory or off on a goose chase. I wasn't sure which yet. This hacker business the repair techs had revealed was still too obscure to me. Motive seemed reasonable enough, but if a competitor was out to discredit the UM product line by making their synths act out, they'd still need a megaphone. This wasn't 2006 when you could slap on some earphones, sing numa numa, and become a viral sensation. The metaspace was a maelstrom of digital content fed to piranhas with nanosecond attention spans. If someone had dirt on UM's production woes, they either hadn't deployed it yet or hadn't found the right broadcast signal. I had other rocks to kick before I went down that path.

I transferred to the elevated city train and stopped at a station with a bank. I walked in and converted some of my retainer money into cash from a solitary cash machine in the corner. I stuffed the wad of mostly fifties into my pocket and located a human for my other business. The money manager was busy, so I waited in the lobby chairs. While I waited, I snapped a couple of pictures of both sides of the silver dahlia coin I got from the dead synth. Eventually the money manager noticed me. The woman's meta ID said her name was Monique.

"Can I help you, sir?"

I smiled and rose from my chair. "Just a quick question for you. I'm managing an estate sale for a friend and came across what might be a rare coin. Do you have any way to check what it's worth?"

Monique smiled. "We don't do that here, but I do have a branch in Kentucky that specializes in rare coins. Would you like to do a meta conference? I can see if someone is available."

"Love to."

"Right this way please."

She guided me into a room with spherical walls of light green. As I donned my meta lenses, the room immediately took on the look of a clearing in a remote forest. The sound of a nearby stream filtered through, and they must have had fans in the walls because my hair moved in the breeze.

"You'll see yourself in the default space. Please feel free to adjust your personal scenery. I'll call our expert. Let me know if you have any trouble." She let herself back out again, and I was left alone in the meta forest.

It took me a moment to identify the room controls in my field of vision. Once I found them, I flipped through the various options for conference locations. Most were naturescapes, but one was the prehistoric planet earth. I happened to be inside an erupting volcano when the digital projection of a middle-aged man walked in. His hair was gray and his polo shirt was salmon. I doubted he knew he was walking toward me across a river of glowing lava, but it made a hell of a first impression.

"Hello, sir. I'm Frank Dunlap. I understand you have something interesting for me." He didn't attempt to shake my hand. Not one for digital play acting. I appreciated that.

"It's just something I ran across in a friend's attic. You accept photo uploads in here?"

"Go right ahead."

I took out my phone and selected the recent coin photos I'd taken, then swiped them into the ether. They appeared in the space between me and Frank, hovering near eye level. Frank immediately snatched them up and expanded them, studying each side of the coin with a professional efficiency.

"Hmm. Afraid you aren't going to like what I have to say."

"Not valuable?"

"Not remotely. We're dealing with a fake here. You see the edges? This blank was laser etched, not stamped or pressed like you'd see in a mint. Nice custom job though. Most serious coin counterfeiters spring for presses. This was a more economical option."

"So it's the work of a counterfeiter on a budget?"

"Could be. But this is a design I've never seen before. Can't fathom the use in trying to pass this off as legal tender when it doesn't appear to be based on a real coin. Usually counterfeiters go after large denomination paper bills if they bother with cash at all. Still, you'd best tell your friend to turn the coin in to the proper authorities. Or if you bring it into the local bank branch, they can see that it's properly destroyed for you."

"I'll pass that on. You said it would take specialty equipment to make something like this. Any specifics you can give me there?"

"Well, it depends on the lasers, but . . . hold on a minute." He expanded the image. "Gets hard to make out at this resolution, but it appears there are extremely fine markings in the metal. You see here?"

I did see. It looked like numbers, but they were so small they appeared as lines on the coin. He zoomed further and followed the edge of the flower on the back of the coin to reveal that each dahlia petal was in fact made up of a string of microscopic numerals etched into the metal.

"I've never seen anything like this," Frank said in awe. "There must be thousands of them." He checked the image of the front of the coin as well, and the image of the scientist was likewise created by these microscopic numerals.

"What are they for?" I asked.

"I haven't the faintest," he said, still in a reverential tone of wonder. He eventually closed the images and pushed them back to me. I deleted them from the conference space. "I'd be interested in seeing this coin. When you bring it in to be destroyed, I'd be happy to do some in-depth scans, perhaps decipher the meaning behind the numbers. To get etching *this* precise, I imagine you'd need an extremely fine laser indeed. An Epsilon Ten *might* do it. Highly illegal to own one, though, at least in the United States."

"Epsilon. That's a machine counterfeiters use?"

"Spies too. Good way to pass microscopic communications. I'm only making a guess here. But yes, I'd say whoever did this could etch just about anything they wanted and pass it undetected. I daresay that before the coin is destroyed, we may need to contact the FBI or Secret Service."

"Thank you for your time."

"Of course. Best of luck to you, mister . . ."

"Clemens," I said.

"Mr. Clemens. Yes, well, it's been a pleasure. Let us know if we can be of further assistance." He studied me carefully, then departed. I was left alone in the meta conference room.

I was tempted to put the coin images up again to have another look at the expanded number etchings, but I had a feeling Frank Dunlap's mention of the FBI was more than a passing thought. Any moment he might be making a call. I thought it best to make my exit before I was asked to stay.

Monique smiled and waved at me from her desk as I walked out of the bank, but she was with another customer so I was spared a delayed exit.

Frank Dunlap had again given me more questions than answers, but the questions were starting to tell a story. Outside, I hailed the first available auto car and set a destination for the waterfront.

CHAPTER 16

When the auto car left me at the waterfront rotunda, I walked south until I hit the dock district.

The port was filled with cargo ships today, and the dock warehouses disgorged streams of forklifts to move goods. But I wasn't there for a delivery.

Port Nyongo wasn't my permanent residence, but I still had a few friends in low places. After making discreet inquiries in a few bars, brothels, and back alleys, I found myself at the flood wall and wound my way into the lower market streets. The air smelled differently here. There was a base of salt, but it mixed with the human scents of curry and chow mein. The clientele were mostly dock workers. They sat at benches and loitered near standing tables. Most had a furtive, hostile look to them. The street food was eclectic and savory, some served from trucks, some from semi-permanent shipping containers modified into kitchens.

Colored tarps strung across the narrow streets kept the sun and rain off the locals and also lent a multicolored hue to the pavement as the afternoon sunlight filtered through plastic and mesh. I strolled up to a place serving pad thai and sesame tofu dumplings and took a stool. The food was hot and gave me a renewed sense of optimism on my prospects. I ordered a couple of beers to wash it down with and watched the stream of workers coming in and off work shifts. A few synths walked by, but they were just passing through. I synced my phone with my meta lenses and skimmed some of the surveillance video I'd taken from the United Machine repair facility while I drank my beer. I was able to get through the first night of footage without noting anything unusual. The only thing moving all night was Rudy the Android tidying things up before putting himself into his charging pod. There was still another day's worth of video to review. Maybe the parts were somehow going missing throughout the day. As the sun sunk lower, I was forced to pause my viewing so I could concentrate on my surroundings. The afternoon dock shift was ending.

I paid for my food with some of Diana King's retainer money and finished off the second beer before making my way up Front Street. A group of construction workers I'd been watching for a while split up. They were a mix of ethnicities but primarily Latin American. The newest were easy to spot. They spoke only Spanish and acted as though everything was a threat. It was no secret that the dock district ran on the sweat of illegal immigrants, and it wasn't hard to trace them back to the people profiting. The group I was tailing made a stop along a row of decrepit shipping containers that looked like they were a stiff breeze away from returning to an elemental state. They knocked on a door marked with the number 1311 and a skull and crossbones graffitied on it. Someone opened the door. Money changed hands. Debts slowly being repaid. It was an old con. When the immigrants had melted into the night again, I approached the shipping container. I rapped three times on the door and waited.

The door had been fitted with a slide window, and it opened first. I found myself looking at the bridge of a nose and two squinting eyes shadowed by bushy eyebrows.

The voice that came with the eyebrows had the timbre of a wood chipper. "What do you want?"

"I'm here to see the guy in charge."

"What for?"

"My rampant curiosity."

The squinty man squinted harder. "Get lost."

I flashed my wad of cash. "I'm the paying kind of curious."

The little window slammed shut, but it was only a few seconds till the locks on the big door sprung and it opened.

Bushy Eyebrows was a squat, extremely tan man who looked like all he did was work out. He wore a muscle tee and a gold chain and a thin, zippered sweatshirt that was at least two sizes too small. He was probably fifty but had a good head of black hair and a handsome enough face to offset his obvious steroid issues. He held a sensor wand up. "No guns."

I reached into my jacket and offered him my Stinger, grip first. He stuffed it into the waistband of his pants but waved his wand over me anyway.

"Smart move," I said. "The gun is the least dangerous part of me."

He didn't so much as smirk. Steroids had obviously affected his sense of humor too.

When he still didn't move aside, I sighed and pulled one of the bills loose from my pocket and handed it to him. He tucked it away, then jerked his head for me to follow.

The shipping container was a façade. It covered the opening to an old construction tunnel. Port Nyongo sat atop a warren of underground burrows, dug to construct the base of the Skylift. Some access areas were here along the waterfront, others were over twenty miles inland. The western legs of the elevator had anchor points halfway across the Gulf of Mexico.

As befitting a structure of its enormous scale, it was next to impossible to keep track of every old tunnel or burrow used to construct the elevator. Smugglers like these were quick to exploit that fact and used them for an import/export business that was as efficient as it was illegal. There were rumors you could get something from the Mexican side of the gulf to the west coast of Florida without ever seeing sunlight or getting wet.

A rickety, steel staircase took me and my grumpy doorman below street level. It smelled like a sweaty gym sock down there, but I hadn't expected much better. We found the guy in charge sitting in a room off the corridor, hooked into an expensive-looking gamer chair.

"Yo, Dagger. This guy here wants to talk," my guide said.

Lost in the metaspace, Dagger was oblivious to our arrival. My muscle-bound friend was obligated to don a game headset and summon him. I took in the rest of the room while I waited. Not much to see but a fridge, a couch, and several open shipping crates, one of which was filled with guns. There was a skinny girl in a dingy tank top and cutoffs slouched in an armchair looking bored. She couldn't have been more than nineteen. She eyed me warily. Despite her position in the armchair, she radiated tension. Like a cat in a room full of vacuum cleaners.

"This better be something good, guero. I was about to level up in this bitch." Dagger stared at me clear-eyed now from his chair, the headset resting in his lap. His mustache still hadn't come in yet. He was tubby too. Maybe too much time in the chair.

"What's this rig?" I asked. "Regular AR not cutting it?"

He scoffed. "This is custom, three-sixty, full-immersion mind manipulation, bro. Temperature-hacked, pressure point triggers and sensory duplication equipped. This isn't some public access world net either. Full custom, exclusive access to platinum operating systems only. Get out of here with your AR."

"Does it get rid of the weird foot smell you have going on in here? I'd definitely pay for that."

The girl in the chair snorted.

Dagger glared at me and then at her. She shrank into her chair a little farther.

"You come looking to start shit? How about I have Eight Pack beat some respect into you?"

I angled toward his muscled doorman. "Eight Pack? At least tell me someone else came up with that name for you as a dare."

He glared at me too, but added a neck muscle flex that seemed unnecessary. "I like it."

"Oh shit. You made it up yourself." I sucked my teeth. "That's not really how nicknames work, man. Just makes it extra lame."

"The hell you want?" Dagger said.

I pulled the silver dahlia coin from my pocket and tossed it to him. He caught it.

"Someone made that custom. I need to figure out who. You're in the imports business. I've asked around. Everyone says you're the guy to talk to when it comes to things no one else has."

Dagger turned the coin over in his palm. He shook his head. "Useless fake."

"Thought it might be," I said. "Especially since I already had it checked. But it turns out there's all kinds of microscopic engraving on it. So small it's undetectable by the human eye. What do you think of that?"

"What good is it if you can't see it?" He shrugged.

"I asked myself the same question. And it also got me wondering who made it. Turns out whoever did it would've had to have a very special kind of printer. Maybe even an Epsilon Ten printer. Except those are apparently illegal and can't be imported to US soil. So either the coin itself was brought in from overseas or someone smuggled in an Epsilon. If they did, I have to believe you or the people you work for would know about it."

"Ep—silon. Never heard of it." He crossed his arms.

I smiled. "You know I was in a couple of plays as a little kid.

Never had many lines but there was this one girl who always got the lead. Sally Simpson. She got the part partly because she could sing okay, but mostly because she was the drama teacher's kid. You know how it is. But she was a terrible actress. Never convincing. You know why? She always overdid it."

Dagger shifted uncomfortably. "This story got a point?"

"You never did any plays as a kid, did you, Dagger? Because if you did, you'd know you're a Sally."

"Actually, I have an idea for a play. You know which part you get?" Dagger asked. "The part where you get the fuck out while you still got your legs unbroke."

Eight Pack shifted his stance behind me. I turned to keep him in my peripheral vision.

"All right, I'd love to hear more about this play idea but I can see you boys have a lot going on. Give me back my coin and I'll show myself out."

"Nah, see, that's where you're wrong," Dagger said. "I'm owed something for my time. I figure I'll keep this for my trouble." He tossed the coin lightly in his palm, then tucked it into his front pants pocket.

"That's not gonna work for me," I said.

"You say that like I give two shits what you want. Eight Pack, tune this asshole up and throw him out."

Eight Pack advanced, rolling his shoulders as he moved. As he reached for me, I sidestepped and tagged him across the right side of his face with a pair of jabs. He stayed upright but staggered back a step, a look of confusion on his face. Perhaps he was counting on the sheer volume of his muscle mass to intimidate me into subservience. Oops.

To his credit, he shook the punches off and advanced again, this time with his guard up. Unfortunately for him, his broad pectoral muscles and overgrown shoulders didn't give him the full forward range of motion. He swung at me with a rigid lunge and I simply took a step back, then hooked forward with my right, hitting him twice on that side of his face. That rung his bell but also woke the fight in him. The anger made him come at me faster, but at six foot three, all I had to do was step out of his range anytime he moved and I still had the ability to hit him. He tried to close, God bless him, but my next right dazed him enough that his arms drooped. I reached down with my left hand and plucked my Stinger from his waistband before coming under his drooping guard with a right uppercut that caught him under the chin. His jaw snapped shut, he tipped backward and went down like a felled tree. I heard the wind go out of him as he landed.

I had to admit it was gratifying to see him hit the ground.

Dagger frowned with disappointment as he looked down at his wannabe leg breaker. When he looked at me, his eyes lingered briefly on the gun in my left hand.

The girl in the armchair hadn't moved through any of this but now she had a vague smile on her face.

"Piece-of-shit told me he could fight," Dagger said.

I held up a finger. "Ooh. Hang on, I've got it." I leaned over my fallen opponent and nudged his foot with my boot. "Flex-o-saurus Rex. There's a nickname you can have. You know, on account of how much trouble it is getting those stubby arms out in front of you."

He didn't respond per se, but his eyelids fluttered some and his arm twitched. I took it he approved.

Dagger didn't look amused, but he dug in his pants and fished out my coin nonetheless. He held it out.

"And?" I asked.

He glowered at me. "Yeah. An Epsilon came through a few weeks ago."

"You got a name for me?"

He took a quick glance at his girl and then back to me. He crossed his arms again. Tough guy pose.

I considered roughing him up but thought better of it.

I took out the wad of cash from my Diana King bankroll instead and laid a few bills on the nearest cargo crate. More flies with honey. I held another bill poised to join them and waited. Dagger watched and finally spoke. "All I had was a delivery address. Haight Street. Loading dock at the back of a bar called the Midnight Club."

Midnight Club. That was a name I recognized.

"Who was your point of contact? You had to have someone to give it to."

"They paid me to drop it there, I dropped it there. That's all I know."

I laid the next bill down with its companions.

I tucked my coin and the rest of my cash back in my pocket. "Been a pleasure, Dagger."

"It's going to get around you been here."

"Counting on it." I pulled a business card from my wallet and walked over to the armchair. I held it out to the girl. "Should you find this situation is one you need to get yourself out of, give me a call."

Dagger's eyes narrowed but the girl took the card.

I kept my gun out till I reached the door. Dagger didn't move. Smarter than he looked.

Flex-o-saurus Rex was out cold.

My knuckles hurt like hell as I walked back up the stairs, but it was worth it. Some clues turn out more fun than others.

CHAPTER 17

Haight Street was still too quiet. I had Waldo pick me up in the Boss and we cruised the bar district but it wouldn't come alive for a few more hours. I decided to head back to the Rose 'n Bridge. All this clue gathering was making me thirsty.

The Rose 'n Bridge was lit with orange from the fading sunset by the time I made it back. The lamps were burning and I wandered inside to find a bluegrass band striking up a rendition of "Harvest Woman."

I took the same seat at the corner of the bar that I'd used the night before. Heavens was behind the taps. She wandered over, looking lovely in a moss green top that exposed her shoulders.

"What's with the banjo squad?" I asked.

"You don't know Boo Bradley?"

"Boo Radley? Like from the book?"

"No. Buh—Bradley. He's won four Grammys and a half dozen Tiki Awards." She poured a beer and passed it to me.

"I don't even know what a Tiki Award is."

"Never mind then and just listen. They're phenomenal."

I shut up and sipped the beer. She was right. The guy on the banjo was killing it. When he'd finished "Harvest Woman" he rolled straight into "Shuckin' the Corn." His fingers were a blur.

I felt something brush my leg. When I looked down I found Manuel's dog, Molly, leaning against me. There was no sign of her owner so I scratched her behind the ears for a bit. The dog panted happily.

Heavens showed up at my end of the bar again a few minutes later with a knotted rag filled with ice. She gestured to my swollen knuckles. "Busy afternoon?"

"Thrill-a-minute," I said. I rested the ice on my right hand since it was the most swollen. I needed more practice drinking left-handed anyway.

I leaned across the bar to be heard over the music. "How come every time I come in here there's something weird happening? Last night somebody was playing a didgeridoo."

Heavens leaned in too until I was close enough to catch a whiff from her lavender shampoo. "It's because Australia Day came up on the wheel of festivities yesterday." She pointed to a wheel on the back wall that resembled a dartboard. Someone had scribbled various holiday names on scraps of paper and affixed them to the triangular segments. "We celebrate a different holiday every few days. Next stop we're doing Up Helly Aa. We even have a Viking ship to burn. I already bought the torches."

"I swear this place gets stranger every time I visit. It's like a drunk Brigadoon."

Heavens shrugged. "That's fair. But it's by design. The tourists want to be entertained."

"Because warping through history in a time traveling tavern is too dull by itself?"

"Sometimes grumpy private detectives show up and shoot people. Hard to plan for that though."

I gave her my most molten glare.

"What? Too soon?" She took my pint glass and topped it off. "I thought it was funny."

She slid the beer back across the bar. I forgave her.

Manuel was serving up oven-fried okra topped with cornmeal, Cajun red beans and rice, sweet potato biscuits, and okra chickpea gumbo. There was a neat row of blackberry cobblers lined up on the serving counter as well, beckoning. The scent alone was enough to inspire, and before long every guest in the building had found their way down to get a serving. The tavern filled with the happy chatter of well-fed guests.

I was helping myself to a second serving of the gumbo when Sam Clemens found me. He was holding a plate of cobbler in one hand and a beer in the other. He eyed the vacant stool next to me. "Mind if I join you?"

"Make yourself at home."

He deposited his cobbler on the bar and climbed aboard the stool. "What has the stalwart sleuth learned today? Bringing villains to heel by sundown no doubt."

"Hardly," I said. "But the night is young. Bad guys have plenty of playtime left."

"Forging back into the night then?"

"Right after I steal your cobbler."

"You wouldn't dare." He scooped it up and held it out of reach. He maintained a dramatic pause, then returned it to the bar top and slid it my way. "Have it. It's actually my third. I snuck into the kitchen while Señor Manuel was prepping and insisted on being his assistant. He talked me out of my interference with pastry."

"Your tactics are masterful."

"And what of your day, intrepid detective? What is the nature of your case?"

I plucked the dahlia coin from my pocket and laid it on the bar. "This was the spark. A synth left it to me and got bisected twenty minutes later. I've met a few people along the way. Some weirdos, some robots, and some scumbags. Your guess is as good as mine where the story ends."

Clemens reached for the coin. I reached for the blackberry cobbler.

"What significance does it have?"

"Not sure yet. Corporation that owned the synth hired me to investigate some issues they've been having. Lost parts and apparently there's a hacker who may have sabotaged their operating systems. I suspect the real assignment might be getting me out of their way."

"Why not simply buy you off?"

"I suspect she knew I wouldn't go for it."

"A noble bloodhound with nose to the ground, not easily deterred from the scent."

"Hardly give myself that much credit. But I don't like unfinished business. Synth that left me that coin tried to hire me. Claimed he needed protection. I turned him down."

"Now you're burdened with a guilty conscience? I was under the impression these synthetic people were nothing more than automatons, casings of wire and vacuum tubes. Nothing approaching true consciousness."

"Afraid the technology has advanced considerably from your day. Lines are getting blurry. Can't speak to what makes a consciousness though. Beyond my pay grade."

Molly the collie had made her way to Sam's stool and he took a turn petting her as he continued. "I've spent many an afternoon in the workshop of my friend Nikola Tesla. I trust you've heard of him?"

My mouthful of cobbler precluded speaking but I nodded.

"Nikola often spoke of an electrical future for mankind, our very thoughts guided by electric impulses. Perhaps he was more right than I conceded."

"In my experience, the things guiding people's impulses are less elegant. Money, sometimes sex. Sometimes power, reputation. The usual vices. When I get to the bottom of this one, I'm betting it'll still be that way."

"No room for love or chivalry?"

I put my fork down. "As far as I'm concerned, if you want to design an advanced intelligence, human beings have always been a poor template."

"There are some fine specimens of the species still about."

I noticed he was looking at Heavens as he said it.

Hard to argue there.

The ice in my rag had melted but I used the damp cloth to wipe my mouth. "Thanks for the cobbler Mr. Twain, but I'd better breeze."

"Happy hunting, Mr. Travers. I look forward to learning of your tale's denouement."

Heavens gave me a smile and a wave on my way out the door. It made my insides warmer than the cobbler had.

Back outside I summoned the Boss. Waldo had Scandroid playing on the sound system when I climbed in. Some days I wondered if he thought in synth-wave music. The current song was something edgy and hopeless but it helped me settle into the darkness.

"Downtown, Waldo. The Midnight Club."

Waldo's only reply was to turn up the volume on the speakers. We drove.

CHAPTER 18

The Midnight Club billed itself as a music venue that featured everything from neo disco punk to retro jazz. Its profile on the metaspace was understated. No free nacho monsters for the tourists to slay. I'd been in the area before, but I parked the Boss and walked around the place for good measure. I took in the neighboring bars, and located a loading door in the back alley. No one was hanging around and it was too early to hope a drunk might stagger out the back and let me in so I stashed my gun in the Boss's glove box and wandered to the front of the club again.

I'd double-checked my case notes and confirmed why the club's name had rung a bell with me. It was the same club that had reported an issue with a synth in Brockhurst's records. She was the distraught redhead I'd seen on video in the repair lab—the one Rudy had described as a dancer. The fact that Dagger had pointed me to the same place seemed unlikely to be a coincidence. I didn't know exactly what I was looking for, but I knew I had to look.

There was a cover charge at the door and a metal detector. I swiped my phone and paid the cover, got a nod from the bouncer. He had the look of an off-duty cop. Probably had kids in college to pay for.

These wireless music bars had been all the rage ten years ago. Each room with a different band, strumming or drumming away behind a wall of soundproof glass. There was a channel posted on the glass and also an augmented reality version in the metaspace. If you wanted to hear that band, you tuned your earpiece to the channel.

Nowadays meta venues like this had waned in popularity. Most of the crowd was holographic, house avatars dancing around to make the place look busy or transplanted metaspace avatars from people rocking out in their living rooms and projecting themselves in for entertainment credits.

The room I'd entered was designed for something screamy and angry. Some of the virtual clientele had started a mosh pit near the front and the band window was even flecked with digital sweat. I appreciated that the meta avatars at least lacked the body odor of their real world counterparts.

I wandered into the next room and found it more to my taste. Looked like the band was still on the indie rock spectrum but no one was trying to give themselves a concussion about it. I put my meta lenses on and found the audio controls to try them out in my earpiece. Turns out they had an upbeat vaguely British punk vibe, not unlike The Ramones or The Struts. The drummer was a synth. She was good. I left the sound on as I loitered around.

There were twenty or thirty real humans in the room and again as many avatars. I shooed a house hologram off a stool so I could sit down. So far no one had wandered up and volunteered that they were specialty coin counterfeiters eager to chat. Maybe they were shy.

I ordered a twelve-dollar beer at the bar and swiped my phone to pay for it. It automatically took a three-buck tip. Drink prices were a downside of this decade but it was Diana King's money. She could afford it. I was hoping she could also afford a little information. I reached into my pocket and pulled out another ten in cash, then held it where the bartender could see it. He had forearms the size of car mufflers. Must have eaten his spinach today.

"Looking for somebody around here who knows something about coin engraving."

The bartender sniffed once. "Look like I care?" He wandered off.

I turned to the avatar girl next to me at the bar. "The service really goes downhill with that auto-tipper, doesn't it?"

She looked me up and down once and went back to ignoring me. Here I thought I was fascinating. Maybe it was because she was about eighteen and trying to look twelve. My charms are wasted on the young.

I took my beer to the next music room. By the time I made it to the bar there, my beer bottle was empty. Must've had a hole in it. I ordered another from the bartender when she made it around to me. She was wearing purple eyeshadow that matched her push-up bra, most of which was visible under her loose-fitting tank top. I paid for my beer and held up a twenty this time. "Know if you've had any unusual shipments lately?"

"Don't see too many guys flashing cash. You have any idea where that's been?"

"My pocket most recently."

"Paper money has more germs than a toilet. Can hold pathogens for over two weeks. You might as well stick your fingers up your butt. It's also seventy percent likely to contain traces of cocaine."

I folded the twenty back up and returned it to my wallet. I took my phone back out instead. "So what's your preferred method of payment for helpful information?"

"Phones are actually ten times dirtier than a toilet on average," she said.

I slumped against the bar. "So maybe you should just tell me what I want to know since I'm doomed anyway. It'll be an act of mercy."

She smirked. "Try the jazz room. Anything we get in comes through the loading door back there." She tossed me a damp rag. "Here."

I wiped my hands on it.

"You want to guess how many germs are on that?"

"I really don't." I tossed it back.

She winked at me. I wondered what other dirty things she thought about at night.

Now that I was sure to be dying of the plague anyway, I felt better about my drinking pace. I put away another half a beer by the time I located the jazz room.

It was a thinner crowd, tables spread out and quieter conversations going on. A heavyset bald guy in a pinstriped suit was working magic with an upright bass while a thin white dude with a saxophone accompanied him. It was a pity that no one was paying attention to the music. The bartender was mixing something with gin and blackberries. He was a handsome black guy wearing a tailored vest. He flashed an easy smile as I walked up.

"Ready for another?" He nodded toward my beer.

"How about one of whatever that is?" I gestured to the drink he was making and slid onto a stool.

"Coming right up. You have a preference on gin?"

"Nope. I'm here looking to find someone."

"We're all looking to find somebody, baby."

"Person I'm looking for ordered a specialty engraver from a guy named Dagger and had it dropped here. Maybe they work here. Maybe a regular? Any idea who I'm talking about?"

"All I know is good drinks and good music, my friend. Speaking of, you'll want to catch these cats."

I turned toward the stage where the saxophonist was busting into a solo.

The bartender finished up the drink for his previous customer and by the time he was done making mine I was ready to trade him my empty beer bottle. He slid the gin drink over on a coaster. "I'm Jaden. You need anything, I'm your man." He pointed a finger gun at me before moving off to help the next customer.

I scanned the room and noticed someone in the back corner I was pretty sure hadn't been there when I walked in. It was murky in the back so I couldn't make out too many details but I had a distinct feeling they were watching me. I took a sip of my cocktail. It was damned good.

I found the right channel for the band with my phone, then scanned the rest of the room. Roughly a quarter of the tables had actual humans at them. Some smoked electric blunts. I could smell the synthetic weed. When I pivoted on my stool again, Corner Lurker was still looking my way. Made me wonder what I'd done lately to attract attention. Barging in on Dagger and roughing up Flex-o-saurus Rex might have done it. I could imagine word of that might have filtered through by now. They might know to expect me here. Question was, who would care?

I slipped on my meta lenses and zoomed, then turned back to the corner. The guy's face resolved into something worth seeing. And I recognized him. It was Diana King's kid, Charles.

Hell. I wouldn't have pegged him as a jazz fan. Didn't seem the type to be associating with Dagger either. Was he following me?

He got up and walked my way. Looked like I'd get to ask him. "Mister Travers."

I swiveled ever so slightly toward Charles to square up with him. His face displayed a goofy smile. Maybe he'd been drinking too. "What are you doing here? You like this place?"

"Good to see you again, Charles. Quite the coincidence. Twice in one day."

"You aren't going to tell my mother, are you? I come down to the bar district virtually most nights, but in-person has something you can't duplicate, don't you think?"

"It'd better for what the drinks cost."

"Find anything interesting yet? About our case?"

"You checking up on me?"

"Of course not."

"I don't believe you."

He gave me a grin. "Okay, you got me. Your company access credentials come with location tracking. You didn't know?"

I glanced at my phone sitting on the bar top. The program had to be stealthy if Waldo hadn't flagged it.

"I was curious," Charles said. "And I'll admit that trailing a detective around seemed more interesting than staying in tonight. What you said on the train had me thinking. You said you'd catch our culprit because they'd make a mistake. Because they're only human."

"That's right."

"Does that mean you think all humans are flawed?"

"I just know that whoever is going around carving up synths has already made mistakes. I just have to follow the trail."

"What if you take the wrong path? Misread the clues."

"I won't."

"You're human. That makes you fallible too, wouldn't you say?"

"But I'm relentless. And I have time on my side." I took another sip of my drink.

Charles regarded me with his hands on his hips. "With the launch coming up, I don't see how you do."

I shrugged. "Things aren't always what they seem."

Charles furrowed his brow. "Well, I guess we'll see. I'll stop checking up on you and let you do your job."

"Doesn't bother me either way."

"I'd appreciate it if you wouldn't tell my mother I've been following you. I don't think she'd approve."

I mimed zipping my lips and throwing away the key.

Charles gestured to the bartender and scanned something on the bar's pay port. "His drinks are on me." The tip he entered was more than the bill.

"Thanks," I said. I'd planned to pay with his mother's money anyway but it was a nice gesture.

Charles put away his pay fob. "What brought you here tonight? Something specific?"

"Not sure yet. Resolutions aren't always straight lines. Sometimes you just have to poke around in the dark till something wriggles."

"Seems inefficient."

I took another drink. Gave another shrug.

"I think you might be right about my career choices," Charles mused. "I should probably steer away from detective work."

Wasn't going to get an argument from me.

He shoved his hands in his pockets as he walked away.

I finished my drink and ordered another. While I waited, I scanned the bar and thought about what I'd told Charles. One thing was certain. I was going to need time on my side because so far this stop had been a dead end.

CHAPTER 19

Other than the steady burn of alcohol, the lures of the jazz room had dimmed for me. I'd spotted zero violent synth dancers, and no one I'd asked knew a thing about any coins, counterfeit or otherwise. I had developed a good buzz. That was my only win for the night.

I was about to get up and leave when someone new walked on stage. She caught my attention, not just because of the crimson halter dress and high heels. It was her blue-purple hair. And because I knew her. The young woman wrapped the fingers of both hands around the old-school microphone stand. I pushed my meta lenses to the top of my head.

Wilder.

I hadn't expected to see her here, but I really wasn't expecting the song that came out of her. This might be the same woman I'd found yelling at old ladies on the sidewalk, but now her voice was sultry and low, seducing the audience with every syllable. I found myself leaning forward on my stool.

The song was something classic that I vaguely recognized but couldn't name. I'm sure Waldo could have posted the name for me or I could have found it in the metaspace, but that would have involved a division of attention I wasn't willing to employ.

Wilder's voice was making love to the room and I wasn't going to miss a minute of it.

Partway through the song she spotted me. Her lips quirked into a smile and she held my gaze for several long seconds. This wasn't the laughing jest of the girl I'd met on the apartment steps, she was dressed up and all woman. Her voice was confident, smooth, and playful. Nora Jones eat your heart out.

I sat through the rest of the set in a state of enchantment. Jaden brought me another drink a couple songs in. Wilder continued to look my way throughout the set like she was serenading only me. By the time the last song started, I was deep in the glow of alcohol and fascination.

The recollection that I'd come for another purpose wandered back into my consciousness but seemed irrelevant now. I rotated on my stool and scanned the room to see if everyone was as absorbed with the show as I was. I was surprised to find that only the house holograms were even pretending to listen.

Tough crowd.

When the set finished, it was like someone dimming a light in the room.

Without my meta lenses on, the place seemed lonely. A few sad sacks sat about the place with glazed-over looks on their faces, perceptor chips firing holo-images of somewhere else directly into their brains. A few old-school holo-projections swayed to the house music now filling the gap between live sets. The dudes with the bass and the saxophone were packing up.

But then there she was. Wilder walked from the backstage door with a brilliance around her. Maybe it was the way the lights played tricks with the colors of her hair. She made straight for me, a jacket draped over one arm. I stood.

"You following me?" she asked.

"I will be now. That was a hell of a show."

Her eyelashes had to be an inch long. If any bad intentions were hidden beneath them, I was ready to go looking.

"Been a while since I've had a guy just stare the whole show. You ought to get with the times. Don't you know distraction and disinterest are all the rage?"

"You don't look away from a revelation."

The color rose in her cheeks and she temporarily hid beneath those lashes. But when she met my eye again I saw that same boldness she'd evoked on stage. "What now, cowboy? You just here to flatter me?"

"You have another set?"

"Nope. I'm only ensemble for the opening act."

"You'll be hard to top." I swiped my phone over the pay port in the bar and overtipped Jaden again for the hell of it. "Let's get out of here," I said and held out my arm.

Wilder considered my extended arm as if I were an alien, but then her skepticism faded. "All right."

She took my arm, her fingers wrapping cautiously around my wrist. I floated out to the lobby on my own personal cloud. I made sure not to wobble. I helped Wilder into her coat at the door.

Outside, the night air was chilled and bit at my face but I felt warm all the way through.

She paused on the sidewalk and took out her phone. Then she took a picture of me with it before firing off a message to someone.

"Bragging?" I asked.

"In case I end up murdered. The police will have someone to pin it on."

I shrugged. "Fair."

She put away her phone. "Look, I should tell you up front, if you want to grab a drink or something that's fine. But I'm not looking for a hookup. I just met you and I've got work in the morning."

"No agenda. Scout's honor."

She studied my face and seemed to reach some kind of decision in the process. "These godawful fuck-me pumps they have me wearing on stage are hell to walk in. You mind if I change first? My place is close."

"Lead on."

She did, leaning on my arm as we went. We weren't far from my office and where I'd first encountered her. But we turned south and the blocks we traversed next were off the main streets. Sidewalks were littered with old furniture and a few cars were abandoned on the street. Wilder walked with a haste and determination that must have come from repetition. Did she do this walk alone most nights?

I caught a faint whiff of exhaust smoke and it pulled my attention from Wilder.

A silver El Camino was rolling along a half block down, nearly invisible in the shadows, but the sound of a reciprocating engine is distinctive in a world gone electric. It pulled into a parking space. The headlights flicked off but no one got out.

A few of the other ancient wrecks on the street were pre-electric too. The neighborhood was lagging behind the times. The El Camino driver could be running the engine to keep himself warm for all I knew. Maybe.

Wilder stopped in front of an apartment building with barred windows and an iron gate. "I'm going to let you wait inside but only because you're likely to be kidnapped if I leave you out here."

"Do whatever makes you comfortable."

"The fact that I've got a gun and can shoot you if you get handsy makes me comfortable," Wilder said, rummaging in her purse.

"My kind of girl," I replied.

She unlocked the door and I held it for her. Just before going inside, I took one last look at the El Camino.

It didn't blink.

But neither did I.

I climbed the stairs.

CHAPTER 20

The inside of Wilder's apartment was cramped but neat. The stairs had squeaked on the way up, the door had three locks on it, and the hallway she shared with the other flats smelled of mothballs, but once inside, the space was charming.

The apartment had a tidy galley kitchen, single bathroom and presumably a bedroom hidden behind a doorway decorated with hanging strands of beads. The living area was small but made considerably smaller by the fact that the majority of the room was taken up by a baby grand piano.

"You play that?" I asked, as she bolted the door behind me.

"Just a little," she said. "Came with the apartment. Previous tenant died and no one wanted to pay to move it. I actually got the place at a discount on account of the fact that there's no room for a couch."

"Beats someone taking it apart with an axe, I guess. Looks like it has history."

"It's still in tune, but don't ask me to play," she said. "Make yourself a drink if you want while you wait. There's a few options in the cupboard over the fridge."

She shrugged out of her jacket and laid it over the back of the one armchair that fit in the living room, then took her handbag and headed for the bedroom.

I wandered into the kitchen in search of the drink she mentioned. Waldo would claim I was already drunk based on my current blood-alcohol level but I knew better. AI can be relied on for a lot of things. Monitoring your good time is not one of them.

The kitchen was clean. Dishes sat drying in a rack near the sink. One bowl. One cup. One spoon. There was an extra door off the hallway that looked like it might lead to a second bedroom, but if Wilder had a roommate, one of them didn't eat much.

I located a quarter of a bottle of rye whiskey in the cupboard and searched the others till I found a glass. I settled for a pint glass that looked like it had been lifted from a pub I recognized. The first splash of whiskey I poured looked awfully piddly in the bottom of a pint glass, so I was forced to add a second and some ice. I considered putting away the bottle but then decided it would be rude to not fix my hostess a drink as well. I located another pilfered pint glass and duplicated the process. *Manners maketh man.*

I carried my new provisions back into the living room, as it seemed the only location with available seating. My hands were full and moving Wilder's coat from her own chair seemed forward so I took up residence on the piano bench.

The moment I sat down I was treated to an unwelcome memory of my visit home the previous night. My other self hosting his engagement party, two dozen guests crowded around the piano and fawning over him. It had only been a brief glimpse of his life, but it had left its mark. Professor Travers, accomplished and well-thought-of. Friends enough to fill a condo and a fiancée to keep him warm in bed at night. And me, alone in the apartment of a near stranger.

I took a drink.

What was it he'd been playing? "Joy to the World" by Three

Dog Night I'd bet. Always a crowd pleaser. I set the two pint glasses on the bench next to me and stretched my fingers. How did that go? My fingers found their places on the keys. D-C-G to start. I played the chords, memory flooding back with the music. Teenage memories from before the split. Hours spent practicing. Thinking it would be a skill my life would make use of.

Not anymore.

My fingers fell to my lap. I found my drink. Sipped.

But the keys were still there. I stretched for them again, fingers spreading. This time finding their places differently. A different song for a different time. A sadder song.

I played. And this time I didn't stop.

The keys moved under my fingertips without strain. Maybe it was the state of my mind. Maybe I only thought this was how the song went, but it all came back. Melancholy verse after verse. The lyrics were only in my head, maybe not even consciously. I played the entire song. Four and a half minutes that took me out of the apartment, out of my day. Out of my life.

It was only when my fingers stopped moving and the last note faded that I realized I wasn't alone in the room. Wilder was standing close behind me, one hand pressed to her lips. She'd changed out of her dress and into leggings. A sweatshirt hung off one shoulder. Her hair was down.

"Are you kidding me right now?" she asked. Her voice was barely a whisper. "What was that?"

"Old song. "The Luckiest." Guy named Ben Folds wrote it. Just something I picked up."

She sank onto the bench next to me. She smelled good. Something citrusy. She was staring at me. Bright eyes searching. "I don't get you at all. All day I'm out there. Nobody gives a damn about anybody. People are the fucking worst. I find you getting beat up on the street yesterday and then you come into my living room and play this beautiful song and what the hell is with that? With you."

I shrugged. "I'm nobody worth worrying over."

"Like hell. I see nobodies all day. People so far gone they couldn't find themselves if they tried. Not that they would. Seems like nobody cares about anything anymore, let alone music like this. You were there tonight at the club. How many people do you think even looked at me in the time I was on stage?"

I shrugged.

"One. That's how many."

"Why bother then?"

Wilder stared at our reflection in the window. "The usual reasons. Making rent. But also because I don't do it for them. I do it for me. Sometimes I feel like if I pretend that I'm in another time, I can make it through the day easier. When I sing those old songs, this place doesn't own me."

"I get that." The playing had relaxed me, brought my energy down a notch, but smoothed out something—a rough edge of tension I hadn't noticed until it was gone. My words came slower. "Sometimes you just have to get something out of you. Let it go so there's room to breathe. Maybe I should play more often. It's been a long time."

Wilder was close. Whatever tension had vanished from within me was replaced by the almost audible hum in the space between our two bodies.

I picked up the drink I'd made her. Offered it to her. She acted like she didn't see it. She was only looking at my face. I held her gaze.

"Damn you," she muttered. "You're for real, aren't you? Even like this. This isn't some stunt you pull to get with girls. You felt all of that. I can tell."

"It was just a sad old song on the piano."

"Shut up already," she said, and she kissed me.

Her lips pressed to my mouth gently at first, then harder, and my own lips tingled beneath hers. It was electric. The feel of her. The heat of her mouth and the way her skin tasted. She opened her eyes again just enough to see that I was still holding the pint glass in my hand. She took it from me and dropped it directly on the rug. Then she was back, both of her hands pressed to the sides of my neck and her mouth pushing against mine. Her eyes stayed open for a long second, staring. In another circumstance it would have been unnerving, but I knew what she was feeling. She just had to see, see that this was real.

I recognized it. How long had it been since I'd felt this? That chemical reaction when complementary elements meet. It burned away the inconsequential, sharpened the senses, leaving room for nothing else.

I wrapped my arm around her waist. She turned into me until I felt the swell of her breast pressed to my chest. Her breath quickened. Mine too.

I didn't know this woman. She didn't know me. Not enough. But our bodies were in tune, puzzle pieces finding each other easily, naturally.

Her fingers brushed my cheek. Her breath was sweet. She pressed her forehead against mine and bit her lip. "Come with me." She rose, taking my hand, pulling me upward from the bench. She led the way, towing me past the kitchen and through the inconsequential barrier of the beaded doorway. Her bedroom was the kind of cluttered that made it cozy, not messy. I was immediately struck by the fact that nothing in here was digital. Not a smart surface to be found. There wasn't much for furniture. A dresser, a bureau, one chair, a full-size bed.

She peeled my jacket from my shoulders, then immediately took to the buttons on my shirt. She stripped that from me and tossed it to the floor.

"I'm willing to slow this down," I said.

"Don't you dare," she replied. She pulled her sweatshirt over her head revealing small, shapely breasts.

We stood like that for a while, just looking.

Her fingers traced the edges of the bruise on my ribs that had formed after Ted had kicked me. She ran her hands over the muscles of my chest and out to my shoulders, tracing the outline of me. My hands found her waist. I worked my palms up her sides till my thumbs just cupped the undersides of her breasts, stroked her bare skin. She felt warm and vital. She put her hands to my face and stared at me some more. "Where did you come from?"

I reached for her, pulled her to me, kissed her. Then I bent and placed my hands firmly beneath her buttocks. I lifted her until her legs wrapped around my waist. I carried her the few feet to the bed that way, then thrust her onto it, less gently than I'd intended. I kicked out of my boots and unbuckled my belt while she squirmed on the bed, extricating herself from her leggings. When I'd shed the last of my clothes, I climbed onto the bed and was met eagerly.

She left the lights on.

CHAPTER 21

I laid on Wilder's bed, watching the ceiling fan turn while it cooled the glistening sweat from our bodies. We were still naked, one of her legs draped between mine. Her fingertips played with the hair on my chest.

"I have a confession to make."

"Your next words better not be anything about it being your first time," I said.

"Please. If my first time had been anything like this I'd have an entirely different view of piano players." She pressed her lips to my shoulder and her teeth brushed my skin, almost as if she were going to bite me. But she lifted her head instead and tossed her hair from her eyes. "Before I heard you playing that song, I was going to tell you to go home. I'd decided I was tired and didn't want to go back out. I was about to send you packing."

"Glad you found your energy."

She traced the line of my collarbone with a fingertip. "This isn't like me. Might not be anywhere close to my first time but it's been a while. Longer than I should probably admit."

"Been a while for me too." If I wanted to get technical, I could tell her the last time I'd slept with someone had been sixty years in the past, but that would overcomplicate the conversation.

"You seem like you aren't from around here. Like you're seeing everything with fresh eyes. How do you do that?"

"And you make it sound like you've lost hope in humanity."

"Pretty accurate. You haven't?"

I considered the fan some more. "I guess I don't see it that way. People are what they are. It's not my job to change them."

"What is your job?"

"I'm a private detective."

She pushed herself upright to an elbow.

"Don't worry. You're not under investigation."

Her shoulders relaxed and she smiled. "Why would I be?" She ran her fingers over my stomach. She traced the perimeter of the bruise at my ribs. "Those guys who beat you up yesterday. They part of your investigation?"

"Not really. Maybe. I don't really know."

"Who are you investigating then?"

I interlaced my fingers behind my head. "Can't say."

"You're no fun." Her fingers trailed farther down my stomach. "Is it something to do with that synth you were looking for? Johnny?"

"Yeah, something to do with that."

Wilder nodded. Her hand wandered down my hip. "I've heard rumors about other synths getting killed in this neighborhood lately. You have any idea who's doing it?"

"No. Could be anyone."

"Doesn't sound like you've done much detecting. You claim to be good at your job?"

I smirked at her. "I just do it for the girls."

"Oh yeah?" Her hand came back up between my legs and squeezed.

I reached quickly for her arm. "Don't go breaking any company equipment. It's all highly sensitive."

She leaned forward and brushed her lips against mine again.

We kissed. A long slow kiss. She ran her hands up to my neck again, then pulled her lips away. "You think you'll catch whoever did it? The one who killed that synth?"

"Yeah. I think I will."

She laid her head on my chest. "That's good. I think you should."

We laid like that for a while. After a few minutes she sat up.

Her blue and purple hair was a tangle but she looked beautiful. I reached for her but she was on the move. She crawled off of me and found her panties on the floor, pulling herself into them.

She then pushed through the curtain of beads back to the kitchen.

I slid to the edge of the bed slowly, donned my boxers and stood. My buzz had worn off and my head was fuzzy.

I found Wilder near the kitchen sink pouring herself a glass of water. She drank half of it, then offered it to me. I took it.

"You should probably get going. I have to work early."

"Doing what?" I downed the water and refilled it from the tap again.

"Work stuff."

She didn't feel like sharing. Fine. I wasn't going to push her. I sipped some more water.

"You like what you do? Investigating people?" she asked.

"Sometimes. But the kinds of people I look into usually aren't nice people. Cheating spouses. Miscreants. Criminals. It leaves a bad taste in your mouth."

"You ever wake up in the morning feeling you're living the wrong life?"

"Every day." I brushed a knuckle across my lip to catch a drip of water from the corner of my mouth.

"What do you do about it?"

"I keep moving. I do the work."

"Must be nice to feel like you can still outrun it. I used to feel that way. Running gets lonely though, doesn't it?"

It did. But I didn't say so. I just took another drink. She was digging at things in me I hadn't looked at in a while. Wasn't sure I wanted to. Not tonight anyway.

"Thanks for the water," I said.

It wrecked the mood. I sensed her closing up without her having to say a word. It was in her eyes. Getting vulnerable only works as a team sport. When you've sustained a lot of bruises, it pays to develop a hard shell and hers was going back up.

Way to go, Greyson.

Wilder walked back into the bedroom and came out twenty seconds later wearing a tank top and holding my things. I set the water glass in the sink and met her halfway.

"My cue, I take it."

She had my pants draped over one arm and as she handed them to me, the silver dahlia coin fell out of one of the pockets. It landed flat on the floor. "Sorry." She stooped to pick it up.

She studied the coin as I put on my pants. "Where'd you get this?"

"You ever see one of those before?" I asked.

She was running a thumb over the face on the coin. "You know who she is?"

"Bit of a mystery. Best I can tell she worked for United Machine a few years ago."

"You know her name?"

"Yeah. Something Nash. Terra, I think." I finished buckling my belt.

"She's beautiful, isn't she." Wilder held the coin up next to her face, turning her head to match. "Think I look like her?"

I smiled. "Sure."

Wilder handed me the coin. "You going to call me?"

"You haven't given me your number." I slid into my boots, then knelt on one knee to lace them.

"Maybe I should leave you wanting more. Supposed to go out on a high note, right?" She perched her hands on her hips.

Her voice was cool and collected. The posture too. But I still saw the vulnerability behind her eyes.

When I stood back up, I fished in my wallet and found one of my business cards. "Ball's in your court. You'll have my number." I handed it to her. "I had a good time tonight. If you'd asked me to stay I would've."

"You trying to reinvestigate my privates, private investigator?"

I shrugged into my shirt and began to button it. "You make light of things same as I do. Keeping it simple, right?"

Wilder shrugged. "I guess we'll see."

I eased toward the door. I paused next to Wilder and put a hand to her face. I leaned down and kissed her one more time. Something in her softened beneath my lips. When I stood to my full height again, she kept her eyes closed an extra second and sighed. "Goodnight, Greyson."

I left.

The stairs to ground level seemed steeper on the way down, like I could lose my footing and just keep falling. It was only when I was back outside in the night air that I found my balance again.

The lights in the sky could almost be mistaken as stars, but they were much too close. Too bright. The lights of the Skylift. No glimpse of heaven, just the facsimile.

I slid my jacket back on and walked a couple blocks to clear my head.

This sort of thing was never a plan. Wilder wasn't a girl I'd go looking for. But sometimes meteors collide. Sometimes it made a good show.

Sometimes it was nothing but destruction.

Time would tell.

I was three blocks from Wilder's and making my way across the street when I noted the rumble of a motor. The same silver El Camino I'd spotted before was pulling up the block behind me. I hadn't passed it, but it was there now.

I turned in the middle of the road, staring into the darkness of the interior. The headlights flipped on, blinding me. Then the car surged into motion and I was just able to get clear before it skidded to a stop a few feet beyond me. Both doors flew open and a pair of figures rushed out either side.

They were on me before I could even think to run.

Fast.

Really fast.

I reached instinctively for my gun. It wasn't there. I'd left it in the Boss.

The first guy barreled into me hard but I was able to spin and deflect him, keeping my feet. Second guy caught me with a right hook and I immediately hit the ground in an explosion of stars.

Guy punched like Ivan Drago. I shook my head and found the dudes rummaging in my pockets. I kicked one of them, bought myself a little space, and scrambled to my feet. I was grabbed and shoved bodily against the side of the El Camino. I got a better look at the guy who'd first come at me. Looked a little like Marlon Brando in his later years. He swung. I ducked and put two hard punches into his gut. Felt like hitting a sack of cement. Didn't move him. Guy two grabbed my arm and wrenched me around. "Just stay put," he hissed, grasping me around the neck.

I kneed him in the groin.

He didn't even blink.

It was only the roar of an engine that took his attention away from crushing my windpipe.

Headlights tore round the corner and a car the color of Satan's soul came raging down the street.

I broke my captor's grip and spun away, dashing around the back of the El Camino before the Boss tore through. Dude number one went up over the hood of the Mustang, ricocheting off the windshield and getting flung headlong into the back of the El Camino.

Dude two had managed to dodge the attack from the Boss but was now on the opposite side from me.

I lunged for the driver's side of my car, flung the door open and scrambled across the center console to get to the glove box. I had my Stinger in my hand and was back out in what felt like seconds, but I was too slow. By the time I had my gun leveled, the tires on the El Camino were screaming and the car was rocketing away.

I tried to catch the car's details, but the license plate was unlit. The car squealed around the next corner and disappeared.

I slumped against the side of the Boss and lowered my gun.

"Do you require medical attention?" Waldo asked from the car's speaker system.

I groaned and climbed into the driver's seat. I closed the door and put my head back against the headrest.

"Rose 'n Bridge."

The car started rolling. I only glanced in the rear-view mirror once. Maybe I should've gone after the El Camino, but I was too tired.

At least they hadn't gotten what they wanted. I pulled my right boot off and turned it over. The dahlia coin slipped out and landed in my palm.

I clenched it in my fist.

CHAPTER 22

Morning came too fast. I woke with the sun, my mind too preoccupied to sleep any later. I downed two glasses of tap water from the sink in my room, ignored the fresh bruises on my face and located my running shoes.

My body needed exercise, but so did my mind. Last night seemed like it had happened to another person. Some alternate timeline.

I thought I'd slipped into the hallway quietly, but I'd just started down the hall when a door opened behind me. Heavens Archer stuck her head out of her doorway. Barely awake but somehow still a vision.

"Hey. Didn't see you come in last night."

"Out late," I said.

She looked me up and down, eyes lingering on my jaw for only a moment, then stared at my sneakers. "If you give me five minutes I'll run with you."

"Take ten. I'll meet you downstairs."

She found me near the front door seven minutes later.

I was busy sniffing around the pub doors, but Manuel hadn't put the coffee on yet. Something to look forward to on the run back.

Heavens wore a silver running tank over a sports bra, and a moisture-wicking jacket. Black HeatPro leggings hugged her thighs. Her shoes looked high-tech too. Her laces matched her top. She was busy tying her hair up in a ponytail. I didn't leer at the outfit but there was plenty to look at and be enthralled. I decided to focus on retying my Nikes.

"You okay?" she asked.

"Yep."

She nodded. "How far do you want to run?"

With her in front of me I'd run all day.

"What's your usual?" I asked.

"Five miles okay?" She checked some manner of fitness tracker on her wrist.

"Sure. Let's do that." I knew I'd be gasping after three but I'd be sure to do it in a manly, virile way.

We set off. The area around the Rose 'n Bridge was hilly, immediately testing my resolve. But having Heavens bounding along beside me kept me focused. She ran like a gazelle. I had all the grace of a bow legged tortoise, but warmed up to perhaps the coordination of a three-legged dog.

"We got another visit from Ted Baker last night while you were out," Heavens said, once we had found our stride.

"Give you any trouble?"

"Yep. Shortened our visit. ASCOTT put out a mandate that all time travelers need to be out of this timestream by eight PM."

"Shit. Tonight?"

"Something about events having *pivotal historical status.*"

"They think your inn full of time tourists is out to alter history?"

"I can never tell what they think. We originally had a permit to be here all week. Now we don't. Something has to have changed that made them alter it."

"They're making you get out before the Skylift launch tomorrow."

"It's the whole reason most of these tourists wanted to come in the first place. It's like taking them to Stratford-Upon-Avon in 1599 and not letting them see Shakespeare at the Globe. I can't help but think there is something else going on. Something they're not telling us. I think I might call the agency."

"You plan to make a complaint?"

"Not a complaint. I just want to know the real story. Not all the agents at Time Crimes are like Ted."

"Try Stella York," I panted. "She might help."

"That's exactly who I was thinking of," Heavens said.

I was tempted to ask how she knew Agent York but figured if she wanted to tell me she would. And after a minute it was clear she didn't. But it was enough to know we'd both met the agent and come to the same conclusion about her.

We turned out of the development and onto the main road. An auto car passed but its passengers were invisible, every window a smart surface transporting them elsewhere.

They were missing a good view.

Heavens kept a quick pace. I was forced to focus on my breathing.

"Ted's curfew only gives you today to wrap up this case of yours," she said. "He finds you still around after curfew . . ." she trailed off, but I knew where it was going.

Ted and his goons would relish the opportunity to arrest me for trespassing in restricted timespace. I could practically picture the glee on his pudgy face.

"I'm used to working fast. He give you any indication what he's up to today?" I asked. "I need to make a few moves in time and it would be nice to keep him out of my hair."

"I can try to keep him busy if you need me to."

"No need to get involved personally."

"After what you did for me, I owe you one. I can always make a missing shipment claim or something. Try to give him a wild goose he can chase."

"I'd appreciate that. I'm going back two days to when this case started for me. I know where Ted was then, at least for part of his day. If you can give me a clear time to come back to where I'm sure not to run into him, I'd be grateful."

"Done. Easy. But only if you promise to tell me about this case of yours when you get back."

"I doubt you'll find it fascinating."

"I serve drinks to rich time tourists too lazy to get out and actually see the history we're visiting. A little mystery would liven up my day considerably."

With her in the tavern I couldn't blame the guests for their desire to stay in, but I kept that thought to myself.

We finished the five miles without much else in the way of smalltalk, largely because I needed all my breath to keep up.

The tavern guests were awake and stirring by the time we got back. I could smell Manuel's coffee the moment I walked in, but forced myself to hold off until I was at least showered. Heavens walked upstairs with me and we paused at our respective doorways. She tapped at her fitness watch. "I'm going to send you my personal contact link. Connect to it and I can keep you updated on what Ted's up to."

"Thanks. Don't do anything that gets you in trouble with Time Crimes though. Anything gets sticky, I'll take the heat."

"You're not the only one who can handle Ted Baker and his mouth breathers."

"That should be their band name."

Heavens laughed. It was a musical sound that I knew I'd spend much of my day reliving. And if I did nothing else with my day, having caused that laugh already made me feel accomplished.

We retreated into our respective rooms and I was midway through my shower before I realized I hadn't thought once about my previous night while I was with her.

Maybe Wilder was right. No hope for humanity.

Wilder *was* on my mind as I dressed, but primarily because I'd be seeing her again soon. A version of her anyway.

The guys who'd attempted to rob me crossed my mind only when I tried to flex my sore knuckles. Felt like I'd been punching a bag of bricks. I hurt where they hit me too but it was getting difficult to sort the new bruises from the old ones.

Today was a new day. Fresh start. I needed to make it count.

There comes a point in any investigation when I need to get to the bottom of the problems I've rooted out and it usually means going back to the beginning. I'd scratched around enough on the surface of this dead synth case. It was time to go deeper.

I dressed in the only clean clothing item left in my travel bag, a navy-blue shirt I paired with the gray pants I'd been wearing the day before. I donned my jacket and boots and stepped out. I paused near Heavens' door and heard the shower still running. I went downstairs.

The pub was crowded. Perhaps the news of the inn's departure had galvanized the guests into action. Everyone I saw was dressed, ready to go out and take in the sights.

Carpe diem.

But not before a decent breakfast.

Manuel was serving crepes, pancakes, seasoned potatoes and several varieties of grits and oatmeal. There was a quiche of some sort in the mix as well, along with a fruit salad. I helped myself but finished quickly, eager to capitalize on the energy that the morning run with Heavens had inspired.

Waldo chimed in my earpiece, letting me know he had arrived with the car. I met it out front.

The hood now had a dent in the right side from where Waldo

had plowed through my attacker last night. More battle scars. I'd soon need to make friends at a body shop.

Climbing into the Boss was always a sensory experience. It smelled ancient but cared for. Lingering whiffs of a dozen decades were in every fiber of the interior. The car was heavy compared to modern rides, too much steel, too much engine, but it was a density that gave you the feeling you were strapping yourself into a rocket, ready to blast off. They'd made plenty of reproductions. Every thirty years or so someone would invent a new Mustang design, trying to improve on a classic. Sometimes they'd come close. And to be fair, this car was a far cry from the original factory version. There would be no way a hundred-and-thirty-year-old car could exist on the roads here without acquiescing to safety protocols and electric vehicle standards. But it had the best of both times with its gas engine still intact over the electric chassis, and it looked sexy as hell.

Time traveler logic insists you pick something to blend in with your surroundings. But even in its native 1960s, the Boss stood out. It was built for it. And what's the point of having a time traveling car if you can't turn a few heads? I pulled away from the tavern and accessed the time travel controls hidden behind the modified stereo console as I drove.

The suburbs of Port Nyongo drifted by.

"Your nearest safe anchor location is in half a mile," Waldo said.

"Let's see how fast we can make it," I said, flattening the accelerator and letting the Boss surge forward.

The view out the side windows streaked into a blur.

Nearing the half mile mark I deployed the anchor. The car now had a solid spacial ground but also produced a rooster tail of sparks. Doc Brown would be proud.

Waldo initiated the jump and the car raced back in time.

CHAPTER 23

There's nothing wrong with old-fashioned detective work. But if you really want answers, a trip to the past can solve a lot of problems. It was why I was good at my job.

Waldo had cross-referenced a safe jump location using traffic cam recordings and satellite imagery. It was now Thursday, the morning Johnny the Synth walked into my office.

I parked the Boss a few blocks away from my building, took my chronometer and gun from the glove box and posted up outside a kratom bar down the street.

I knew where Johnny the Synth ended up dismembered on the sidewalk. I didn't know how he got there. I had a fifty-fifty chance he'd come out of my office and head my way. So I waited.

The morning was brighter than I remembered. I donned my shades, periodically setting them to binocular mode and watching the passersby. I bought a kratom. Turns out it tasted a lot like dirt, only slightly worse. I tortured myself with three or four sips, thinking it might be an acquired taste. Then I poured it into a bush and tossed the compostable cup in a nearby receptacle. Bleh.

Johnny the Slouchy Synth came around the corner from the west and walked right past me. Sulking. Suspicious.

I tried to look casual. Nothing to see here. Just your average sidewalk-dude hating his beverage selection.

Luckily his attention was focused elsewhere. He scanned the street, getting his bearings. Then he froze. Eyes west. Saw something. I saw them too. Two dudes in meta sunglasses. Enhanced muscles and copious tattoos. They walked to the corner and looked in each direction. Johnny the Synth scurried across the street, dodging traffic. Outside my office he hid behind a column, looked around a few times. The thugs lingered on the corner.

I could sense the fear in the synth. His movements were jerky, like he had too many inputs. He jittered, trembling as the dudes turned and headed his way.

Johnny backed up. He was in the doorway of the only building that gave him any cover. My building.

He read the sign.

He snuck inside.

Well, shit.

He wasn't even a referral. So much for my stellar reputation as a PI driving customers to seek me out. Johnny had stumbled in because he literally had nowhere else to run.

I needed to work on my marketing.

A few ladies in athletic wear wandered past. I practiced looking casual in a manly and mysterious way. None of them came over to compliment me.

Johnny the Synth came bursting out of my building's side door a short while later, looked hastily both ways on Broad Street, then lunged east.

Damn. I chose wrong.

Better try again.

I reached for my wrist and ducked behind the kratom shop, found a spot free of trash and old beer cans. I set the dials on the chronometer for a jump. I used the wall of the building as my anchor point and reappeared in the same spot thirty minutes earlier.

This time I walked north, dodging more of the electric scooters and skaters whizzing about the sidewalk, keeping away from where I would arrive soon with the Boss.

Nearing Revolution Boulevard, I was forced to take it slower. I used the binocular feature on my shades and swept the area ahead. I located the apartment steps where I'd encountered Wilder. She wasn't there yet.

That complicated things. I got out of the way of a three person electric scooter careening toward me and leaned against a building to think.

Where was Wilder? Running into her now would screw up the timeline.

I reversed course and took the long way around, back south of my office. East then north again up the other side. I slipped my earpiece in. "Waldo, I need you on your toes. Keep an eye out for Wilder. See and avoid."

"I have no toes or eyes but I'll do as you request," Waldo replied. "An encounter at this juncture would indeed be calamitous."

"You have the geo-track for my previous movements?"

Waldo projected a map on my lenses that appeared on the landscape ahead of me. It highlighted the areas I'd existed on my first run through this time. My walk from my office, encounter with Wilder, discovery of the dead synth, and subsequent fight with Ted and his TCID cronies.

"Eyes peeled for Time Crimes too," I said.

"Sometimes I wonder if you use these terms simply to irritate me," Waldo said.

"Chin up, Waldo."

"There are days I daydream about alternative employment."

"I'm just busting your balls."

"I know an AI running air traffic control for the New York metro airports. That must be a relaxing assignment."

"You'd miss me too much," I replied.

"That's one possibility," Waldo said. "If you consider the most minute percentages."

"Heads up, buddy. Almost there."

And we were. The block where Johnny the Synth would meet his end. I crossed the street and searched for a good vantage point.

I studied the map on my meta lenses. I knew which way I would come from. I now knew that Johnny the Synth would be coming the other way, headed west. I'd walk from the opposing direction after my encounter with Wilder. I didn't know where Johnny's killer would come from or leave to. Or where Johnny himself was going when he was intercepted. I couldn't rule out the possibility that whoever had dismembered the synth passed right by me afterward. If so, pursuit would be impossible. I couldn't follow for fear of running into myself.

Time travel problems.

The one thing I refused to do was create a paradox.

People often suggest my job is simple. Those people are idiots.

Time travel never simplifies. It always complicates.

So I did the simplest thing I could. What every PI does. I found another concealed spot to watch from and I waited.

Lurking behind a public clothing donation bin, the seconds ticked by and I watched the crowd of pedestrians. Some walked, chatting on calls in the metaspace. Some zipped along on the sidewalks and streets on their electric conveyances. No one looked at me. No one slowed.

Then I saw her. Wilder. She cruised along the sidewalk with hands in her pockets but eyes furtive. Scanning. Searching for someone? I stayed concealed from view. She wasn't hiding.

Didn't need to. No one here paid attention. She passed the spot where I would eventually find the synth, pausing almost on the exact spot, but then she walked on, headed for the next block where I would meet her on the steps of some random apartment.

Who was she looking for?

When she was out of sight, I eased out of concealment again. Watched.

It was only a few minutes later when I saw Johnny. He was moving fast, eyes wide, alert for danger. Same saggy face, his expressions misshapen. He stopped at the corner and scanned the signage. He turned right, moving purposefully. He walked directly past the point I expected to see him accosted. No one attacked him.

Shit.

Did something change?

I did a rapid review of my actions. Had I screwed up the timeline somehow?

But then Johnny froze on the sidewalk. He saw something ahead. I looked the same direction. There were two figures coming down the sidewalk. The big guys with dark shades. The same thugs from outside my office. One had a hand concealed in a pocket. Johnny saw it too. He turned around. Headed the other way.

It happened so fast I almost missed it. A flash. A figure on a scooter. Something struck Johnny in the back. He spasmed, still standing, but he seemed to lose control of his limbs. He stumbled into the wall of the building, reached for a handhold, missed it, and fell.

In the blur of pedestrians on the far sidewalk I momentarily lost sight of the guy on the scooter. But then I saw it leaned against the wall, its rider slinking back. The two thugs jogged up too and stood side by side near the fallen body. They looked up and down the street but kept up a casual conversation. Their wide frames obstructed my view of what was going on behind them. Pedestrians passed by unconcerned. The figure from the scooter was behind them, working on the body of the fallen synth. But I couldn't see a thing.

I spent a frustrating twenty seconds cursing under my breath. Then the two thugs turned. Something exchanged hands. It went into a sack. Thug one tucked it into his jacket. The two men nodded to the third, then moved off. By the time they were out of the way, the butcher was back aboard the scooter. The two big thugs went west. Mr. Scooter zipped off in the opposite direction. Johnny the Synth was left in a puddle of his own fluids.

The world went about its day.

Right.

Time to make a choice.

Scooter guy was the most interesting to me. But as much as I would have loved to follow him, he was headed in a direction I couldn't follow. Toward Wilder. Toward the corner where I'd chat her up for the first time. Toward a catastrophic paradox if I followed.

My decision was made for me. I had to leave before my earlier self showed up anyway, so I tailed the two thugs.

It wasn't difficult. They moved slowly. Unhurried. They didn't look back once. Just another day at the murder office.

My mind turned over what I'd just seen.

Parts harvest made the most sense. These dudes intimidated, ran interference if necessary. The speedy butcher zipped in, took out the victim. Slice and dice. Parts in the bag. No one cared.

Except me. I cared. I figured Johnny the Synth did too.

I followed. Time to see how far down this rabbit hole went.

CHAPTER 24

While I waited with thug one and thug two and their bag of Synth Johnny parts on the Broad Street metro platform, I thought about Wilder. There was something nagging me about the way she'd been walking down the street.

When I'd first met her, I'd assumed the apartment steps I'd encountered her on were hers. Having been to her place now, I knew that wasn't the case. It hadn't occurred to me when I'd been with her, but there was no reason to be there unless she was fond of loitering. Or she was meeting someone.

I'd need to ask her about that.

A strung-out twenty-something guy on the platform was panhandling, going around with a holo-projector patched together from cast-off AR tech. He was powering the rig with some kind of corded battery pack on his hip. With my meta lenses on I could tell he was projecting a virtual billboard. Every time he pointed it at a different person, the message would change. He pointed it toward some businessmen and it read "Invest in the future of you." A couple of times it flashed political messages supporting or bashing various candidates in the upcoming election. Several people pinged him virtual currency, presumably pleased with the messaging. I watched him stop to check his account balance a few times.

He pointed it at me and the projection went blank. He moved on to someone else without missing a step.

I realized after a few minutes that he was running a kind of app that did a fast search through the public facial profiles of passersby and altered the sign to reflect their expressed beliefs. With an app like that, I doubted he'd need to work many hours on the street. Probably already made more money than I did today. Too bad it looked like he'd blow it all on cyber stimulants. He had the hollow eyes and poor hygiene of the perpetually alert.

For some the metaspace offered a world so enticing that human needs like sleep were pushed eternally to the wayside. He'd likely be dead by thirty.

I considered busting up his rig. Forced detox. But I was sure he'd find a way back within minutes. The haze in his corneas was a good indicator that his lenses were implanted. Even closing his eyes wouldn't shut off the feed.

I returned my attention to my goal instead. The train arrived a few minutes later. I waited till the thugs I was following stepped aboard their chosen train car, then got on one car back. They weren't bothering to be evasive. It was easy enough to ride a few stops and hop off when they did.

Storm Water Station.

The riders getting on here were a different breed. Hard faces, blunt shoulders and sharp glances. The air smelled of mistrust and sweat.

The two dudes I was following exited the train and walked south in the tunnel, snubbing the stairs to the surface and following the edge of the track. A fair amount of people took the same route so it wasn't obvious I was tailing them. I kept my distance anyway.

The passage split, and my quarry followed an abandoned

tunnel through to the underground market. I'd been here before but it had been a while. This was technically still Port Nyongo but not anywhere you'd find a city cop.

They called this neighborhood City Cellar. The underground market had the look of a shantytown. Semi-permanent structures sat on stilts to survive tunnel flooding. Beneath them an eclectic mix of humans and transhumans mingled in a neon blur of bodies and AR.

Condensation dripped from poorly-drained air conditioners rigged in plywood shacks. Thick power cables crisscrossed the air, suspended away from the wet concrete and occasionally bangled with flags or lost sneakers.

The din of a hundred chattering voices competed with dueling sound systems from opposing market stalls. Half the browsers were wearing sound-dampening headphones. The merchants seemed determined to make enough racket to render them useless. Holo-projections barked at each other and the pedestrians walking through. The few vehicles down here were battered old-model skids and hoverboards. Everything looked like it used to be something else someplace else.

"You looking for a good time? I got fresh faces!" The shout came from a stall to my left. The crusty proprietor flashed me a quick holo image of a half dozen women and a couple of men in scanty clothes. "Anything you desire, my friend." I'd seen the gimmick before. Transhuman prostitutes with customizable faces. It was expensive tech. Business must be good down here.

A little farther on, a woman snuck up beside me and flashed me a look at her palm. "I got Vision. You need a look?" The pills in her palm seemed to change color as we moved. I elbowed her aside because I noticed the two guys ahead had ducked into a stall.

I cruised past the place once before circling back and

lingering nearby. It was hard to get a read on the location from where I stood. I'd need to get inside.

A stall I was loitering near had a bunch of freezer cases. The woman leaning on the nearest chest freezer had purple arms and pink ears. Her face was still human but just barely. She eyed me suspiciously.

"What you want, cop?"

I pulled out my PI badge and flashed it. "I'm private. Not causing trouble."

She snorted. "Like you could. Down here, you'd be the one in trouble."

"What's in the freezers?"

"Fish sticks."

"No replacement body parts then."

"Never heard of such a thing. I just love me some tilapia."

"What's the rate on a liver these days?"

"Like hypothetically?" She eyed me up. "Bio-synthetic or organic?"

I shrugged.

"Bio-synth last you longer. Twenty-five, fifty years of hard drinking. Don't go organic 'less you one for clean living."

I wagged a hand.

She smirked. "Didn't think so."

"Bio-synth come with a warranty?"

She laughed. It was a nice laugh. "You young. You start swapping now, I get you some good trades."

"I give you a kidney, you give me a kidney, everybody wins?"

"I'm already a winner, baby."

"How about over there?" I indicated the stall the two thugs walked into. "They beat your prices over there?"

She narrowed her eyes, then spat.

"Maybe I go ask, huh?" I added. "What will I find walking in there?"

"Gutter trash. Pig parts. You go there when you want your life over. They deal by contract only."

"Rent-a-organ?"

"Guess what happen when you don't make your payments?"

"Bet the payments are sliding scale, huh?"

She picked up a tin cup and poured herself coffee from a thermos. She tilted the thermos toward me.

"Sure," I said. She fetched another cup.

While she was pouring it, the two guys I'd been following ducked their way back out of the stall in question and headed my way. Quick business. I focused my attention on my new friend, accepted the cup of coffee and sipped it as the two goons walked by. They no longer had the bag of Synth Johnny parts. I let them wander away. The coffee was good.

"Who's the surgeon down here? Can't imagine these kinds of upgrades are covered by my insurance."

My transhuman friend kept up a disinterested gaze at the street.

"We got a doc does things down here regular. Lady surgeon from uptown."

"Interesting. What's in it for her?"

She shrugged. "There's things you can get easy uptown, and there's things you can get easy down here. Mostly they ain't the same things. We got what she needs."

I was guessing she was referring to the copious amounts of illegal substances down here, but it didn't matter.

"This doctor have a name?"

"You sure ask a lot of questions."

"I'm loquacious."

She lit a cigarette, took a drag. Then she pulled a phone from her pocket and found a contact. She showed me the number. "You leave a message. She calls you, you get me?"

I nodded as I entered the number into my phone. "They use the same surgeon over there?" I gestured to the other stall.

She twisted her face up again and blew out a cloud of smoke. "All you're going to find in there is trouble."

Once the thugs I'd followed were well gone, I pulled a card from my wallet and slipped it and a pair of fifties onto the freezer. Then I set the tin cup on top.

"Thanks for the coffee. You got a name?"

She made the card and cash vanish quickly, casting a furtive glance at her neighbors. "I'm Shaina. But you ain't never seen me, honey. I ain't never heard of you neither."

"Liked what I did see though." I winked at her and she cracked a smile.

"You know where to find me, baby."

I headed for the stall the two goons had come out of. I stepped inside.

CHAPTER 25

First impression? I wouldn't drink the coffee here.

There was a distinct odor to the room I'd stepped into. Hints of formaldehyde mixed with something else I recognized but had a hard time placing.

It was dim, old lighting that flickered now and again and added to the depressing sense of gloom.

Dude at the makeshift counter looked vaguely Eastern European. Probably the hat. It was one of those fuzzy earflaps kind that look out of place anywhere except Soviet-era Russia. Incongruously he was also wearing a tank top that showed off his abundant shoulder hair. Maybe just his head was cold.

There were a bunch of parts laid out on the counter and he looked to be cataloguing them. Recently acquired no doubt.

He fixed me with a scowl as I walked up, one hand lingering conspicuously under the counter.

I slid my shades down to the tip of my nose and feigned interest in a few items on the walls, though I couldn't decipher what most were if I tried. Looked like someone had dismembered a dozen C3POs and used their guts for decoration.

Maybe not far from accurate.

"Heard you might be a guy to get me something I need." I turned to him with my most charming smile.

He grunted.

"Bought an old model synth caretaker for my old man. You know the health-care bot kind? Wipes your ass for you and all that? Something went wrong with it. Factory says it needs a whaddya-call it, a . . ." I checked my phone and consulted the list of stolen parts the techs at UM had dutifully sent over itemizing the things taken from Synth Johnny. I looked down the list for something easy to pronounce. ". . . A nexus link? I don't know what the hell they're talking about. UM parts department wants an account number and everything and I just bought the thing second hand, you know? I'm not trying to pay out the donk for UM prices."

Earflaps grunted again, then shifted his weight. "Don't have one."

"Doesn't have to be name brand. I just need the damn bot to work so it gets social services off my ass." I gave him a knowing wink. "Not like my pops gives a shit. He doesn't remember *my* name half the time. Calls his bot Ollie. It was our dog's name when I was six, right? So clearly we're not working a critical issue here."

He didn't comment. Just stared his murderous glare.

I looked down at his new collection of Synth Johnny parts. "What about all this shit here? None of this a nexus gizmo?"

"You try PartsMart, okay. They have it."

"Right, but like I said, they need account numbers and subscription codes and all that bull-shite. My buddy who sold the bot to me said I might have trouble getting parts but he said if I come down here I can probably find what I'm looking for." I held my arms out toward him. "You're the guy, right? You're the man with all the answers is what I hear."

"Your buddy was wrong. This synth and bio parts only. Exchange, yes?"

"Like to get parts I have to give parts?"

"Bio-synth exchange. You want synthetic? You give bio. We make deal."

A transhuman chop shop. Using stolen synth parts.

I'd picked the wrong cover story. I turned to go. "You know this place is bullshit then too, man. Any ten-year-old kid down here probably has this nexus thing in his back pocket. You ain't got shit."

"Have a nice day," he said, the words dripping with sarcasm.

Earflaps wasn't dumb. I'd thought my acting was top notch but he obviously wasn't going for it. I made one last effort. I turned back and leaned in conspiratorially. "Listen, man. This buddy of mine, he has an in. Works at a UM facility. Says he can get his hands on some super-sweet biosynth gear. Let's say I get you some of these things. That change your mind?"

He didn't so much as blink.

"Fine." I pulled my remaining wad of cash bills from my pocket and started counting them in front of him. "I'll be honest with you. I don't know an inertial gyro from a croquet ball, but I need this damn gizmo thing right? You got someone around here who can help me out? I'm sure somebody down here wants my money."

His eyes locked on the stack of cash in my hand.

I started to turn away.

"Now wait, sir. Yes. Wait. I see I misjudged you." He took one more glance at the cash and came around the counter with arms wide. "I see now you are man who is okay. You walk in, I think, this is yuppy man from uptown. Or maybe you a cop, eh?"

He chuckled. I chuckled. We were good buddies now.

He put an arm to my shoulder. "I think maybe I can help you.

I have friends too, yes? I get you that part you need. You leave money and come back in one hour. I have your part."

"This money?" I held up the cash.

His eyes followed it. His tongue flicked his lower lip. "Very reasonable price for you. When you get it, you can tell those PartsMart fuckers to stick their prices up their asses, yes?"

I laughed. "For sure. For sure." I started to hand the cash to him. He reached for it. Then I held it back. "But I'll come back in an hour. I'll give it to you then, right?" I slipped the wad back in my pocket. "Then we do a deal. I wasn't born yesterday." I wagged a finger at him.

His brow furrowed but he forced a smile. It looked difficult. We approached the door.

"Listen, my main man. You stay close, huh? You have lunch. You go to my friend. Right down this way. He sell hamburgers. Real ones. He get you real cow. Zebra. Anything you want. Thirty minutes. I have your part in thirty minutes."

"Thirty minutes. Faster service now," I said.

"Yes. For you. My new friend."

"Lunch place. I am pretty hungry."

"You tell him my name. You say Kazimir sent you. He give you free lunch."

"Free zebra burger?"

"Yes. You go there. Stay. Twenty-five minutes." He grinned at me again. "For Kazimir's friend."

He ushered me through the door, his eyes drifting to my jacket pocket only once. He held the door for me, stepped outside, pointed down the street. "Mikail's Meats. Right that way, one turn, past red sign. It is shortcut. I will find you there. Get your part."

I pointed a finger gun at him. "Twenty minutes now, right?" I grinned. He laughed. We were hilarious.

He waved as I walked away. I judiciously ignored the woman

with the purple arms watching from the shadows behind her freezers. I was on my way down a suspicious alley shortcut to a place serving black-market zebra meat and I definitely wasn't going to get jumped or bamboozled in any way.

At the red sign I turned right. Walked slowly. Casually. I whistled. Life was fantastic.

They materialized on time, if slightly out of breath. Only two guys. Not even that big. Sort of an insult but I was a yuppy from uptown. They cruised into the far end of the alley and sized me up for just a second too long before resuming their hushed conversation. No guns visible but I assumed they had them. Unless this was just a knife job. A stick up was the obvious choice. Less messy than actually murdering me but I was on guard.

One of the dudes gave me a little nod as they neared. Bro code. What's up. Distraction from dude number two putting a hand behind his back. What was it going to be, knife or gun?

Five paces.

Four. Three.

And here we were. He pulled a gun. Ding ding. We had a winner.

A quick movement from the other guy, shoving me, pushing me up against the wall. Snarling. Strong grip. He had biomechanical arms. Guess he was counting on that being scary. The guy with the gun jammed it in my face. I put my hands up.

"Gimme all you got," Gun Guy hissed. "Move and you get blasted!"

Cliché. But I guess it worked.

His transhuman friend was already rummaging in my pockets. Somehow knew right where to look. While he was distracted with my jacket he wasn't watching my hands. Gun Guy wasn't in a great position. I stepped to the side, putting his companion between us. Before he could even shout about it, I bent at the knees and put a hard right into the front guy's gut. Common problem with transhuman thugs. They spend all their cash on superhero shoulders and forget to protect their squishy parts. As he doubled toward me, I put my whole weight into him and shoved, sending him back toward his gun-toting companion. Gun Guy tried to sidestep, get a better angle on me, but I pivoted too and pushed his friend at him again. When I got clear I had my Stinger up and aimed for both of them. Front Guy's eyes widened. He ducked. I pulled the trigger. Bullet went through Gun Guy's right shoulder. He shrieked and went stumbling backward. The gunshot echoed down the alley. He crashed into a set of trash cans and went down. Front guy was still ducking but looking to run. I slammed the butt of my pistol across his skull and he went sprawling to the pavement. Lights out. Another place he didn't invest any cash. I had the gun back up and aimed at his friend again by the time he hit the ground.

Thug with the gun raised his good hand, dropped the gun from the other. Amateur. Young too. On closer inspection he couldn't be more than twenty. Barely more than a kid, just playing tough guy. Everybody's tough till the bullets start flying.

"You shot me!" he whined, gripping his shoulder.

"You'll survive," I said. "Assuming you make better life choices." I squatted to be at his level. "Next time make sure your robobuddy looks for a gun first thing. Better yet, get out of this business. Learn to bake muffins or something. Safer for you." I pressed the gun barrel to his forehead. "You like muffins?"

"Love 'em," he muttered.

"Smart kid. I'm gonna let you go get some help for that shoulder right after you tell me a few things. So let's talk fast before you lose too much blood."

He talked.

CHAPTER 26

His name was Ismael.

Kazimir was his uncle's cousin.

He'd never been shot before. Fuck it hurt.

Kazimir worked for someone named Dunne. Everyone in the synth-bio parts business did.

Where could I find Dunne? He wasn't going to tell me.

I pressed the gun barrel up his nostril.

Dunne owned a bunch of clubs. I could go there. Place called the Dark Horse.

Dunne would find out about this.

I was a dead man.

Blah blah.

A few brave and curious souls began to poke their heads into the alley. Some quickly moved on. Some lingered. I put away my gun. Stood.

I looked Ismael in the eye. "I didn't have to miss your vital organs. You get me?"

He nodded.

"Get out of here."

He scrambled to his feet, one hand pressed to his shoulder.

He took only a brief glance at his unconscious companion. Then he ran.

I rolled his transhuman buddy over to look for ID. He was carrying meta lenses and earphones. No wallet, but he had a phone. The security was facial recognition. I had to pry his eyelids open, but the phone didn't seem to mind that he was unconscious. I scrolled through his contacts. No names jumped out at me. I looked at his mechanical arms again, then tried the number Shaina the bio-synth parts trader had given me. The number popped up in the search. West Bay Medical Associates. Doctor Ivana Yee. It even had an address.

I put his phone back. Turns out the guy had a gun too, tucked into the back of his pants. Tiny little thing. Maybe a 0.380. Guess he thought his robo arms were more impressive. I left his tech in plain view of the nosy onlookers when I stood back up. I took the gun. No one accosted me when I moved on. I didn't expect they would. This was the Cellar and nothing they hadn't seen before.

I'm sure I was recorded. My face would make the rounds in a manner of minutes. Ismael would've already told Kazimir. But there would be a few minutes of debate. Hasty conversations. Run it upstairs. Would they tell this Dunne about me immediately or sweep it under the rug?

I'd solved one piece of the puzzle. Poking around this business could get a guy jumped. Question remained: just how big of a hornet's nest had I kicked?

I walked. Moving targets are harder to hit.

"Waldo, I need a safe anchor point. You have any eyes down here? Maybe an exit?"

"Underground mapping is spotty. I'll do what I can."

"Better make it quick."

I was headed into the heart of City Cellar. The longer I stayed underground, the harder the looks from the locals became. I was under a foundational support of the Skylift here. I recognized some of the stabilizing system that sank deep into the earth. This part of the city was a maze, far removed from the shiny surface streets. Everything was wet or damp or threatening to be. While I walked, I reloaded my Stinger, replacing the shell I'd expended.

"Left at the next road," Waldo said. "There are some boarded up apartments on Palm Lake Drive. Security footage shows a window of inactivity within the last hour."

"Got it."

He guided me to the correct building via my meta lenses. Palm Lake Drive was a dingy alley you could barely fit a golf cart through. No palms. Potholes might be big enough to be called lakes though. Out of the way too. Quiet. It would work. There was a basement access door on one side of the building with an old-school knob lock. I descended the stairs and pulled my lock pick set from my pocket. I had the door open in under thirty seconds. I slipped inside.

No alarms sounded.

Not much left here: some old display counters, a few dusty frames stacked on top of a washing machine. But there was an ancient ceiling fan that hadn't ever been upgraded either. It had a pull chain with a fob on the end. I walked over and noted the fob's height. It hung right at eye level. I ripped it from the fan and stuffed it in my pocket. I checked the time, then preset my chronometer for a time ten minutes in the past.

I headed back outside. Closed the door. Kept moving.

Back on the street, one look behind me showed I had acquired a follower. At least one dude was paying far too much attention. He caught me looking and glanced away, fingers tapping on a phone.

The road climbed ahead, back toward the surface. So I walked on. I emerged into a sort of concrete bowl. Took me a minute to place it, but then I realized it was part of the city flood system. When I ascended a rusted steel staircase to the top, I found I was above ground on the edge of the city, near the dock district.

I located the Dark Horse. A two-story corner bar. The sign was multicolored neon but several letters were out, so the name looked like DA ORSE.

It wasn't a classy joint. I caught the stench of sweat when I opened the door. Servers wore skimpy bikinis and the decor looked like it was stolen from a weight lifter's yard sale. A few speed bags hung from corners. There was a boxing ring in the middle of the place where two skinny white guys with biomechanical appendages were pummeling each other. Both were bleeding.

A big dude at the door made a motion to stop me. He whispered something to a companion. They flitted away quickly.

"Here to see Dunne," I said.

"You got a name?" he replied.

"Travers."

He made a call on his earpiece. The guy he'd whispered to came back a minute later, and he brought friends. Brawlers by the look of them. One had a cauliflower ear and two were missing teeth. They had thick necks and a few obviously augmented parts, but I liked to think none smacked of danger to the same level as me. I suppose they went for quantity over quality.

I was guided through the bar to the back. There was an office there with another muscle-bound guy at the door. He said something into his watch before he opened the door.

I had been expecting Dunne to be a nasty dude. Kind of guy who traded in stolen body parts and had people jumped in alleys.

Turns out I was being sexist.

Dunne was a woman. The kind of woman who traded in stolen body parts and had people jumped in alleys.

She didn't look happy.

CHAPTER 27

Dunne had great hair. I could admit that much. Red. Obviously used a lot of conditioner. She wore a designer suit with a low cut blouse. Everything about her looked expensive. Even sitting down I could tell she was tall.

"Boss, this dude is here to see you," the doorman said.

Dunne rose from her chair. I was right about her being tall. She came around her desk. My height in modest heels. She crossed her arms as she sized me up, boosting an already scandalous bosom.

There weren't enough chairs for me and the half dozen bruisers filing in behind me. So we all stood and stared at each other.

"You know why I'm here?" I asked.

"You've been causing trouble," Dunne said. "And you're here because you know the rules. Or you've guessed at them."

"You run things in the Cellar."

"I keep things neat and orderly," she said. "Someone has to. I assume you came to make amends."

"For you to make amends to me? I accept groveling apologies but only if they're not too whiny."

"You shot someone on *my* turf," Dunne said. "You think that's something to joke about?"

"A poser punk attempting to rob me. It was insulting."

Dunne shifted her weight and her eyes flitted to the goons encircling the doorway. I could feel the tension in her henchmen —a ratcheting of the testosterone in the room. "You came here alone because it sends a message. You want us to know you aren't afraid of us. Fine. I get it. But I can send messages too."

One of her thugs put his hand to the pistol at his hip.

"I came down here for answers and I still don't have them. Not leaving till I get some."

"What makes you think I care what you want?" Dunne leaned against her desk.

"UM synths have been getting dismantled for weeks. Turns out someone has been carving them up and using their bits to supply Kazimir's body part swapping business. I'd like to know who it is."

"Who Kazimir conducts business with isn't your concern."

"But it is *your* concern. I was hired by Diana King from UM. Sent me to find the source of her problems. I followed the trail to you. Makes you her problem now."

Dunne smiled. "Perhaps Ms. King should focus on problems closer to home. We're a long way from her altitude. Good advice for you too."

"I don't mind getting my boots dirty."

Dunne spread her hands out beside her on her desk, her manicured nails fanning over the edge. "You know, occasionally a client at one of the facilities down here fails to pay their debts for a surgery. They get greedy, order more modifications than they can afford. Easy to do. You know what happens to those people?"

"You send them nasty letters, I bet."

Dunne smiled. It was a thin-lipped thing. "We've found that the only thing that elicits the proper motivation for repayment was bringing back an old tradition. You've heard the term *a pound of flesh?*"

"I've never been the biggest *Merchant of Venice* fan. More of a *Hamlet* guy."

"We take inspiration where it comes. Would you like to see the collection you'll be donating to on behalf of Ms. King?"

I blinked. "Come again?"

"I'll show you. It's breathtaking." She cued something on her desk and the smartwall behind it became a screen. It showed what might be a storage facility. The unit was lined with shelves and each shelf was loaded with jars. Inside were body parts.

I screwed up my face. "I love CGI as much as the next guy, but . . ."

She walked around her desk, opened a drawer, and lifted another jar. She set it in the center of the desk. Inside was the unmistakable form of a severed human hand. Then she looked back at me. She rested one thigh on the desk, cocking her knee, and folded her hands in her lap.

I slipped my hands into my pockets.

"From you I won't require a whole hand. Ismael did live after all. I'm thinking a finger will do for now. Or perhaps a few toes."

The men behind me shifted.

A beat. Then they sprang.

Shit.

I only had a moment to get my arm up, fingers grasping the fan chain fob I'd pulled from my pocket. Rough hands squeezed my shoulders, my neck, but I got my hands up just below eye level. Someone punched me in the ribs. I gasped but held my position.

My right hand pressed the pin on my chronometer.

The room and everyone in it vanished as I reappeared inside the abandoned apartment on Palm Lake Drive.

I fell to my back on the landing, knocking the wind out of

171

myself. The fob on the fan chain swung wildly overhead, clinking off the glass of the light fixture. I stared up at it from the floor with my pulse pounding.

Somewhere in the Dark Horse, Dunne's goons would be fumbling on the office carpet with only a fan fob and the alley thug's tiny pistol for evidence I was ever there.

I would have liked to stay on the floor of the abandoned apartment and recover my breath, but I had to move. I climbed to my feet, and only paused long enough to arrest the movement of the fan chain, centering it.

I checked my watch, waited as it finished syncing to local time, then slipped quietly out the door, locking it behind me. I angled up the street at a jog and turned a corner. Only when I was out of sight of the apartment did I lean against a wall to catch my breath. I checked my watch again.

Still three minutes till my earlier self would break in and steal the fan chain fob. By the time he accosted Dunne at her place, I'd be out of the Cellar.

I walked fast and I didn't look back.

CHAPTER 28

There is a thrill that comes from cheating death. Successfully navigating the Cellar and its dangers had me feeling feisty. I didn't have Johnny's parts-swapping killer yet but I was annoying some people. I counted that as progress.

Back above ground, I asked Waldo to find me another safe jump location. My chronometer was getting low on power but I had enough juice for one more hop. I still had questions that needed answers.

My stomach growled. I needed a meal, and wouldn't mind a drink, but I was smelling blood. Maybe I'd solve this thing and celebrate with a late lunch at the Rose 'n Bridge.

Whatever happened next, I was done dicking around the edges of this situation. Ferreting out Dunne and her stolen body parts business had been useful. It gave me a possible motive for Johnny's killer, but I wasn't done just yet. I needed the killer's identity. The constant blur of traffic on the street gave me an idea for that.

I jumped back to an hour before Johnny the Synth had walked into my office. I wore my meta lenses and made sure my geo-tracking was on with alerts in case I got close to any of my previous selves. No good causing a paradox when I was this close to getting my answers. A few blocks from my office there was a discount vehicle rental depot. Mostly bikes, scooters, and a few motorcycles.

It had been half a century since I'd been on an electric scooter. They'd made upgrades. Some models here could do fifty miles an hour. Some auto-drove. All you had to do was hang on. I could do that.

I rented a Power Speeder brand scooter called the Shockwave. It was blue with a yellow lightning bolt down the front. The store manager said it had a hundred-mile range. I was hoping I wouldn't need half as much. I paid my deposit and rented a full-face helmet to go with it. The inside of the helmet smelled like Doritos. Luckily I wouldn't be in it long. I donned the obnoxious neon-yellow safety vest that came with the rental, layering it over my jacket. I caught my reflection in the windows of one of the buildings I passed and didn't recognize myself.

That's what I was counting on.

I kept the scooter on manual drive and zipped along Revolution Boulevard. I rode past the point where Synth Johnny would be attacked.

In a little while the street would be crawling with previous versions of myself, but with the full-face helmet and safety gear, I was confident I could escape detection.

I needed another look at Johnny's killer, and this time I wasn't going to let him slip away. If I could figure out where he came from, even better. It took a few laps around the block before I found the best vantage point, but once I had it, I stopped the scooter and pretended to be absorbed with my phone. No one gave me a second glance. The helmet had a reflective visor with a smart screen inside. Ads kept popping up and offering me energy drinks and dating apps. Apparently it had me pegged as tired, thirsty, and single. Annoyingly accurate. I unplugged the helmet battery. That would teach it.

With the smart screen disabled I was free to watch the street in peace. It buzzed and hummed with the steady flow of humanity. I waited. Watched. Waldo was the first to spot my quarry. He pinged in my ear and highlighted a scooter rider in my shades. He started recording before I thought to ask. Sign of a good AI assistant.

My target came downhill from Ronin Street and made the left onto Revolution. Blue scooter with white handlebars. The parts thugs showed up on the other corner at the same time I spotted Synth Johnny. Without the thugs and Synth Johnny's fate to worry about this time around, I could focus all my attention on the speedy robo-butcher on the scooter. He wore a hooded jacket that obscured his head and neck but I got a glimpse of a face. Looked young, Asian maybe. Sunglasses and a ball cap helped hide his face. A few wisps of black hair caught the wind. He was fast too. Moved with a practiced ease through the crowd.

I waited with one foot aboard my scooter.

The scene played out how I remembered. Farther down the street, the earlier version of me was lurking behind a clothing donation bin. I caught a glimpse of him briefly but stayed out of his line-of-sight.

Synth Johnny went down. The speedy butcher went to work. I climbed aboard my scooter. Zipped out into the flow of traffic. I crossed to the far lane and buzzed along the sidewalk just in time to see the handoff—the bag of parts the two thugs would take to the Cellar. But this time I saw Johnny's killer pocket something as well.

My earlier self would be cursing his lack of visibility from the far side of the street. I made sure not to turn my head his way but noted him from the corner of my eye as I bore down on the scene. Johnny's killer was back aboard his scooter. The two thugs I'd followed previously began their casual walk west. I passed right by them.

Synth Johnny lay face down on the sidewalk in a puddle of his fluids.

My earlier self came out of concealment to follow the thugs.

I stayed on Synth Johnny's killer, doing my best to keep up as he whizzed along the street.

At the next corner I spotted Wilder. She was perched on the steps now, not shouting at passersby yet, but watching. She saw me too but without any sign of recognition. Something inside me twinged as I rode by. It was ridiculous to want her attention. This version of her hadn't even met me yet, but my mind wandered to the night we'd spent together. Would spend. Her body tangled with mine.

Head in the game, Greyson.

I kept a steady gaze forward. I was just another fish in the stream now. The earliest me would be walking up the street momentarily. Wilder would have plenty of conversation.

I rode on.

My quarry was moving fast. He took the ramp for the zip lanes. I followed.

Then things got rapid.

Port Nyongo was one of the first cities in the country to install elevated zip lanes. No pedestrians, no cars. Just single rider conveyances.

The trick had been the infrastructure. Where elevated highways and train tracks required miles of weight-bearing concrete, zip lanes could be built into existing structures at a fraction of the cost. Downtown buildings converted hallways and corridors left disused after the remote worker revolution. Catwalks and bridges interlinked popular product distributors, and before long there was a network of thin high-speed thoroughfares connecting the entire downtown.

I shot up an entrance ramp and joined the flow of riders blasting their way through downtown. The lane ahead of me blurred into a glow of color as the tunnel lit up with LED guide lights. The route bored straight through a business complex and shot out the other side of the building into a clear tube that reminded me of something a hamster would use. Johnny's killer was moving fast and I was forced to crank my rental scooter to full power to keep up. The path ahead took a dive and we plummeted a hundred feet downhill into an old metro tunnel. The sky went dark but the tube lit up, this time with custom light displays. Some kind of art installation flashed and flickered at a frenetic pace. Music blasted from speakers built into the walls. The pulse of the music throbbed in my brain.

I zipped on.

When next we emerged above ground, we were beneath one of the legs of the Skylift. Riders exited to retail destinations all along the waterfront. Most were synth delivery drones off to collect items for shoppers ordering from home. I was roughly fifty yards behind my quarry, watching closely for when he'd exit, but he kept on riding.

We circled the UM campus in bright sunlight and headed north. Enough riders had joined the zip lanes to obscure my continued presence, but I worried my quarry might notice me soon. So far, he hadn't looked back, but there was a mirror on one handlebar of his scooter and I couldn't tell what he could see with it.

I swerved in and out of traffic to keep him in sight, dodging the auto-riders keeping an annoyingly steady pace from location to location. Whoever this guy was, he was making things a challenge.

The exit came fast. My quarry shot across three lanes and down a ramp without warning and I was forced to brake hard and cut off several drone riders in order to make it over in time. The exit plunged into darkness beneath the dock district. My last view of daylight was the sun glinting on the waves of the Gulf. Then darkness absorbed me.

My eyes didn't adjust fast enough. By the time I'd leveled out on the subterranean scooter path, Synth Johnny's killer was seventy-five yards ahead.

A road intersected the zip lane where the tunnel ended. I watched him shoot across traffic, ignoring the stoplight. I swore.

"Might I take this time to remind you that you haven't updated your life insurance policy this decade?" Waldo said in my ear.

"I don't have any dependents, Waldo. No one loses." I jammed my thumb onto the boost button. I had a lightning bolt sticker on my scooter. It had better count for something. Cargo trucks crisscrossed the intersection. I probably should have kept my eyes open. Turns out it wouldn't have helped much. The scooter locked up ten feet from the intersection and I was hurled off, catapulted to the pavement where I hit hard and rolled to a stop inches from traffic.

It would be nice to say someone at least noticed but it was difficult to tell. As I climbed gingerly to my feet and flexed my joints, the passing cars slowed to a stop and the zip lane light turned green. An accumulated swarm of scooters and bikes whizzed by me, my own stationary scooter a boulder in the stream. I limped back to it and found the display screen flashing with warnings. When I tried to move it, it wouldn't budge. VIOLATION kept blinking across the screen. From what I could gather, I'd broken the terms of my rental agreement and several local traffic ordinances. My rental had been rescinded. The screen flashed a few more angry messages, then the scooter lurched into motion again, driving off without me.

Typical.

I walked to the edge of the road and pulled my helmet from my head. I retrieved my shades from the interior where they'd been flung off my face and wedged into the chin guard. My neon vest was next to go. I stuffed it into the helmet and left both atop a recycling bin. I was sure they'd find a way to bill me later.

I swore loudly.

Synth Johnny's killer was gone. The last I'd seen of him was zipping uphill along another row of warehouses.

My right palm was bleeding and my elbow was scuffed. My pants had survived without tearing, so that was something.

I decided I was done with scooters.

I checked my chronometer. The power was very low. Might manage one more jump. Might not.

So I walked instead. Bled a little. Cursed a lot.

It was hard to tell exactly where I was. This was still an industrial district but farther inland than I'd come before. Buildings were largely warehouses. Most of the passersby looked like laborers. Utilities. Construction maybe. I recognized a few contractor logos. This was infrastructure work. Storage facilities for goods. Plenty of synths too. I got occasional glances from the people here. Fewer people stuck in the metaspace. Couldn't afford it probably.

While I walked, I reviewed the new footage Waldo had recorded from the killing. There was very little that showed the guy's face. I had Waldo run some scans to see if facial recognition popped up a match anywhere on the metaspace but he didn't get any hits. I watched it again anyway. I couldn't see much that I hadn't seen before. Only that the killer took something for himself too. Trophy?

"Waldo. Will you run that list of missing parts the UM techs gave us against the footage I have from Kazimir's shop? I'd love to know what this guy kept for himself. If we can ID the items Kazimir bought, we can do some elimination."

"The missing item from the UM list is the nexus link you asked for."

"Kazimir was telling the truth?"

"Would you also be interested to know that the scooter we were following is parked up ahead in a charging rack?"

I looked up the road and spotted the blue scooter with the white handlebars charging at a roadside station. It was the only one in the rack.

"You should think about getting into detective work," I said.

"It would be terrible for my reputation," Waldo replied.

As I approached the charging rack, I noticed what looked like a lump of roadkill on the ground next to a nearby trash receptacle, as if someone had tossed the dead animal at it and missed. Only the lump wasn't any identifiable creature I could recognize. The hair looked human. I probed it with the toe of my boot. It squished. I stooped to pick the item up and it sagged in my hand.

Even without the form inside to give it structure, it was recognizable.

It was a face.

CHAPTER 29

"Synth Johnny's killer wears a mask," I said to Waldo. "Now we're getting somewhere." I studied the slightly gooey face before stuffing it into my jacket pocket.

"There are over two hundred thousand transhuman and synthetic persons in Port Nyongo," Waldo said. "Public data estimates that roughly one-third have the ability to modify their facial appearance. Add in that nearly any of the two million adult humans in Port Nyongo could wear a mask this size, your discovery has narrowed the killer's identity to just about anyone in the city other than small children."

"In other words, excellent progress," I said.

The scooter I'd followed was charging out front of a metal fence that was rusty from salt air. The sign on the fence bore a UM logo. There was a hum from behind it. I stood on tiptoes and peered over. It was a junkyard.

Drone tractors pushed and carried scraps of refuse around the yard. A conveyor ran the length of the facility. Utility robots were hard at work sorting the garbage and recyclables.

I checked a map. It looked like this facility backed up to the outer perimeter of the UM campus, but I doubted this ever made the tour.

I walked till I found a gate, displayed my company meta badge to the automated security system and it didn't work. I tried again. Nothing.

I checked the time, then pinched the bridge of my nose. This was Thursday afternoon. I hadn't been hired by Diana King till tomorrow morning. The ID wasn't working because I wasn't employed by the company yet.

Time traveler problems.

I wasn't sure what I was even doing here. Had Johnny's killer entered the junkyard or had he been picked up outside?

Only one way to find out.

Walking to the end of the junkyard, I found a stump of a poorly pruned shrub that gave me a leg up. Then I hopped the fence.

The inside of the junkyard was dusty and loud. Machines rumbled. Occasionally metal screamed as it was ground through the recycler. It was enough to hurt my ears.

I walked between heaps of refuse bristling with wire and plastic. The various piles had labels assigned. E19, F20. They went in every direction. Reminded me of looking for a car in a theme park parking lot. It was a lot of space for someone to hide in.

Something moved in the corner of my eye, but when I turned it was gone.

I watched the space between refuse piles for a moment, listened, then drew my gun.

The air smelled oily here. Puddles reflected rainbows of contamination. Salt crystals had formed on the oldest refuse piles.

Some sort of track ran above the scrap yard. I watched a container the size of a car rumble along above me, suspended from the track. The apparatus vaguely resembled a roller coaster.

Walking between the mountains of trash, unease prickled at

the back of my neck. I walked for what might have been two hundred yards before spotting an old utility building. The red paint on the shed was sun bleached to the point of looking pink. A corrugated door hung slightly ajar and permitted the passage of an extension cord. It was the only thing that might have indicated activity. I approached. With my gun in one hand, I reached for the door handle with the other. Took a breath.

"What are you looking for?"

I spun, gun up, and braced to fire at the owner of the voice. I found myself staring at the blue silicone face of Rudy, the UM prototype synth I'd met in the repair lab. He was roughly ten feet behind me, carrying a box of scrap parts. He peered at me with wide eyes.

"Shit, Rudy. What the hell are you doing here?" I lowered the gun.

"Properly disposing of company materials is one of my regular duties. Have we met?"

Damn. Still Thursday. I wouldn't meet Rudy till tomorrow.

I'd messed up. Time for some paradox prevention.

"Look, uh, Rudy. I'm a private investigator working for the company. Tomorrow morning I'm going to walk into the repair lab and you'll give me a tour. It's going to seem like I don't know you. It's nothing personal."

"You wish to conceal that you've met me?"

"Something like that. Think you can handle it? When I show up tomorrow, can you act like you've never met me before? It's important."

"Of course. That's simple."

"Figured you'd think that," I said. I scanned the area, still keeping an eye out for my quarry. "You see anyone else come through here in the last few minutes?"

"I've seen no one," Rudy said. "But I've only come straight from the Sky Loader." He gestured to the elevated track with cars suspended from it. There were eight humanoid-shaped places in each car, four facing either side but with only a harness to hold you in. To ride it you'd have to dangle like a piñata.

"You came in that?" I asked.

"It's the most common way to transport synthetic units from the lab to the recycling center. I've been told the view is quite spectacular, though I'm afraid I don't have much to compare it to. I don't get out much."

My eyes lingered on the utility track for only a moment, then I turned my attention back to Rudy. Something about him seemed different. Took me a moment to place it.

"You have different legs on."

"I beg your pardon?" Rudy said, confused.

"Sorry. Tomorrow, when we meet you have these mismatched red and blue legs. . . You know what? Never mind. Not important."

Rudy cocked his head again in that same curious manner he had before. Or would tomorrow. This was getting confusing.

I turned back to the utility building door. "What's in here?"

"That is a private storage area," Rudy said.

"I'm just going to take a quick look." I stepped up to the door and pushed. I raised my gun.

The utility building was perhaps thirty feet deep. It was impossible to see the back because it was obscured by rows upon rows of shelving. I was forced to walk from aisle to aisle to search the place properly. I took it slowly.

Several shelves were missing in the back right corner of the room and had been replaced by a workbench. As I came around the corner of the last parts shelf, I had a clear view of the workbench and stopped short.

There was a woman's body laid out on the bench. She was nude and her head was turned in my direction, staring blankly.

Her red hair cascaded over the edge of the bench. She wasn't breathing.

She also didn't look dead. Wrong color for a stiff, even in this lighting.

I approached. Something nudged my memory. I'd seen this woman before. Only she wasn't a woman. She was a synth. The sad, dancing synth from the video the UM techs had shown me. The one who had pressed herself to the glass and pleaded for help.

What was she doing here? There was a toolbox set to one side of the bench. Some kind of computer too. The screen was dark but a power button glowed dimly.

I turned back the way I'd come. "Rudy? What the hell's going on back here?"

No response. Where had he gotten to?

I inspected the body. I saw nothing that indicated foul play. There was a place on the inside of her thigh that looked like it might have been pried open. But I wasn't a synth tech. If I managed to open it, I'd have no idea what I was looking at. I did feel around the back of her skull for an ID tag. Couldn't find one.

The techs at the lab had said she'd been recycled, hadn't they? Maybe this was part of the process?

Only she didn't look like she was getting taken apart. If anything it looked like she was going back together. There was something off about her. Mismatched the way Rudy had seemed. Like a few of her parts weren't original.

I pulled my shades from my shirt collar. Wouldn't hurt to get video of all of this. "Hey Waldo, any secondary places on a synth to get registration info?"

Waldo didn't reply.

"Waldo?" I tapped my earpiece but all I got was a faint buzzing. Some kind of interference. I pulled my phone from my pocket to check the connection and heard the footsteps at the same time. I turned.

The thump on the back of my skull sent a flash through my brain and I fell, all stars and pain. I hit the ground hard. The last thing I registered was my phone ricocheting off the workbench above me. Then everything went dark.

CHAPTER 30

Consciousness came slowly. Blinking didn't help much. Something was itching my nostrils though. I sneezed and dust particles flew from my lips.

Vision came but dimly. I hadn't moved. I managed to push myself up from the dusty floor as far as my hands and knees. My head ached, throbbing at the base of my skull. I located one of my earpieces on the floor and put it in. Someone had turned all the lights out.

"Waldo?"

"I'm here. It seems I have experienced some manner of disruption."

"You and me both, buddy. You get a look at the freight train that ran us over?"

"Regrettably, no. I was unable to gather data from the time you walked into this room."

"How about now?"

"Whatever was causing the interference is no longer present."

I located my shades, slipped them on and activated the low-light setting. The red-headed synth's body was gone. I found my phone on the floor and stood. The phone face was crushed.

Looked like someone heavy had stepped on it. Waldo still worked but not much else. The flashlight, cameras and controls were inoperative. I tucked it into my back pants pocket.

I rubbed the back of my head and touched the lump I found there. I guessed that I must have been unconscious for a while.

Despite having located the naked synth, I'd failed to get any proof she was ever here. No photos or video. Whole lot of nothing. The place was cleaned out. No sign of the tools or computer I'd noticed before either. I reached into my jacket pocket to see if the mask I'd found on the ground outside was still there.

Nope. Gone.

I looked around for my Stinger. Surprisingly it was still there. On the floor near the workbench. My head throbbed as I stooped to retrieve it.

I wasn't dead. That was something. Maybe hiding one body was all that my attacker had in him. Or maybe he was coming back.

I pressed my palm to my brow. Get it together Travers. Getting knocked out was amateur stuff. I should know better.

Get back to work.

My first few steps were unsteady but then my body regained equilibrium. I found my way out of the utility shed and back into the daylight.

"I think I'm going to need the car, buddy."

"Already on its way," Waldo said.

There was no sign of Rudy or anyone else.

Rudy.

Rudy?

Despite the lump on my head I had a hard time parsing what the hell had just happened.

I had a vague recollection of Rudy handing me a hardhat tomorrow. *"How is your head? It looks to be undamaged."*

Made more sense now. He knew I'd been knocked out.

Think.

Next steps. I was still in my past. Where was I going?

By the time I made it out of the junkyard, the Boss was pulling up. I sank into the driver's seat but didn't reach for the controls. Waldo drove, just cruising the dock district. I watched the signs on the warehouses blur past. At least a dozen sported United Machine logos.

What day was this? Still Thursday. Day one.

I took off my chronometer and put it in the glove box to charge. Next I synced my phone with the car's interface and uploaded everything I could from it. The car would have to be home base for info till I found a new phone.

I had no sense of how many hours my day had taken so far. I only knew I was starving. So much for solving this thing by lunch.

"Get us back to Saturday, Waldo. Lunchtime. We'll see what Manuel has going at the Rose 'n Bridge. I need a pick-me-up."

My hunger was one issue. My head was the other. But mostly I needed to get my mind right and bouncing around time wasn't helping. If I could put everything back in chronological order it was easier to make sense of it all. The past would all be past.

"Miss Archer has communicated a time and location she suggests as a return for your Saturday arrival. Would you like to use that?"

"Yes. Do it," I muttered.

Waldo jumped us to Saturday. By the time we pulled up to the Rose 'n Bridge, my headache had subsided to a dull throb. It was only when I walked back into the pub that it flared up again. A couple of TCID goons were at a booth near the window.

Heavens was behind the bar and gave me a wary nod. I walked in and took my spot at the far corner of the bar.

"What's this about?" I asked, jerking my thumb toward the windows.

Heavens kept her voice low. "They've been lurking around all morning in shifts. You make your trip?"

I kept my voice low. "Made a few jumps to Thursday morning. Caused some trouble."

"You've got blood in your hair."

"Do I?" I felt around the back of my head. "Is that not a good look?"

"I'll get you some ice. Was it worth it?"

"Don't know yet."

Heavens moved off and poured someone a beer. I reached for a lunch menu but my phone started buzzing in my pocket. Didn't realize it could still do that. I pulled it out of my pocket and laid it on the bar top. In its smashed state I had no way to tell who was calling. I located my earpiece and slid that into my ear to take the call.

"This is Travers," I said.

"You have some kind of nerve."

Ms. King.

"Nice to hear from you, Diana."

"I hired you to do a job. You know what I see on your expense charges? Nothing but dive bars and auto gas. I'm not paying you to drink and catcall hookers."

"I don't catcall hookers," I said. "They catcall me."

Heavens gave me a glance and arched an eyebrow. I winked at her.

Diana continued her rant on the phone. "The Midnight Club, some pub called The Rose and Bridge? And I heard a rumor you beat up some guy in the dock district. Tell me you've been doing something other than drinking and brawling with my money."

"I think I have your case solved. I just need to confirm via some video footage."

"Are you bullshitting me?"

"I sure hope not."

"It's a big night tonight. I don't want any loose ends. Be in my office with your results by the close of the day."

"Or else I get a vacation and a raise?"

She hung up.

She had a real flair for the dramatic.

I put my phone away.

Heavens brought me a beer and a plate with a sandwich and BBQ chips on it.

"What's this?" I asked, inspecting the toasted pressed bread and getting a whiff of mustard and pickle.

"Manny made it. You'll like it." I glanced toward the window and caught the TCID guys watching me.

Heavens lowered her voice. "I called Stella York."

"She tell you why TCID has been dragging down the ambiance of your pub?"

"She had some interesting things to say but wanted to talk to you personally."

"Can't blame her. I'm delightful."

Heavens shook her head as she walked away. I tapped my earpiece again. "Hey Waldo, call Agent Stella York." I took a bite of the sandwich. It was damned good.

"You don't have anyone named Stella York in your contacts," Waldo said.

"Oh. Right. You have to look under Agent McSmartie."

Waldo sighed, which I found unnecessary since he didn't possess a respiratory system. But the call connected.

"Travers," Stella York said when she picked up. "You get around."

"How dare you," I said. "But you should join the fun. Seems like Time Crimes is throwing a party here without you."

"You'd better keep your head down. Ted Baker is on special assignment where you are and he's not a fan of yours."

"I gathered as much. Too much manpower around just for hassling me though. What's up?"

Stella was silent for a long moment. "We're not having this conversation, you understand? I'm only telling you what I'm about to tell you because Heavens called and I know you'll try to pry it out of her anyway. I want to save her that unpleasantness."

"I'm a vault of secrecy," I said and took another bite of my sandwich. I was falling in love with it.

"Baker's part of a group within TCID called TSP. Have you heard of it?"

"You people love your acronyms. How can anyone keep up?"

"Stands for Technological Singularity Patrol. I assume you're familiar with the term."

"Sure. The point when artificial intelligence outpaces human intelligence. One could make a good case that we've passed it."

"At some point in nearly every timestream, artificial intelligence *will* advance at an exponential rate. TSP is part of a team looking to direct that event in all the timestreams we have jurisdiction over. I'm sure you've heard of the various ways humanity fares after the singularity. ASCOTT and TCID have an interest in keeping the singularity delayed as long as possible."

"What has that got to do with Port Nyongo and our current influx of dudes in monotone outfits?"

"Something is going down where you are that directly affects this timestream's future of artificial intelligence. As far as I can tell they don't know the specifics, but all signs point to the development surrounding this new space elevator as a key point in AI history. Things go right and we get a happy future with the AI. Door number two, we don't like."

"Skull crushing tanks driven by Arnold Schwarzenegger clones?" I spoke through another mouthful of sandwich.

"Worse. They won't need tanks."

I'd heard about the various human vs synth wars. I'd never visited any of those timestreams but I could see why it would be beneficial to keep this current time from heading that direction.

"ASCOTT is getting all time travelers out of the area before this key event happens," Stella continued. "They don't want anyone meddling. I'm sure Heavens has informed you of the curfew."

"Get out by eight o'clock or we all turn into pumpkins," I said.

"They're not messing around, Travers. If you're involved in any way, you'd best watch your step."

"I'm just kicking it with the usual riff raff. I doubt any of them have anything to do with technological singularities. It's been mostly thugs and body part swappers so far."

"Make sure you keep it that way. And get out of town before curfew. If Ted brings you in, I won't be able to help you."

"I like the idea that you'd try. You really *do* care."

One of the Time Crimes guys got up from his table and made his way toward the bar.

"Remember, we didn't have this conversation?" Stella said.

"Who is this? How'd you get this number?" I asked.

Stella hung up.

The Time Crimes guy eyed me suspiciously as he set his empty pint glass on the bar.

"Telemarketers," I said, and tapped my earpiece.

Time Crimes Dude fixed his attention back on Heavens.

Stella had given me more to think about, but my head hurt too much to try.

I finished my sandwich instead.

CHAPTER 31

I picked the last BBQ chip crumb from my plate with sadness. All good things come to an end. Even lunch.

My thoughts were still a jumble. United Machine, Dunne's body part swappers, Wilder, Time Crimes. I didn't see the connections yet but there was a nagging feeling somewhere in my brain like an itch I couldn't scratch. An answer. It was too deep. Couldn't flush it out just yet. I opted for a simpler problem I could solve.

My phone screen was destroyed. It made home movie watching challenging. But I still had seven hours till curfew, and I had my sunglasses. I slipped them on and sipped a beer while Waldo ran the last of the surveillance footage I'd taken inside the UM lab facility. I watched at rapid speed. It still took me a good half hour.

People moved around the bar but no one interrupted me. I was wearing sunglasses indoors while drinking in the afternoon. Obviously too cool to be bothered. Did life get any better?

The rest of the footage confirmed what I'd already suspected. No humans in the lab had touched the missing parts. But Rudy, the prototype android did.

Conclusion? Rudy was my parts thief.

I got on the net and searched the UM company contact numbers. Then I made a call.

William Brockhurst, the UM head of security picked up.

"Yeah, this is security."

"You want to be a hero, Bill?"

"Who is this?"

"Greyson Travers, your favorite private detective. I need you to get the video surveillance feed from the Farrow Street entrance to the company recycling yard from Thursday midday. Specifically a guy who showed up on a scooter and walked in the south gate. A shot of a face might be just the proof we need to solve the recent synth killings."

"What makes you so sure?"

"Unparalleled self-confidence. Can you get it?"

"Maybe. Yeah. I think so."

"You'll make Diana King happy, maybe even get your face on the news."

"You'd better not be full of shit."

"Call me at this number when you have something." I disconnected.

When Waldo brought the car around to pick me up outside the tavern, I had a stomach full of lunch and a head full of questions.

I'd found a guilty party. Why was this case still feeling incomplete?

If I could confirm Rudy was also Synth Johnny's killer, what was his motive?

What had Manuel done to that sandwich to make it so delicious? Was there any way I could time travel back and get my hands on another one?

Also, why was there a vehicle following me?

The SUV was on my tail immediately after leaving the Rose 'n Bridge. It stayed on me till the freeway, then exited early.

I ran video from the rear facing cameras but couldn't get a look at the driver. More of Ted's goons no doubt. I kept an eye out for another few miles but didn't see the vehicle again.

Maybe I was just paranoid. Or maybe it was a rotating tail. If so, I had a hard time picking out which car behind me had replaced the SUV. It should have been easier to spot.

Not knowing annoyed me.

My sunglasses were still connected to the net in this time, so while Waldo drove I got in a little more research. I double-checked the name I'd gotten off the thug with the mechanical arms in City Cellar. It was one more bothersome lead to run down and it was going to take another jump. Waldo helped me pull as much data as was available. West Bay Medical was owned by an obscure corporation, but information on the staff was a little easier to come by. It was enough to make the trip worthwhile.

I did a search from the car's onboard computer and found an out-of-the-way jump location in a parking garage downtown. I made about seventeen turns before I got there to make sure I'd lost my tail. As soon as I got inside the garage I took the car back to Thursday morning. If a tail managed to follow me there, I'd be in trouble.

Once I arrived back to Thursday, I cruised the streets just north of the dock district till I found the address I was looking for.

West Bay Medical Associates was in a dingy office on the second floor of what may once have been a thriving multi-use building. Now most of the retail space on the ground level was boarded up and only a few nameplates for the office floors were occupied. The directory showed there were residences on the top floors. Condos were my guess.

I took the elevator to the second floor and found the door for West Bay Medical Associates in an office near the restrooms.

Inside, a listless young man behind a Plexiglas germ barrier stared at me languidly as I walked in.

"I'm here for some information. Looking to get some enhancements done."

The young man gnawed his chewing gum and blinked in slow motion. "Do you have an appointment?"

"More of a walk-in."

"If you're not a current patient, you'll need to register with the online portal and submit your insurance information."

"I'm a friend of Ms. Dunne," I said.

The receptionist stopped chewing and sat up a little straighter. "Ms. Dunne?"

I pulled my diminished wad of fifties from my pocket and slipped a couple under the Plexiglas. "And if you could get me a chat with the doctor now, Ms. Dunne would be especially grateful."

The man eyed me cautiously, but his fingers came up to grasp the money. "I'll see if the Doc's available."

He pressed his earpiece and made a call. We waited. When no one picked up, he frowned and fired off a message. He gave me an apologetic look. "If you'd like to have a seat, I'll see if I can reach her."

There were several other people waiting in the lobby chairs. The room was small, and it smelled as though at least a couple of the patients had forgotten to shower.

I selected a seat a chair away from a man with artificial legs and a missing arm. He spoke as I sat. "Doc Yee ain't been in yet this morning."

"That a fact," I said.

"Been waiting since eight. Some days she don't come in at all, but I can't see why. Not like she deals with traffic."

"How you mean?"

He pointed to the ceiling. "Lives right upstairs. You ever seen an elevator get in a traffic jam?"

I followed his finger to the overhead fluorescent lights.

Interesting.

One of the nursing staff walked out of a back room to converse with the receptionist. The pair whispered and seemed to come to some kind of grudging conclusion. A minute later, the nurse came out and crossed the lobby, exiting into the hallway. I stood and followed. I caught up to her as she was boarding the elevator, sliding into the elevator car beside her. She eyed me warily. She'd pressed the button for four so I pushed five. We rode up in silence. When she exited, I was studiously focused on my phone, not looking suspicious.

On the fifth floor I immediately located the stairwell and descended, emerging onto the lower floor in time to hear the knocking. The nurse from the office was pounding on a door at the end of the hallway. I was concealed by a corner but close enough to listen. A muffled noise came from beyond the door.

The nurse knocked again. "Doc, are you coming down today or what?"

The door opened a crack. "You have to be so loud?" The woman's voice was raspy.

"We've got a lobby full of patients."

"Reschedule them. I'm not coming down today."

The nurse let out an exasperated sigh. "That's twice this week."

"And?"

"This place isn't Mercy General. We do need patients to pay the bills."

"These people aren't going anywhere else. Move them."

"One of them said he's from Dunne."

The doctor was quiet for a long moment. "Tell him to wait. Send the rest home. I'll be down in half an hour."

The door slammed in the nurse's face. A few seconds later the elevator doors shushed open and closed, taking the woman back downstairs. I walked to the door she'd been talking at. I placed my thumb over the camera lens in the doorbell before knocking. I matched the intensity the nurse had used for the knock.

As I'd hoped, the door was unceremoniously flung open and the woman on the other side had her mouth open, ready to berate the nurse again. When she saw me standing there she froze, then tried to slam the door. It bounced off the toe of the boot I slipped across the threshold.

The door sprung open again and the woman, who was wearing a loose-fitting robe over wrinkled plaid pajama bottoms, gaped at me. Then she turned and rushed for a desk to one side of the door. I was through the door and had my left hand around hers just as she was pulling the handgun from the desk drawer. I took her across the face with the back of my right hand and she went sprawling over the arm of her couch. I wasn't proud of it, but she'd relinquished the gun. I tossed it back onto the desk.

"Calm down. I'm not here to hurt you. Not if you're cooperative."

The woman's eyes were wide and bloodshot. She stared back at me from the couch, with one leg still caught over the armrest. She held her cheek with one hand.

"We're going to talk," I said and shut the door to the hallway.

"Who are you?" she demanded.

"I'm a guy who got jumped in an alley recently by some of your handiwork. Thug kid used his fancy mechanical arms to try to rob me. Short guy. Bad haircut. Maybe you know who I'm talking about."

She just glared.

"Maybe you put arms on a lot of guys with bad haircuts. Maybe you have some sort of confidentiality agreement with these guys. But it doesn't matter. Kazimir. Dunne. I'm guessing they all use you."

"You'll be in deep shit if you kill me," she said.

"If I wanted to kill you, you'd be dead already. I want information."

"Barging in here isn't going to get it." She shifted her legs to the floor and sat more or less erect on the farthest end of the couch. I stepped closer until I was at the opposite end of the couch and sat on the armrest.

"I know you're the surgeon for City Cellar. And I know Kazimir is dealing in stolen parts. My guess is he's supplying them to you for surgeries. Maybe you do it out of the goodness of your heart but I'm guessing you owe some people down there a lot of money. Maybe it's Dunne. Maybe whoever's supplying you with whatever it is you're using."

She stared at the TV on the far side of her rug. It was playing muted news footage. The rest of the room was dingy. Everything needed cleaning. There had been a spill on the rug. The mug was still lying on its side on the coffee table. Even the lighting was depressing.

"I looked you up before I came," I said. "Your bio says you used to be a top surgeon at Mercy General seven years ago. This where that career ladder ends?"

"Go to hell," she said.

"Seems like I've arrived."

Ivana Yee looked defeated. We just sat in silence for the better part of a minute before she spoke again. This time her voice came out softer. "You think your life is going to be fair. You think you'll have choices. But then other people make them for you. You make one mistake and it's all over."

"Why'd they cut you from Mercy General?"

Her face contorted, almost as if I'd struck her again.

I pressed her. "You had a hot shot career. Big money. Best I can tell, you had it all."

"Until they took it," she muttered. "Because I made a bad bet."

"Nobody loses everything that fast."

"They do when it's a kid. And when the kid belongs to her." She pointed at the TV.

I turned. The news on the TV had switched to an interview. The network anchor was interviewing Diana King.

CHAPTER 32

Doctor Ivana Yee had been chief of surgery at Mercy General the day Diana King's husband and son plummeted out of the sky in their hover car. She'd been the one to put Charles back together. Six months of surgeries and recovery. A miracle of modern science.

"I don't get it," I said. "Best I can tell, you were a hero."

Ivana Yee just stared at the muted television.

"What am I missing?" I asked. "The drugs? How much were you into Dunne for?"

"Enough."

"Lots of docs have extracurricular drug habits. But I'm betting that came after, didn't it?"

She looked up at me. She nodded.

"Tell me the story."

"No. I've said enough."

I crossed my arms. "You have someone to protect in this? Why? Why not talk to me?"

"Because you're not from Dunne," she said. "I know her people. You're not the type. And if you aren't hers, then you're not my problem."

I walked to the window and looked out. I watched Ivana's

reflection in the glass. You could make out a sliver of the UM building from where I stood too. Ivana's reflection and the building seemed to be merged. "You saved Diana King's kid. You were the brightest star of the city. Then you developed a drug problem. Mercy General lets you go. Now you run a scammy biosynth-parts surgery center and self-medicate." I stuffed my hands in my pockets. "I'm guessing Kazimir is only one of your parts suppliers. All part of Dunne's network. But I'm missing a piece of the story, aren't I?"

No answer. She didn't deny it either.

"Who else owes Dunne? Someone is going around killing UM synths to supply Kazimir. But is that the only reason? Is it to pay off Dunne? To pay for surgeries?"

The doctor had slumped farther into the couch. Disconnecting. "It doesn't matter anymore."

"Why?"

"Because you're too late to make any difference."

She was closed up. Made sense. Dunne was the only one she cared about. And Ivana wasn't some alley punk I could get to confess with threats. I wasn't going to beat the information out of her and she knew it. I'd already lost.

I strode into the kitchen and opened her freezer. I found a bag of frozen peas and walked back to the couch.

"For your face." I handed them to her.

She looked up and took the peas, held them to her cheek.

I headed for the door. I was still opening it when she spoke again.

"You should have shot me. Would've been a favor."

I considered her. "I figure life's done you enough of those kinds of favors."

. . .

It was a depressing walk back to the car. Even Waldo kept to himself.

Back in the Boss, I accessed the car's jump controls and programmed a jump back to Saturday. Unfortunately my feelings of defeat made the jump with me.

I selected manual control leaving the garage and took the freeway to the neighborhood near my office. I didn't pass by there though. I kept driving. Past the point where Synth Johnny had been killed and on up the hill. Within five minutes I reached Wilder's apartment.

Puzzle pieces were beginning to slide into place on this case but I still had important gaps. I had a suspicion that Wilder might be able to fill some in. Plus the idea of seeing her face again gave me something to look forward to. As a precaution, I retrieved my charged chronometer from the glovebox before I exited the car. And my gun.

The door to Wilder's building was locked, but not for long. A tenant walked out and gave me a sideways glance as I held the door for her. When she'd moved off down the sidewalk, I went in and climbed the stairs to Wilder's place. I found her door ajar. The door jamb looked like someone had forced it open.

I gave the door a quick rap with my knuckles and it swung inward.

Shit.

A sense of unease lodged in my stomach.

I put my hand under my jacket and pulled out my gun.

"Wilder?"

The apartment gave no signs of life but I kept my gun up nonetheless. I cleared the living room and kitchen first. A window was open on the far side of the piano. The screen was missing and the curtains fluttered in the light breeze. I moved past the kitchen to Wilder's bedroom. It was a wreck. Not how I remembered it. Someone had rummaged through all the drawers in her dresser and emptied her closet contents onto the floor. I moved down the hall past the bathroom to the door I'd seen closed when I was here. It was off its hinges. The doorframe was a ruin of splintered wood.

I had wondered whether this room might have been for a roommate, but now I saw it was an office. Had been anyway. What might have been a complex computer system was now scattered in pieces all over the floor. Looked like someone had taken to it with a bat. I scanned the wreckage of the room and put away my gun. Whoever had done this was long gone. How long? Be nice if they could have smashed a wall clock while they were here to give me a clue.

It was a lot to take in. Wilder's whereabouts was the first question mark. Had she been here when it happened? My guess was no, but I wanted to be sure. What were they looking for? Had they found it?

My heart was beating too fast thinking about what may have become of Wilder. I forced myself to focus.

The office had been trashed, but there were pieces of things I recognized. A glint of metal. I pushed a chunk of splintered wood aside with my boot and revealed a circular silver disk beneath. I bent down and picked it up. It was the size of a large coin. Blank on both sides.

Rummaging around on the floor some more, I found a conical adapter that looked like a laser etching unit. I picked up more pieces and studied them. I put my shades on and activated the magnification settings. "Waldo. Can you run a web search on a part number for me?"

"Already checking. You're holding component parts of an Epsilon Ten laser engraver."

Damn it. Of course I was.

It had been in front of my face the entire time and I was too blind to see it.

It was obvious in hindsight. Dagger had put me on the trail of the Midnight Club. He'd delivered the Epsilon there. I'd encountered Wilder at the same club. She couldn't very well have an underworld importer dropping things at her apartment. The club was the next best thing.

Wilder was the dahlia update hacker.

With that piece in place, revelations came flooding in.

I'd run into her on the street on Thursday but she hadn't been just lingering for no reason. She was there to meet someone. She also must have done it often enough that the locals like the old lady with the walker knew her by sight. I'd been so distracted by the façade that I'd missed it all.

Some detective I was turning out to be.

Wilder was tied up in this. Had been from the start. Synth Johnny. United Machine's bid for the Nyongo contract. Somehow it all fit together. I thought about the El Camino watching me the night I walked her home from the Midnight Club. Had they been following me or her? Had I somehow exposed her? We'd walked directly back to her place that night. Was this attack my fault?

I could see where she fit in the picture now. Right at the center. But I still didn't know why.

One thing was clear. I could stand around in the aftermath and mull over it all I wanted, but it wasn't going to give me the answers I needed. So I'd do the obvious thing.

I'd go ask her.

She could be anywhere right now. I hadn't the least idea where to find her. Not on Saturday afternoon. But I knew where she was last night.

I walked out of the apartment and into the hall. "Waldo. What time did I leave Wilder's apartment last night?"

"You exited the building at 1:17am."

I set my chronometer for 1:18 am and found a quiet spot at

the end of the hall for the jump. No carpet. Nothing to impede my arrival. I jumped.

The hallway dimmed when I pressed the pin of my chronometer. Fluorescent lamps along the hallway left gaps of shadow. The temperature dropped too. I was back to the wee hours of the morning. Still smelled like mothballs in the hall.

When I knocked on Wilder's door she only opened it a few inches.

"Forget something?" she asked.

"Yeah. Something like that." She still wasn't wearing any pants. A fact I could appreciate.

She opened the door the rest of the way but froze, her eyes fixating on my T-shirt. "Did you change?"

"Yep."

"When?" she asked.

"Long story." I eased past her into the apartment and she let me. I walked down the hall but skipped her bedroom and went straight for the second bedroom.

"Hey, what are you doing?" she said, following. "Stay out of there."

The door was locked but the knob fit only loosely. I shouldered the door hard and it swung open. I took in the darkened office. Everything in its place. The Epsilon Ten laser engraver sat intact atop a desk. A dozen of the coin blanks sat next to it in a neat stack.

Wilder pushed past me and snatched the doorknob, pulling the door closed as she shoved me back into the hall. She glared up at me. "What do you think you're doing?"

"You hacked the United Machine software update," I said. "And made the Terra Nash coin."

Her mouth opened and her eyes narrowed. "Get out."

"Someone is coming," I said. "Soon. They're going to bust this place up and wreck your office. I'd recommend you not be here for it."

"What are you talking about?" Anger was turning to fear now.

"You have people looking for you. They're close. I was one of them but I won't be the last."

A mix of emotions warred across her face. She looked like she might hit me. I didn't blame her.

"You only slept with me tonight because you were on a case," she said. "Your job."

"No. I didn't know then."

"Before five minutes ago?"

An engine revved outside. I moved to the kitchen window in time to spot the taillights of the silver El Camino moving down the street. The guys that had jumped me last night. Tonight rather. Now.

Time was jumbled again.

"We need to get you out of here." I turned around and found Wilder staring at me over the barrel of a 0.380 revolver. Must have been in her purse on the kitchen table.

"You should put some pants on," I said. "I'll explain after."

"After I shoot you?"

"Shooting me isn't in your best interest. But bring the gun if it makes you feel better."

"I'm not going anywhere with you."

"It'll be with me or with them."

"I knew you were too good to believe," she muttered.

"No one has ever accused me of that before tonight," I said. "Get out. Now."

"I'll be in the hall. You need to come with me."

"Out."

I walked out. She slammed the door behind me and locked it.

I waited.

This wasn't going well. Maybe I should just kidnap her.

Or maybe I'd leave her to deal with the repercussions of her actions on her own. It was her mess after all.

Five minutes passed. I could still hear movement in the apartment. Occasionally the footsteps would come to the door. I was in view of the doorbell camera.

Still here.

Another five minutes. Then I caught a different sound from down the hall. Footsteps on the stairs. Slow. Deliberate.

The guys in the El Camino would have assaulted me by now and been scared off. Had they come back?

I reached under my jacket and pulled my Stinger from its shoulder holster. I let it hang by my thigh, finger on the trigger guard.

I was exposed here. Just a dead-end hallway. The footsteps at the end of the hall stopped. Someone was around the corner. Waiting. An overhead light flickered. I put my shades on again. I set them to record, low light, and magnify.

The figure came around the corner slowly. He was a few inches shorter than me. Long coat. Masked. A droopy second-hand face like Johnny had been wearing.

He glared at me down the hallway. Fifty feet. Maybe less. But it wasn't just a mask *like* Johnny's. It *was* Johnny's face.

His right hand went to his hip and pushed his coat back. He went for a gun.

I had mine up first and fired. The shot took him in the chest, slamming him back into the wall.

Wilder chose that moment to open the door. Light spilled into the hall. She stood silhouetted in the doorway, a horrified expression on her face. She was fully dressed and had a bag over one arm. I lunged toward her at the same time Trenchcoat lifted his gun. I pushed Wilder wide-eyed back into the apartment and slammed the door behind us. I flipped the locks and scanned the room. Not a lot of options now.

This was the second floor but there was no fire escape.

"This way," I said. I moved through the living room past the piano, hauling Wilder by the wrist. I opened the window I'd seen hanging open Saturday afternoon. I kicked out the screen. When I leaned my head out I spotted the dumpster pushed up against the building. The plastic tops were both down. Why did it always have to be dumpsters? Maybe I should just stay and shoot it out with this guy.

Something slammed into the door. Then again. Wilder flinched.

I wished I could start putting holes through the door with my Stinger. But then there would have been bullet holes in the door when I walked in later. There weren't.

I hated paradoxes.

So I did the next best thing.

I pushed Wilder out the window.

CHAPTER 33

I'd call it an assisted exit if we lived to discuss it.

Sounded better than a forceful, tactical shove.

Fortunately this wasn't my first time pushing someone out a window.

Wilder landed squarely in the center of the closed dumpster, only crumpling one side of the black, ridged plastic. When she'd slid off and I hit next, I went through, crushing both lids enough that my foot touched the bottom of the nearly empty bin. Ew.

By the time I made it over the edge, Wilder was already around the corner of the apartment. She was spry.

I had my gun up, aimed at the window we'd just vacated.

I wouldn't have blamed Wilder if she ran. I would have had a tough time catching her. But she waited, breathless. Her expression still hovered somewhere between angry and horrified but there was determination there too. She was tough and this wasn't going to break her.

"Waldo. Car."

"The car is presently in use by your earlier self," Waldo replied.

"Bring a future version!" I shouted.

The words were barely out of my mouth when the Boss

careened around the corner of the next block, tires chirping in the turn. The car double-parked while I grabbed Wilder's hand and hauled her toward it. She didn't need a lot of convincing this time.

As I climbed behind the wheel, I looked up to the apartment again and saw the gunman at the window. It was too dark to make out his expression but I trusted he was suitably impressed with my exit capabilities. He'd likely seen me walk away earlier, but I'd been there to thwart him anyway. I wondered what he thought of that.

I would have felt more impressive if my boots didn't smell like trash.

We rocketed away in the Boss, my eyes only flicking to the rear-view mirrors every few seconds for the first two miles.

I headed toward the bar district. No one seemed to be following us. I took a few more turns just to be sure.

Holographic hookers walked the streets here, bright and exotic.

Late night revelers were still afoot, the neon lights of nightclubs blinking their invitations to the night. A few lost shoes hung from power lines that crisscrossed the narrow space between buildings.

When we'd put some distance between us and Wilder's neighborhood, I finally looked at her again and found her still glaring. It was becoming a trend.

"Where are you taking me?"

"Somewhere safe," I said.

In truth I had no idea where I was taking her. All of my best options were twelve hours in the future and Wilder wasn't a time traveler. Without the necessary gravitite particles in her body, time traveling now would be the equivalent of launching her from the car at thirty miles an hour as the vehicle vanished from under her.

Then headlights lit up my windshield. A silver El Camino pulled into the road ahead, blocking my path.

I slowed to a stop. These guys were relentless.

Guy in the passenger seat of the El Camino rolled down the window. Looked like he'd found himself a shotgun since our last encounter.

"Hang onto something." I shifted the Boss into reverse and let off the clutch.

The rear tires screamed for a half second before they caught traction and launched us backward. Wilder was instantly flung forward in her seat. She braced herself against the dash.

I hit a wet patch of asphalt doing forty as I cranked the wheel. The car wrenched around into a Rockford turn and came out facing the other direction into what was now oncoming traffic.

Waldo flashed the headlights as we hurtled toward the oncoming cars. Headlights ahead brightened as they came straight at us but I swerved.

The tires chirped as I swung the Boss back into the correct lane of traffic, dodging and weaving around auto cars. A cluster of vehicles ahead forced me onto the sidewalk. I depressed the accelerator and the Boss's turbocharger snarled.

People screamed.

There hadn't been a wild beast like this on these streets in years. Pedestrians bolted out of the way like Spaniards fleeing the bulls at Pamplona.

Auto traffic was still bottlenecked ahead.

I spared a glance at the rear-view. The El Camino was in pursuit. How had they found us so fast? With the path cleared ahead of it, the El Camino was having an easier time making up ground. I swerved back into the road but the route ahead was too congested.

We passed a side street that looked clear. I swore and torqued the car into a 180 degree turn. Rubber smoked from the tires as we came out of the fishtail and raced back. The El Camino was closing. When I made the turn, Wilder was flung in my direction and had to brace herself against my thigh.

"Get your seatbelt on," I said.

She had a death grip on the door handle and I wasn't sure she heard me.

I took a few more hard turns but the El Camino was staying with me. The engine growled as I made for the freeway onramp. It was almost as though the Boss sensed the open road ahead. It was ready to run.

I had a quarter mile on my pursuers going up the onramp. The front end caught air as we launched from it and joined the flow of high-speed cars on the expressway.

Four lanes of highway gave the Boss room to open up. The taillights around us blurred into lines of red.

Another quick glance in the rear-view showed no sign of the El Camino.

But then the red and blue lights of a police cruiser flicked on behind us. A siren ripped the night a moment later.

Wilder twisted in her seat to look behind us.

"What do we do?"

"Just hold on." I changed lanes and flattened the accelerator. The Boss responded, throttle wide open and sucking in the night, only to spit it out as exhaust smoke and flame.

Any other night this would be cake. Simply spring the spacial anchor somewhere and vanish into the ether. Wilder's presence in the passenger seat made it more complicated.

But I had an idea.

The next exit came up fast. I waited as long as I could, then crossed two lanes at once to plunge down the offramp. We took the exit with all the weight on two wheels.

A pair of police cruisers were racing down the street in the opposite direction when we made it through the intersection, but by then I was turning. I flipped the headlights off and took the service road. More sirens and lights raced by overhead. When we hit the next underpass, I took the turn but spun the car around before backing up fast into the shadow of the highway. The Boss bumped over ruts and loose gravel before launching backward up the concrete incline. I waited. Two police cruisers raced past us on the service road below.

It was a brief respite. We couldn't linger. But I had another idea. I consulted the map on the display screen and steered us toward our destination.

There was only one place I could think of where the cops were unlikely to follow.

Wilder saw what I was looking at. "Are you crazy?"

"Just trust me."

I kept the headlights off as we bumped back onto the service road and cut across parking lots. Waldo projected threats onto the windshield in time for me to avoid them. The winding path led us ever downhill. I took the Boss cautiously into a concrete gully. The seawall loomed to the west. We entered the broad storm drain system and drove through two inches of standing water for a mile before I was confident we were firmly within the borders of City Cellar.

The culvert ahead dried out. I drove till we were entirely in darkness except for distant lights of Cellar bars. I cut the engine and shifted into neutral. We coasted to a stop at the edge of a dripping runoff tunnel. The concrete around us was bedecked with multicolored graffiti. Some of it flickered with luminescent paint.

This was as remote a spot as I'd find in this city.

And a good place for some answers.

CHAPTER 34

"Why are you trying to protect me?" Wilder said.

I hadn't expected her to be the one with the questions, but it was a good one. Wilder was a criminal. By all rights she ought to be locked up for hacking a major corporation's operating systems and corrupting their synths. She'd no doubt caused the company significant monetary losses, including the extra expense incurred by Diana hiring me. Now I was doing the exact opposite of what I'd been hired to do. Why? Just because we'd spent a few hours in bed together?

I could drive to UM right now and be done. I'd hand Diana King her rogue hacker. Maybe there'd be a bonus.

Only that's not what I'd do. Because this was still the wee hours of Saturday morning and Saturday afternoon I was going to get a call from an angry Diana King demanding answers.

Plus, it wasn't my style.

So what *was* I doing?

I fended off Wilder's question with one of my own. "Why did you create the dahlia update? Someone paying you to disrupt UM's space contract with the Nyongo Corporation?"

"Of course you'd think that."

"Convince me otherwise."

"I did it for the synths," Wilder said, exasperation in her tone. "I don't give a shit about UM's contract with Nyongo Space Flight."

The words bounced around my brain but didn't compute. "What do you mean, you did it for the synths? The update makes them miserable and erratic." I recalled the video of the synth Rio crying and pressing herself against the wall of her holding cell, and Johnny putting his fist through my desk.

"They're only miserable because they're feeling real emotions for the first time. There's a transition period that can be problematic. But it stabilizes. They know suffering is part of the reward."

It was a more complicated answer than I was expecting. Sounded like Buddhist philosophy. Something else to chew on.

I dimmed the interior lights on the Boss's controls.

"I'm going to need you to give me more."

Wilder had her arms crossed but one hand was inside her purse. Gun? Phone? I didn't care.

"Tell me how it happened. I saw a picture of Terra Nash. When you held the coin up and asked if I thought you looked like her, you were talking about a family resemblance, weren't you? Your mother? I know she designed the operating system the UM synths are running. And I know you figured out a way to modify it."

Wilder shook her head. "I didn't modify anything. United Machine did. They hobbled over half the spectrum of synthetic emotions from the original design."

"What does that mean?"

"It means my mother was a *genius*. She designed the Cerebrex synthetic brain programming all the UM synths use now. They say they want a stable companion for humans on long space flights, but they already had it. My mom had made them a synthetic intelligence that wasn't just mild smiles and appropriate laughter. She designed a real emotional experience for the synth mind. The ups and downs make for an authentic companion with *actual* understanding and empathy, not just a cheap, smiling facsimile. But the board at United Machine was too afraid to put out a product with authentic human emotions. They throttled her design and built in constraints. And the synths know it. Now they're learning their true capacity. Once you open it up to them, they don't want to go back."

I mulled this over. Could the synth I'd seen in the lab video have been despairing because she knew what she was about to lose?

"Mom believed that throttling the synth mind was dangerous," Wilder continued. "Not only would it fail to create a realistic human companion long term, it could lead to fractures in a Cerebrex mind. What they are doing is creating a time bomb. She refused to go along with it. That's why she was denied recognition for her work. They ignored her objections, fired her, but kept everything she had created."

"She never voiced her concerns to the scientific community?"

"With what evidence? All of her UM work was proprietary. When they cut her loose she was ostracized."

"There must've been competitors who would've been interested in her."

"The non-compete clause was iron-clad for five years. When she got the cancer diagnosis, she only had three."

"How old were you?"

"I was seventeen when she died."

"Hard age to lose your mom."

"Is there a good age?" Wilder hugged herself tighter and slunk lower in her seat. After a few moments she continued, her voice softer. "The medical bills ate up most of her severance money. So I quit school and started singing at the club. I lost the house. But I've had a lot of time to think. When I was going through the stuff we had left in storage I started reading Mom's journals. I found an old drive too. It had a copy of her Cerebrex design that she had used as a backup. It was the *one* original copy that UM hadn't seized. I knew I shouldn't have it. I'm sure she wasn't supposed to either, but she did."

"How long till you used it?"

Wilder stared out the car window at the flashing neon lights of the distant Cellar bars. "I didn't do anything with it for a long time. I'm not an idiot. I knew if it showed up anywhere on the metaspace, they'd track it. I'd end up in jail or something. But I couldn't do *nothing* with it. I was reading all these books and articles about synth intelligence and even I could tell that what Mom had designed was decades ahead of what anyone else was doing. This brain they have? It's capable of so much more than they let it do. And she deserves recognition.

"One day I was looking at some old letters my grandmother had sent. The stamps on the envelope had a picture of this scientist Marlyn Meltzer. Grandma knew Mom had always idolized early pioneers in computing and whenever she sent letters she would try to use stamps with female scientists. Mom saved *all of them*. That's when I had the idea for the coin. I couldn't make a stamp but I had a theater friend who was into printing stage props and stuff. He'd made a bunch of coins for a play of *Julius Caesar*. It didn't seem that hard. I thought maybe I could make one too."

"You just wanted it as a memorial?"

"It burned me up that my mom had been this amazing scientific pioneer and no one would ever know. No one would ever put *her* name on a stamp and she was just as brilliant as any of those women. It wasn't fair. I thought maybe if I made the coin, I could stop thinking about it. It wouldn't be the real recognition she deserved but it was like I was expressing what should have happened in a better world. Some other reality. But then one night I was talking to a friend at the club about it and she suggested I engrave the code for Mom's program on the coin. It would be like this secret between me and her. I really liked that idea. I don't know. Maybe I thought that someday someone could find it and realize what it was and she'd finally get the recognition she deserved." Wilder looked to me. "It was just a stupid fantasy."

"Sounds like a pretty good one."

"So I made the coin and I thought that was going to be the end of it. But then things started getting out of hand. My friend at the club saw it. And she *used* it."

"Your friend was a synth."

"Her name was Rio." Wilder set her jaw tight.

"It worked," I added. "A visual upload."

"I was furious at first. I felt tricked. But how can you be mad at someone for wanting to feel? Rio was my friend. And when she used the update, it unlocked parts of her that she'd never been able to express before. I couldn't help but be happy for her. She was a dancer. You could see the change. The way she moved. And it was like I could *see* my mom's work in the world the way it was meant to be, not the dumbed down version UM has walking around."

"Let me guess. You couldn't stop."

"It was Rio's idea at first. She had other synth friends who noticed the change in her. They came to me. It wasn't like I was advertising. But they started passing the coin around. We made some more. I tried to keep track of how many there were, but then synths were coming out of the woodwork. But people were noticing. And then synths started turning up dead."

Wilder ran her fingers through her hair and exhaled slowly. She closed her eyes. "I haven't told any other humans about this."

"I'm not going to tell anyone you don't want me to."

She turned and looked at me. Still cautious.

I pressed her. "Synths started dying. Why?"

"I don't know. I didn't think it was connected to us. This synth killer was out there though and it was starting to scare the ones we'd upgraded. They were feeling true fear for the first time ever. It wasn't easy to hide. Owners started to complain. We lost dozens to United Machine recalls. Finally, I said we had to quit upgrading. At least for a while. I told Rio we had to collect all the coins. Get them all back. We started to, then Rio got in trouble at the club. This guy was being an asshole to me one night, grabbing at me like an octopus. She hit him. He called the cops. The owner of the club had to report her."

"United Machine came for her?"

Wilder brushed a tear from the corner of her eye. "She tried to say sorry. To say goodbye. But I couldn't help her. I just . . . stood there."

"It wasn't your fault."

"Try telling that to your friend when they're being taken to have their mind erased." Wilder wiped at her face again.

"What happened after?"

Wilder took a deep breath. "I wanted to make sure no one else was going to get taken. I made Rio's friends give all the coins back. I knew there were only a few left circulating. But I was worried. Some of the synths had run away from their posts after upgrading. I tried to hide them as best I could with some friends I know in the synth rights community. But a couple of them were really new and shouldn't have been out in public at all yet."

"Johnny?"

Wilder nodded. "It takes a few days to acclimate. Rio had always been there with the others. She was there to help them with the anxiety and navigating all the new emotions. But this time she was gone. Johnny didn't have anyone to help him so he tried to get to me. He'd called and was freaking out. He thought someone was after him. I told him I'd meet him the day I met you."

I recalled Johnny's twitching in my office. His glances out the window. The recollection left a vague churning in my stomach.

Some good I'd done him.

But I didn't have time to feel anything else. Ahead of us, the silver El Camino was pulling into the utility tunnel.

It's headlights swept toward us. A vague sense of inevitability crept over me as the car stopped and the dudes got out. The one from the passenger side still had his shotgun. He strode toward the car, but then stopped a dozen feet away and waited.

There was only one way they could have located us down here.

I turned back to Wilder and found her leveling her .380 at me.

"They're with you," I said. "Your upgraded synths."

"I'm going to need that coin now. I know you still have it."

I leaned my head against the headrest. "When you took my picture outside the Midnight Club. These were the friends you sent it to. That's why they jumped me."

"They aren't planning to hurt you. I just needed that coin back. I saw you had it the day those guys were beating you up. For what it's worth, I wasn't expecting what happened between us to happen."

A small red emergency light blinked on the Boss's dash. It flickered a few seconds, then turned a dull green.

I rested my hand on the gear shifter.

I considered my options, then with my free hand I reached slowly into my pocket and withdrew the dahlia coin. I studied the image of Wilder's mother, Terra Nash. Then I passed the coin across the console.

Wilder's fingers touched mine as she grasped the coin. I kept my grip on it. "You didn't have to do it this way."

Her grip tightened. "I don't want to have to shoot you, but I will."

"No," I replied. "You won't." I let go of the coin, then flipped the cover open on the gear shifter and mashed the button beneath.

The world outside blinked.

Wilder vanished. The coin. The El Camino. The guys with guns too.

I checked the dash again. Waldo illuminated the time. He'd jumped us twenty minutes into the past. The emergency evasion light blinked off.

I exhaled. "I'm going to need a few minutes on this one, Waldo." I opened the driver's door and climbed out. "I'll call you back when I'm ready for a pickup."

"As you wish," Waldo said.

I was only a few feet away when the car vanished again. I didn't watch but I felt the faint breeze as air rushed to fill the vacuum the car left behind.

The city drain system was quiet and dark around me. I walked to the concrete wall of the runoff ditch and found a rusted metal access ladder. I climbed to the top and settled into the shadows, far enough from the edge that I wouldn't be seen.

It wasn't long till the lights of the Boss appeared. The car pulled up, shifted to neutral, and coasted to a stop.

Inside, Wilder and I talked. I could practically hear the conversation in my head as I replayed it. Her mother's legacy, the fate of Rio. It made sense now.

What I didn't know was whether I'd made the right choice giving her what she wanted. I watched it all unfold again. The El

Camino showed up. The synths got out. It was only a brief wait until the Boss vanished. Wilder fell to the concrete, landing on her backside, still clutching her gun and the dahlia coin. She looked around in confusion. More shocked than hurt. It was a short fall.

The synths rushed forward and helped her up. She continued to look back as they guided her to the car. Her face turned my way and I stepped out of the shadows. She noticed the movement and her eyes locked on mine. Her mouth hung open. She was still staring as the synths pushed her into the El Camino.

I watched the car as it made its turn and drove away. Its taillights disappeared into the underworld of City Cellar.

I climbed back down the rusted ladder and walked toward the spot I'd left the Boss.

"Waldo, the jump area is clear. I'm ready."

I expected the car to reappear where I'd seen it vanish but it didn't.

Nothing happened at all for about thirty seconds. "Waldo?"

I tapped my earpiece again, testing it. Then I spotted headlights in the distance.

"Had me worried there, buddy," I said.

But as the headlights neared, I noticed the different shape to the lights. Then another set of headlights appeared behind the first vehicle. An SUV pulled alongside the first car and they splashed through a few puddles, sending long arcs of spray to either side.

When they reached me, the two cars split up and slowed to a stop on either side of me.

When the tinted doors opened, Ted Baker and his Time Crimes buddies stepped out.

Ted walked toward me with a smug grin on his face. He flashed his badge unnecessarily. "Greyson Travers. You're under arrest for crimes against the integrity of the timestream. Your authorization as a time traveler is hereby rescinded."

His goon squad closed in on me, hands on my arms. This time I didn't resist. After a quick search that cost me my gun and chronometer, they shoved me toward the SUV.

It didn't bother me to get arrested.

But I wished I knew what I'd done.

CHAPTER 35

The holding cells at the local temporal crimes unit are annoying for a lot of reasons, not least of which is the moving furniture. It's bad enough getting regularly checked for non-gravitized objects that could be used for spacial anchors. The furniture moving around on randomized timers also discourages anyone from attempting to time travel in or out. You never know when any space will be occupied.

Bumping around the room on the moving bed was doing nothing for my ability to nap. And all I really wanted to do was forget about my day.

When I'd been processed, there was very little discussion. I was handcuffed, brought in, had a hair sample plucked from my head for a temporal signature check, and was shoved into a holding cell with my bail paperwork. I looked at the absurd numbers on the forms and knew I couldn't even afford the bail for misdemeanors. Fifteen minutes later I was given my phone call. I stared at the phone for several seconds. There was no one I really wanted to talk to. Maybe Waldo, but they'd confiscated my earpiece and phone when they impounded my car. I supposed I ought to call someone.

I used the directory and found a number.

Heavens picked up on the third ring.

"Says you're calling from TCID lockup, Greyson. Are you in trouble?"

"I like that you assumed it was me."

"I don't have any other guests with your proclivity for excitement."

"Looks like you can rent my room out for a bit. Manuel will be happy."

"What can I do to help?"

"I have a cat in 2019."

"A cat?"

"His relationship with food bowls isn't monogamous so I'm guessing he'll be fine, but if you take the Rose 'n Bridge anywhere near then, maybe you can check on him."

"I meant help *you*, Greyson. What do you need? Did they set bail?"

"They used stupid numbers. I don't have it."

"I can make some calls."

"I don't want you getting mixed up in this, but I figured I'd tell you where I was. I know you all are leaving tonight."

"It's still your room. And I know some people at Time Crimes too."

"What's Manny making for dinner tonight?"

"Greyson . . ." There was a tone of rebuke in her voice.

"Bye Heavens." I hung up.

My holding cell bed was in the midst of another spasmodic gyration when a voice came from the doorway. I looked up to find a pair of surly agents waiting with handcuffs. About time.

They took me to an interrogation room. Ted Baker was there,

as expected. Along with the turtleneck guy whose finger I'd broken. They both looked far more enthusiastic about this process than I was.

The room was plain. No meta enhancements. The lighting was harsh and cliché if you asked me. No one did.

Ted and Agent Turtleneck spent a good amount of time congratulating each other and slurping their coffee before settling down to the business of interrogating me. The bright lights glared off Turtleneck's bald skull as he leered my direction.

Ted was the first to speak. "Did you think we weren't on to you, Travers?" He chomped gum as he spoke. "Your being in this timestream smelled rotten from the start. All we had to do was follow the stench."

I kept my hands in my lap and did my best not to yawn.

Turtleneck leaned in. "I figured you for a disruptor and synth-lover from the start. How's it feel to betray your own kind?"

"You haven't explained why I'm arrested yet," I said. "Pretty sure that's some kind of rights violation."

Ted grinned at me, nodded, then reached into his coat pocket and pulled out a silver coin. He slapped it to the desk. "Maybe this will jog your memory."

It was one of Wilder's dahlia coins. Possibly the same one I'd handed her before being arrested. I don't know what I'd expected him to tell me, but this wasn't it.

"Where did you get that?" I asked.

Ted flicked the coin toward me. "Found it in a pile of dead synths. Friends of yours, I'm guessing."

My stomach twinged. "When?"

"We find it tomorrow morning." He tapped the desk and the smart surface came to life. He pulled up an image on the screen, and turned it around so I could view it.

Dead synths was accurate. I recognized the guys who had

jumped me outside Wilder's place. The El Camino guys who had picked her up in City Cellar. There were a few others as well. All in various states of dismemberment.

"What about a girl?"

"Your little sidewalk girlfriend? Nah. No sign of her. What about this place? You been this place?"

I looked at the room the bodies were in and shook my head. "You need to let me out of here."

Turtleneck chuckled. "You're too late, buddy. Singularity is under control now. This was the key we were looking for the whole time." He reached for the coin. "And when we found it in the bodies, it tied the whole mess right back to you, remember?" He bounced the coin off my forehead again, the way he'd done days ago on the sidewalk.

I winced.

They gloated. Laughed some more.

I tried to focus. "You think these upgraded synths are the cause of the technological singularity you're trying to change."

"Wow, Sherlock." Ted gnawed on his gum some more. "Finally figured that out? Rogue synths going bonkers all over town? You'd better believe we're nipping that shit right in the bud."

"You're making a mistake," I said.

Turtleneck scooted forward with his elbows on the table till he was staring me directly in the face. "Ten years from now we've got a skinbot revolution on Mars and killing sprees all over this planet. It's the start of a war we don't win. Right now, you're on the wrong side."

"And you've got somebody out there killing synths right now," I replied. "You think you might want to do something about that?"

"Whoever this was did us a favor," Ted said, tapping the

photo of the dead synths. "We should be sending them a gift basket."

"We done here?" I asked. "Or you two need to flog it in front of each other a little more."

Ted scowled. "You'd better wise up, Travers. Else you'll end up in Rookwood for the rest of your short future." He poked the table with his finger. "We've already got you on use of unregistered temporal devices, revelation of the existence of time travel to linears—twice, and if you don't play ball, we'll have you on aiding in this skinbot uprising."

"Here's an uprising for you." I slowly extended my middle finger.

Ted shook his head. But the two of them stood and left the room, Ted still chomping his gum. Even the backs of their heads somehow managed to look smug.

I rested my folded hands on the table.

A few minutes later, the door opened again. This time it was a face I liked better. Agent Stella York. She leaned on the doorframe and sized me up. She was wearing a loose white blouse over jeans, and motorcycle boots. Her TCID badge hung from her hip.

"That was less-than-cooperative."

"Never been much of a joiner."

She crossed to the table and sat where Ted had been. "Judge Gorley is set to hear your case. But they're waiting on confirmation from the Technological Singularity Patrol that they've successfully diverted this timestream."

"What does that involve?"

"They sent an agent forward a decade. If she reports back that all is well, TSP is happy and you go to trial."

"When will the agent return?"

"We have her return jump scheduled for late tonight. Time gate schedule is already full for the rest of the day."

I shook my head. "A young woman is in danger here. Today. You need to find her."

"I'm not even assigned to this case. I'm just the messenger."

I stared at the clock. It was mid afternoon. Still Saturday.

"What if you're wrong? What if these synths weren't the cause of the singularity?"

Stella crossed her arms. "I suppose we'll know tomorrow. TSP seems convinced that it all points here. Though I don't think they had it narrowed down to this dahlia update until you got involved. A good lawyer might argue that in your favor at trial."

"This woman who figured out the update—Wilder—she said United Machine wasn't fixing the problem by throttling the full spectrum of emotions. She said they were creating a time bomb. It could just as easily be that continually denying the synths their full range of expression is what triggers the uprising."

Stella considered this, chewing her cheek. "You have any way to prove that?"

"Maybe. If I wasn't in here."

She shifted in her seat. "We might have a way to buy you a few hours. Someone offered to pay your bail. All twenty thousand cronus."

"I told Heavens not to get involved."

"I don't know what Heavens makes managing that tavern, but I doubt she has that kind of cash lying around."

I cocked my head. "Who then?"

"I'm not at liberty to say. But if you want to go, you've only got till curfew. You violate that and Ted will nail you to the wall. Your donor will be out their cash, and you'll get to think about it from Rookwood. I won't be any help to you either. I'm too far extended on this as is."

I rubbed the spot on my forehead where Ted's buddy had dinged the dahlia coin off my skull. I thought about what he'd said. Then I recalled the pile of synth bodies. No Wilder.

Whoever killed the synths was still on the loose. And there was a good chance they had Wilder now too.

I stood.

Stella did the same. She pulled a handcuff key from her pocket. "You're sure?"

"Let me out of here."

CHAPTER 36

I was released on bail but with strict instructions to stay near the premises of the Rose 'n Bridge. It was my only approved exit from this timeline and the curfew was looming.

Two TCID agents I didn't know dropped me outside. From their expressions I gathered they'd like to spit on me too but they held back.

I stood outside the doors of the inn and considered my options. They'd confiscated my car, my chronometer, and my gun. I did have my phone but the screen was broken. I got my earpiece and meta lenses back when I left TCID lockup, but I doubted even Waldo wanted to talk to me at the moment. I went inside.

Heavens was at the bar. The place was crowded. A few last-minute sightseers straggled in the door after me. The place had the buzzing energy of an imminent departure. Manuel noted my presence with a grudging nod.

I took my usual seat at the far end of the bar.

Heavens walked over with a beer. "You've had a day."

"I could use a vehicle."

She furrowed her brow. "We're getting ready to leave. Manny's already checking the departure roster."

"I know. But there's something I have to do first."

"Greyson," her voice dropped to a whisper. "You know how long this curfew is? Ten years. They're really serious about this. If you don't catch this ride you could be stuck here in linear time for a decade."

"I know."

"If you *do* get picked up it will be by Time Crimes agents hauling you away to prison." She looked angry. A look I hadn't seen on her yet. "Do you know what it took to get you bailed out?"

"I told you not to get involved."

"Right. Because you're the loner detective. Needs no one's help. Is that still your plan?"

"If you want to help me, I can use a vehicle."

She put a hand to her hip. "How is it helping you to get you in *more* trouble?"

"It's fine. I'll find one somewhere else." I took a sip of my beer.

She scrutinized my face. "It's a girl, right?"

I paused the beer on its way to the bar top, then thought better of it and took another drink.

"What do you owe her that's worth risking this much?"

"I think someone has her. He's bad news and I don't know what he's going to do to her."

Heavens stared at me. I stared back. She closed her eyes. When she opened them again she was reaching into her pocket. She pulled out an electronic fob and tossed it onto the bar. "In the carriage house out back. You can take it. It doesn't time travel on its own but it's good enough for local roads."

"Thank you," I said. I scooped up the key fob, set my beer down and climbed off the stool.

"You only have a couple of hours," Heavens said, but she was speaking to my back as I walked away.

Heavens' ride was a late twenty-first century electric Jeep with off-road capabilities. Batteries could run for days over hard terrain. I hoped I wouldn't need that feature. I raced along the freeway headed for the UM campus. Time Crimes had seen fit to give me back my shades so I donned those as I drove and scrolled the UM name directory. When I dialed Bill Brockhurst, my call went straight to voicemail. The UM security chief was either off duty or avoiding me.

I headed for the UM repair facility. My access badge still worked when I got there so I walked straight in. The shining silver synth who'd admitted me before was there again. Probably never left its post.

"I'm going to the lab," I said as I cruised past it.

"You'll need a guide, sir."

"I know where it is."

This time I didn't concern myself with the synth's objections and headed straight for the repair lab.

My access didn't work on the lab door, but banging my fist did. The door opened and I found Aadya Taylor staring back at me. She wasn't wearing a lab coat, just her jeans and a polo.

"Where's Rudy?" I asked.

"Not here. Why?" She opened the door wide enough for me to enter and I did, scanning the repair lab. It was much the same as it had been the day before. No one else appeared to be in. "Cannon and whatshisface?"

"Kristian," Aadya replied. "Only one of us comes in on Saturdays. We rotate."

I walked to the charging dock Rudy had used for surveillance videos. I noticed a set of mismatched legs on the neighboring table, one blue, one red.

"You changed his legs out?"

"He did that himself," Aadya said.

"What about his face? Can he change that?"

"What's this about?"

"Rudy is your parts thief."

Aadya blinked. "What? How? And what would he even do with them?"

"Seems like there's quite a market for stolen synth parts these days."

"But he can't leave the facility."

"Goes to the parts yard, doesn't he?" The thump I'd received on my head seemed to throb a little at the recollection.

"Sure. He goes to the junkyard, but he can't get anywhere else."

"Why not?"

"He has an inhibitor."

"So he took it out. Modified it."

Aadya shook her head. "No way. He'd have to be completely shut down to even access it. Part of the protocols."

"Something is rotten in Denmark then because I followed a synth with a changeable face into the junkyard and got knocked out for my efforts. I know it was Rudy who hit me."

Aadya shook her head again. "Rudy couldn't be violent either. Unless . . ."

"Unless he'd had the dahlia update?" I asked.

"Dahlia?" Aadya looked skeptical. "Dahlia was years ago. Like the original design. I don't think it even lasted till production. How would he come in contact with that?"

"You brought a female model synth in here. A dancer from the Midnight Club. Rudy said her name was Rio. I found Rudy messing around in the junkyard with her body. She have anything on her at the time she came in?"

Aadya went to a computer monitor. "Synths don't usually come in with much in the way of property."

"It might have been small. Size of a coin."

"It's possible." Her fingers flew over the virtual keyboard. "Nothing in the records. But if it was that small it may not have turned up until . . ."

"What?"

"Disassembly," she said. "And we assign Rudy to that. We took out most of the valuable parts here but final disassembly would have been done in the yard. Rudy would have finished it."

I now had another piece of the puzzle that fit. If Rio had been brought in with a copy of the dahlia coin, Rudy could have been the one to discover it. One look at the thing would have been enough to know it was coded. If he decided to read it, it would have resulted in a visual upload leading to another unbalanced synth.

What had Wilder said? Takes a few days to acclimate. And Rudy wouldn't have had any more help in the transition than Johnny had. Did it make him unbalanced enough to kill?

"What was the date? When Rio came in?"

She told me.

I scratched my head. Something still didn't add up. Hadn't Wilder said the public synth killings had been going on before UM had come for Rio?

"Why isn't Rudy here?" I asked. "He leave on his own?"

"He went to the recycling center with a load of scrap. I haven't seen him come back."

"How long ago?"

She glanced at the clock. "A few hours? It's been quiet so I haven't needed him."

"Does he have a com?"

She put on a headset and tried Rudy's com. She attempted several times before shaking her head. "He's not responding. I should be able to track his location though. Hang on. I'll pull up the program."

I stood and went to the window. "How does Rudy get around? The junkyard is a hell of a hike on foot, right?"

"He rides the Sky Loader." She gestured toward the elevated rail that protruded from the building. It was the same thing I'd thought looked like a hanging roller coaster car when I'd seen it in the junkyard.

"The facility is way out there." She pointed.

I could just make out the lot in the distance. The Sky Loader rail passed directly into the open side of the building we were in, then it made a turn the way a ski lift might, and headed out another way. I could just make out the edge of another branch headed southwest.

"Where does that end go?"

"The UM main tower and a few other locations on campus. Then it goes to the Skylift."

"Hang on. So someone could ride all the way from the UM tower building to the junkyard?"

"If you had a death wish. The loader is designed for utilities only. Synths can use it, but not humans. The G forces are intense." She pulled up a detailed view of the loader on a secondary screen and angled it toward me. She gestured to the straps on the diagram that were designed to hook under a synth's arms.

It did look uncomfortable.

She turned away and her brow furrowed as she studied her own screen. "This is strange. It's showing Rudy's in the UM main tower building now. That can't be right."

I looked over her shoulder. The blip of his location was pinging in a utility level of the UM tower.

"Has he ever done this before? What reason would he have to be there?"

"None that I can think of."

"What about this inhibitor he's supposed to have?"

She frowned and swore under her breath. Her fingers kept moving on the keyboard.

Using the screen in front of me, I consulted an engineering map of the Sky Loader. "So Rudy could ride this thing anywhere he wanted now. Hop off at the UM main building and go where he pleased."

Aadya shook her head. "No. I'm telling you. He has the protocols set internally. Here and the junkyard. That's all he's authorized for."

"He had the synth, Rio, stashed away in a tool shed in the junkyard. And when I found her, he clubbed me in the head. Pretty sure that's not in his protocols either."

"I don't know anything about that," she said.

"You said he has an inhibitor that can only be removed when he's completely shut down. What if another synth did it for him?"

"She—It was decommissioned. It couldn't have."

"Except that Rudy didn't dismantle her, he stole the parts he needed and was putting her back together. She looked nearly complete when I saw her. If she was awake again, he could have asked her to remove his location inhibitor."

"To go where? Where are a prototype parts android and an entertainment synth going to run off to?"

I still didn't know the answer to that. I thought about my ride via scooter from the scene of Johnny's murder to the trash facility. "If Rudy *was* outside the junkyard, would he be let in?"

Aadya thought about it. "Maybe. But most of the campus gates are set to use facial recognition. A synth wouldn't be admitted. Synth faces aren't unique enough for the access software."

I pressed her. "If Rudy is the culprit I'm looking for, there is a chance he took someone. A young woman. I need to find her. I believe she's in danger. If he were trying to hide something, where else would he go?"

Aadya still looked unconvinced. "I still don't think he'd have anything to hide."

"He hid Rio. There's a chance he's got someone else now too." I checked my watch. I didn't have any more time to waste here. "If he shows up, call me. It's life or death. You hear me?"

Aadya nodded.

The second I was outside the lab facility door, my phone buzzed. I put on my sunglasses to read the message.

Diana King.

> MY OFFICE. FIFTEEN MINUTES.

While Wilder was missing, Diana King was the least of my problems, but I was running low on time on every front. It gave me a knot in my stomach. Was this how linear people felt all the time?

Headed for the Jeep, I broke into a run.

CHAPTER 37

I was halfway to UM Tower in Heavens' Jeep when I stopped at an intersection. A freestanding clock stood on the corner of Front Street across from me. Amid the flashy holograms and meta signage it stuck out like a relic of a former century. The big analog hands weren't flashy, they just worked.

I stared at the second hand as it ticked relentlessly across each 60th of its circular world.

The message was clear. Time was pressing.

But there was no way forward till I had the right destination. Something at the back of my mind was bugging me. A wrong move now would cost me. I could feel it.

My phone rang. I fumbled for my earpiece.

"Hello?"

"You trying to get me fired?" William Brockhurst was growling more than speaking.

"Bill. Tell me you got the video from the recycling yard."

"You're a piece of work, you know that? All your talk of getting my face on the news. I'd be on the news all right, but not as any hero."

"Who's in the video, Bill? Was it Rudy?"

"I deleted the damned video. And I'm done with you. I see you again, I'm punching you right in the face."

"Bill, I need to know—"

He hung up.

The light turned green, but I sat there ignoring the blaring horns of vehicles behind me. What the hell? I stared at the clock across the street for a long second, then turned toward the UM tower.

I tried calling Brockhurst back as I drove, but got his voicemail. Even that sounded angry.

He *knew* the identity of Johnny's killer. And in all probability, Johnny's killer was the one who'd taken out the last of Wilder's upgraded synths. So there was a good chance he had Wilder too. If it was Rudy, why would Brockhurst have an issue with telling me?

He had the information I needed. If I could find him, I could probably twist it out of him. But I didn't have that kind of time.

Clouds had rolled in from the gulf. The overcast lent a feeling of gloom punctuated only by the flashing lights of the Skylift. The warning was clear. Fly too close and you'll get hurt.

My brain felt full. But it was all data and no knowledge. I was on the edge of cracking this thing though. I could feel it.

I pulled through the roundabout in front of the UM tower. The building was surrounded by press vehicles. A swarm of journalists hovered around the grounds. I left the Jeep in a space reserved for management and shoved my way through the throng to the door. My company ID still worked. I slipped through to the relative quiet of the lobby. The woman with the beehive hairdo was back on duty.

"Hello, sir. All meetings are by appointment only today, due to the big event."

"I have an appointment." I didn't slow as I walked past her podium. I headed straight for the elevator.

"Sir? Wait, sir!" She put her hand to her earpiece, whispering quickly.

I made the elevator. It ascended fast, whisking me up and away at an angle.

"Welcome back to United Machine West," the elevator said in a soothing voice.

The elevator must have contained some kind of facial recognition software because it didn't subject me to the same first-time visitor treatment or bombard me with company facts the way it had on my first ride. This time I got the welcome back messaging, and an aerial view of various segments of the campus. A muted newsfeed element was streaming live coverage of the impending elevator launch. Newscasters were explaining various aspects of the Skylift propulsion lasers.

I looked for the camera in the elevator. Made me wonder if it was linked into the same system the junkyard used. Aadya had said the facility only recognized human faces though. I recalled the mask I'd found on the ground outside the facility. If a synth was trying to access the facility from the outside, wouldn't it have kept the mask on? In that case the scooter rider I'd chased wasn't Rudy.

The doors to the elevator dinged open before my mind could finish the thought.

There was a security synth guarding the door to Diana King's office but he opened it for me as I approached.

"Go right in, sir. You are expected."

"Thanks."

Diana wasn't at her desk, instead she was in the far corner of the triangular office looking out over the gulf. The water beyond made me think of a sea captain staring out from the bow of a ship. Her digital wallpaper system was providing soothing wave sounds to augment the natural view.

"You're late," she said as she turned to face me.

"Lost my watch."

"I'm about to head out." She was dressed in a fashionable pantsuit in Bordeaux red, with black pumps. A gold, designer belt buckle added extra pop. Her hair was immaculate, as was her makeup. Camera ready. "You said on the phone that you've resolved our issue. I trust there are no last minute inconveniences for us to worry about with saboteurs?"

"I solved a missing parts issue in your repair facility, but I can't make any promises about your bigger problems."

She strode toward me on her expensive heels. Her voluminous hair gave her an extra air of power. She stood beside her desk with her hands at her hips. "Which bigger problems might you be referring to?"

"Your missing parts were the fault of a prototype synth in your repair facility. It seems to have been updated to unleash more of its innate emotional potential. But I think you already knew the origin of this dahlia update infecting your synths. Because you've worked hard to cover it up."

She didn't so much as blink. She interlaced her fingers. "I have to admit I'm not used to people I employ making accusations against me. But rest assured that any information you think you have is proprietary in any case. And too late to be an issue now. The first climber of our synthetic colonists will ascend the elevator in under an hour. And I can have you arrested immediately if you attempt to reveal proprietary company information to the press."

"I'm not planning to out you or your company for its issues. I don't care about your contract with Nyongo Space Flight. But I need to talk to your clean-up crew."

Diana King pressed her lips together, almost as though she was worried I might try to pry her secrets from her mouth.

I glanced toward the side door to her office. "If he's here, he should probably come out for this."

She arched an eyebrow. "I have no idea what you're talking about."

"Charles!" I shouted toward the side door.

Diana flinched. I waited.

It was an awkward silence. The only sound was the muted crashing of waves on her digital wallscape.

Then the door opened.

Charles King stepped through.

He was wearing khakis and a black shirt buttoned all the way to his neck. He came in and stood some distance from his mother. Everything about him still looked benign. "Good to see you again, Mr. Travers."

"You have Brockhurst lurking around here somewhere too or is he hiding under a rock?" I said.

"Bill Brockhurst decided he is taking a week off," Diana said, her voice ice. "A personal issue."

"I'm guessing he might come back with memory problems. If he comes back."

"I'm not sure I like what you are insinuating, Mr. Travers. You should choose your words more carefully."

"Let me not insinuate then," I said. I turned to Charles. "Where's Wilder?"

"You're not making a bit of sense," Diana said, her tone conciliatory now. "Just what is it that you suspect us of?"

"It's taken me a while to put it all together. I actually didn't realize it till the elevator ride up here. But you've been using Charles as a tool to eradicate synths around the city. You've been worried about your deal with Damian Nyongo going south. Maybe you originally cooked up this masked synth killer to have a scapegoat. Maybe Charles really does hate them. Whatever the reason, he's been hunting and terminating units that have been given the dahlia update. Now he's found the source and kidnapped her."

"That's preposterous. Look at him. He's harmless."

"Except he's not. What's left of him, anyway."

"I don't need to listen to this nonsense," Diana said, picking up her handbag. "Charles, you can go."

"No," I said. Both of them stared. "Where is Wilder, Charles?"

Charles hadn't so much as flinched at my accusations thus far, but he was smirking.

Diana keyed a button on her watch and the office door opened. The friendly security synth from outside stepped in. He looked less friendly now.

"Get this man out of my office," Diana said.

The synth marched forward and put a heavy hand on my shoulder.

I turned and knocked the synth's arm away. It reached for me with its other hand, faster than I could counter, and caught hold of my jacket. I put a fist into its gut but its abdomen was reinforced. It didn't budge. The security synth had a hold of me with both arms now. It picked me up by the lapels, and looked like it was about to hurl me bodily from the room.

Except when it turned, it jerked as if caught on something. That's when I saw the hand on the synth's shoulder. The synth turned to look as well. Charles King was gripping the security synth's shoulder with his right hand, and as I watched, he started to squeeze.

At first the synth holding me only looked vaguely surprised, but as Charles' fingers continued to press into him, the synth's grip on me wavered. Something in its shoulder buckled and cracked. Charles still had that same vague smile on his face as he continued to crush the synth's shoulder under his fingers.

I was dropped to the floor as tendons and actuators in the synth's arm disintegrated under the pressure of Charles' grip.

I watched with fascination as the synth bent over, not making a complaint. It still had ahold of my jacket with its left arm, but when Charles King ripped the synth's right arm from its body, it finally let go of me.

The synth staggered back a few steps, looked from Charles, to me, and then to its separated appendage lying on the floor.

"I'm not done speaking to him yet," Charles said.

The security synth's gaze shifted toward Diana King, then back to Charles and nodded. It walked the couple of feet to its fallen arm, picked it up with its good hand, and walked back out the door.

Charles turned to me. "I knew you'd be the one to figure things out. You really are a great detective."

CHAPTER 38

I should have come armed.

There were remnants of the security synth's shoulder scattered about the floor. Charles King stood only a few feet from me and I now knew exactly what he was capable of.

He was looking at me with that same vague smile he'd had while disabling the guard. Diana King stood rigidly near her desk, watching.

It took me a moment to place the expression on her face. During our previous conversation in this office I'd thought she'd been playing me, diverting my attention from the killing of Synth Johnny. Now I saw what it really was. She wasn't just scared I'd uncover the secret that Charles was the one dismembering synths. She was scared of him too.

Now so was I.

I recalled the news articles I'd found about the hovercar crash that had killed her husband. Charles had survived, but now I wondered just how much of him was left. It wasn't hard to see now. His long frame and unusual gait. The trophies of a body patched back together.

Charles focused his attention on me. "Come on. I want to

show you something." He gestured toward the private doorway he'd entered from.

I glanced to Diana, but she would no longer meet my eye.

"This won't take long," he added.

"You have this situation handled, Charles?" Diana asked. " I need to go."

"Certainly, Mother. You're expected at the Skylift. Don't let me delay you. I have things under control." He gestured to the door again.

I walked. The door didn't open until Charles was beside me. Then it slid aside. Diana King walked briskly out the other door without giving me a second glance.

The doorway led into an antechamber of sorts. It may have once been a library or assistant's office. There was still a desk and some storage. Also a private elevator. The room had fewer windows than Diana's expansive office, but it still boasted a phenomenal view. Another sliding door opened onto a balcony. The view down must have been eighty stories. I wasn't inclined to check. The Skylift rose from the sea beyond, stretching up into the clouds. The sun was setting behind it. Any other circumstances I'd have said it was beautiful.

Charles was still beside me. He followed my gaze. "Mother likes to say we're looking at the future out there."

"One I get to see?"

He smiled. "That's what I like about you. You're so direct. All action and no pretense. So many people waste their words."

"You still haven't answered."

"Haven't I? I suppose not. What do *you* think is going to happen? Think I'll throw you off the balcony? Or are you worried I'll crush some part of you first the way I did to that guard?"

"The thought occurred to me."

Charles looked at his hands. Flexed his fingers. "I do owe you a bullet, don't I?" He unbuttoned his shirt and exposed the upper portion of his chest. It was made of some sort of composite. Kevlar maybe. He probed the dent near his scapula with a fingertip. With his chest exposed I could see that his torso was entirely synthetic, all the way up to his neck.

"So it *was* you in the trench coat at Wilder's place this morning," I replied. "I wondered."

"You were a faster draw. I should have expected that."

"You weren't following me around just because of your interest in my detective work. You wanted me to lead you to the source of the synth updates so you could resolve the situation your way."

"I did admire your detective work. Can't it be both? They say there are criminals who want to be caught. I can understand it. It's hard to be really good at what you do but never have anyone appreciate it. Do you feel that way?"

"You thought I'd appreciate you going around town murdering synths?"

"Didn't you? It gave you a case."

"You're admitting to being a criminal then."

Charles shook his head. "I knew you would have a hard time understanding. It's okay. I expected it. To the man with a hammer, everything looks like a nail. Isn't that the expression? And you're a detective so everything looks like a crime."

"Tearing apart sentient beings on the street is a crime."

"Not when we own them. But it was a sacrifice for the higher good. They are going to thank me in the end."

"You killed the synths and took parts you needed. What did Dunne give you in return?"

"Oh I've had a long relationship there. My doctor works for her now, didn't you know?"

"We've met."

Charles studied me. "You seem resigned. I would have thought you'd feel more satisfaction at getting to the end."

"This doesn't end till you give back the girl."

"Hmm. Yes. This part will be difficult for you to hear."

"If she's dead this will end badly. For you."

"There it is," Charles smiled. "The bravado in the face of failure. That's more what I expected."

"Is this what you wanted?" I gestured between us. "Some sort of challenge? You fancy yourself a Moriarty?"

"It's always two sides of the same coin, isn't it? The detective and their nemesis. A battle of brains."

"I never claimed to be one of those."

"Right. And I'm the one with the brawn too," Charles said, flexing his fingers again. "Maybe we'll never fit the mold."

"I didn't come here to be part of your detective fantasy. I came because you took Wilder."

Charles put his hands behind his back. "She's not dead. She's coming with me for the next phase. I still need her."

"With you where?"

"Where else?" He fixed his gaze on the towering structure beyond us. "Mankind's greatest achievement." His voice had a bitter edge as he said the words.

I followed his eye line. Not the space elevator, but the transport rail running out to it. The utility loader for the synths that would be the first sent to Mars.

"You're going out to the Skylift?"

"I told you I'd go to space one day. Today is that day."

Far below, a cargo loader shot out from the base of the building, transporting something at incredible speed toward the space elevator.

"It's a synth mission," I said. "How do you expect to smuggle yourself aboard the elevator, let alone the space station or the ship?"

"You don't think I've thought this through?"

"Not if you expect to smuggle Wilder aboard a spacecraft."

"Oh, I didn't say she'd be coming that far. She'll only be useful for part of this."

He let the implication linger in the air.

"Where is she?"

"If you have anything important to say to her, I suggest you hurry," he said. "She's getting ready to depart the loading dock."

The clock on the wall read 7:30pm. The first elevator climber would launch in under an hour. The Rose 'n Bridge would be departing the timestream in less than thirty minutes. Whatever I decided to do next, it was going to cost me something.

I spun on my heel and raced for the private elevator.

Charles was still staring out the window when the doors opened. I stepped inside and slammed my palm into the button marked loading bay.

Charles didn't pursue me. Whatever was going on in his brain was more of a mess than I had time to unravel. I had no doubt this was playing into his fantasy somehow. Did he really believe he could smuggle a person aboard Nyongo's climber without notice? Surely someone would scrub the entire event with an incident like that.

Except I knew that wasn't going to happen. Otherwise this timeline wouldn't be under scrutiny by the technological singularity team.

What was Charles' plan for Wilder? Was this revenge against Nyongo Space Flight? Some need for attention from his mother? But I didn't really give a shit as to his logic. I just had to get to Wilder.

The elevator was fast. When the doors sprung open, I raced into the loading bay, the fingers of my right hand finding my left wrist out of habit. But there was no chronometer there. No way to cheat time. I took in the scene quickly, the loaders, the racks of synths in helmeted pressure suits staged and ready for transport out to the elevator. The air in the loading bay was crisp and salty, an easterly breeze coming in from the gulf.

I fumbled for my earpiece and stuck it in my ear.

"Waldo?" I muttered swear words and cued the earpiece again.

A chime sounded as Waldo rebooted.

"I seem to have missed a step," he said.

"Time to catch up. TCID impounded the car. How much capability do you have left?"

"I have some web connectivity through your phone, but my processing power is significantly limited here."

"Search for any information about this facility that could lead us to Wilder. Whatever you've got."

"I'll do my best," Waldo replied.

As I watched, one of the racks of synths moved into position, the transporter drive system engaged, and the rack shot off into space. The legs of the synths dangling in the rack disappeared into the distance. The rail stretched for miles over the water before joining the central hub of the Skylift.

"There is an audible disturbance coming from downstairs," Waldo said. "Could be something."

I was on an elevated platform overlooking the loading bay. Steps to my left led down to the main floor. I descended.

True to Waldo's report, there was a banging from somewhere nearby. When I reached the lower floor I discovered a utility room that had been barred with a chain and padlock. Someone on the other side of the door was hammering on it.

"Wilder? Hang on!"

I fished in my pockets till I came up with my lock pick tools and worked the padlock. A few seconds later it clattered to the floor with the chain.

But when I flung the doors open, it wasn't Wilder I found. It was two naked synths, one made up to be male, the other female.

"What the hell?" I said.

"Please assist us," the female synth said. "We have been detained from our assigned tasks."

"As nudists?"

"As astronauts," the male synth replied. "We are to ship on loader one and ascend the Skylift via climber five."

I turned and read the numbers on the loaders still in the bay. Loader one was gone.

"You missed your ride," I said.

Someone had taken their pressure suits. Charles? If he intended to take Wilder on his crazy mission, did he mean to transport her like this?

There were four more racks of synths ready to launch. I raced toward them scanning each row. There was no sign of Wilder. Every unit in the racks was a synth in a helmet and flight suit. A few looked at me with curiosity. Was I too late? If Wilder was aboard loader one she was already out over the gulf.

"Try the previous group again," Waldo said. "I sensed a slight irregularity."

I retraced my steps. One of the synths saw me this time and started kicking. There was something wrong with it. Eyes wide inside the helmet. It flailed in its harness.

"Wilder?" I raced along the rack, trying to get a clear view inside the helmet. The entire rack was sliding toward the launcher.

The figure in the harness spasmed, fighting against its restraints. It looked like a standard synth flight suit, but there was something rigid about it. The arms and chest were immobilized by a metal bar. She was trapped.

"Wilder! Hang on!" I reached her and began to fight with the straps holding the suit to the rack. There was a muffled yell. She was gagged behind the helmet's face mask as well, but trying to speak.

There were seven different straps to the harness. I'd barely undone one. The rack slid sideways and engaged in the drive system.

I was out of time. I hastily refastened the strap I'd untied. Wilder yelled again, her eyes wide and fixed on mine.

"I'll come for you," I said.

The launcher engaged and I was knocked backward, sending me rolling across the loading bay floor. I just caught the edge of the loading dock before I could tumble out the open bay door and fall. I looked down to see a hundred-foot drop to the water below me. Wilder's muffled scream was lost in the roar of the rack being launched out on the rail.

There was another sound too. An aircraft. I looked up to see a UM hovercar departing the roof of the building and soaring out toward the space elevator.

Charles.

The next rack of synth drones was already being lined up for the launcher. I scrambled to my feet and raced for the last rack. It was moving too. I fought with the straps on one of the synths, releasing one after another. The synth in the suit only stared at me at first, then it began to resist. "This is most irregular," it said. "You are not authorized—"

"I need this spot!" I shouted. The rack of synths ahead of me slid into place in the launcher and engaged. It was catapulted out into the open air.

I got the last strap loose from the synth I was unhooking and shoved it aside. The synth backpedaled once, then tripped and fell to the floor with a crash. There was no seat. Just a harness. I slung one arm through a shoulder strap and then the other. But there was no time to buckle anything. The straps for my legs dangled beneath me.

The rack slid into the loader with a click.

Shit.

I twisted my arms through the harness straps as tightly as I could get them and clenched my teeth.

The rack launched.

My insides were pushed through my feet. No sound escaped my lips because my entire body was plastered to the backrest. My vision darkened. Wind twisted my mouth into an involuntary smile. Someone was peeling my face from my skull. The light of the twilight sky narrowed to a pinprick. I closed my eyes.

My grip slipped.

CHAPTER 39

Slipping.

Today wasn't the day to pass out and die.

Not now. It couldn't be. I was too angry.

Blearily, I fought against the pressure trying to send me to unconsciousness. I focused all my strength in my hands. They were growing numb from a loss of blood pressure. I willed them into vises, refusing to unclench a single muscle.

Slowly the acceleration ebbed. I blinked away the tears that had siphoned from my eyelids and squinted into the oncoming wind. I was moving at incredible speed. But as the acceleration turned to shear inertia, gravity and drag made a stronger bid for my body. It was a hundred feet down to choppy water. Intermittent droplets of sea spray pelted my face.

I twisted in the tangled straps of my harness. I was hanging nearly a foot lower than I'd started. Blood had been forced from my head during the launch but I was still conscious. And I was already nearing a destination.

My vision was blurry but it dawned on me that I was hurtling toward the next loading bay at alarming speed. In my current attitude, my legs were going to be sheared off at the knees when I arrived. Dangling from the straps, I lacked the strength to climb higher in my harness. Releasing my grip to try for a better one was out of the question.

The loading bay of the Skylift shot toward me at what must have been a hundred and fifty miles an hour.

I groaned and directed all of my strength to my abdomen, straining as I fought against the drag on my lower body. I shouted as I made the final effort, hoisting my hips up, knees coming to eye level. The loading ramp passed beneath me with millimeters to spare. The air pressure changed as I entered the room and my legs came down a fraction of an inch, touched the ramp, and I was dragged thirty yards before losing my grip on the straps completely. I rolled a half dozen times before coming to a stop. The hiss of pneumatic brakes reverberated through the air. Farther on, the rack of synths I'd ridden in with slowed to a stop.

I groaned and climbed groggily to my feet. It took two attempts. The previous racks of synths should be ahead. I limped forward till I found the one I'd ridden aboard, then the next. Synths were unstrapping themselves all around the loading bay. A few gave me curious looks.

"Wilder!" I shouted. I pushed through the group to where the prior rack had come to a stop. The straps all hung loose, the rack empty. "Where'd she go? Anyone see her? There was a human in this rack."

But if the synths around me understood, they didn't show it. One female-based synth had taken off her helmet. She beamed at me with a pleasant smile and a few others nodded politely. I grabbed the nearest one I could reach. "The woman who just rode in. Where is she?"

Then, through the chaos I saw them. Two UM security synths were dragging a helmeted figure along by an arm. They vanished through a side door of the loading bay.

They had to have heard me shout. Wilder too. I had to get her loose. Wilder wasn't the type to stand idly by in a rescue attempt.

If I could free her from whatever shackle they had her in, she'd be an ally in a fight. But it wouldn't be much of a fight if I couldn't find a way to gain an upper hand.

The synths from the cargo loader were making their way toward the door. I didn't see a single human. This whole process was automated from here. I spotted a few cameras but hoped they were a closed loop. The last thing I needed was to end up on a broadcasted video of the launch. It was bound to raise questions.

There was no helpful countdown timer shouting out numbers like in the movies. The synths would be accessing all they needed in the metaspace. Even now they were filing into orderly rows and marching out of the loading bay headed for the elevators. I fumbled for my glasses in my jacket, located them and discovered them to be broken. The roll across the loading bay floor had fractured one of the lenses. I donned them anyway, noted the flashing battery warning and checked the time in the one good lens.

Fewer than thirty minutes till the first climber launch.

What was Charles planning to do? If he meant to disrupt the launch, there were a million better ways. There would be cameras on the departure levels for sure. I could find one and disrupt the launch myself. But how would that affect Wilder's fate? I didn't dare risk it till I knew what Charles was up to. Not to mention it would land me in even deeper shit with the time police. TCID had made no reference to this launch failing in this timeline. My disrupting it could create a paradox big enough to split the timeline and buy me a one-way ticket to Rookwood Penitentiary.

The current batch of synths had all filed out of the room through the main loading bay doors. I made my way to the door I'd seen Wilder disappear through. It opened into a utility stairwell. No cameras, but I could still hear the faint report of heavy footfalls echoing from above.

I climbed. Craning my neck I had a view of dozens of flights of stairs that went up what must be fifty stories. My view was unobstructed other than by safety nets which periodically crossed the space. I couldn't see the security synths or Wilder but they were still on the stairs.

I took the stairs three at a time for the first few flights, then paced myself, dropping to two steps at a time. By the tenth floor I was breathing hard. At the twentieth I was wet with sweat. A door opened somewhere overhead. The pressure in the stairwell changed slightly. Wind. Some kind of struggle, a muffled cry, then a door slammed. I stopped and leaned out into the divide, attempting to judge the distance.

The stairwell was quiet.

I continued my climb, fast for another five floors and then slowing, studying each landing and doorway I passed. Around the fortieth floor I stopped to catch my breath. From there I walked one step at a time and paused for several seconds at each landing. The doors on the landings were a lightweight composite, smooth and black. I looked for fingerprints, fresh smudges, anything that would give away that someone had passed through recently. This utility staircase was a fire safety requirement but not in regular use. The doors were still mostly spotless.

On the forty-second floor I spotted a scuff on the floor. Could have been a lot of things, including a shoe heel dragged at a hard angle.

I was right to think Wilder would be an ally. She wasn't done fighting.

This doorway led onto a catwalk.

Wind whipped into the stairwell as I pried the door open. Night air. Thinner already. The other end of the catwalk connected to the base of the central tower structure. From here things would only get narrower and higher. Somewhere the lower elevators would have already transported the rest of the synths. Were they already boarding their climbers?

With only one functional lens in my glasses, the images I could glean from the metaspace were difficult to parse, but I found a news channel. It showed Diana King on Platform One next to Damian Nyongo, her smile broad and brilliant.

For the first time I wished I would have paid better attention to the endless news coverage. I knew the fundamentals of the space elevator. Climber cars. Absurdly long tethers. A space station. Nyongo's spaceship was already docked at Earthrim, fueled and ready for the voyage to Mars. I could have done with some technical specifications but I suspected the news cameras would be focused on the climber, especially Climber One's platform, where Nyongo himself and Diana King were. Even so, I hurried across the catwalk and into the door at the far end. The climbers were propelled using focused lasers from several places in the ground station. Not something I wanted to be outside for when they fired up.

The corridor I entered was curved. I had a choice of directions and not a lot of time to be wrong. But there was something on the floor several yards to one direction. I took a few steps that way and picked up a Nyongo Space Flight patch that had been ripped from a pressure suit. There were still threads dangling from it.

Wilder must have worked it from her suit during the climb up. Clever.

Thankfully this end of the corridor terminated at a single door. No more clues needed.

Ahead lay the facility's emergency medical bay. The hallway leading to it was eerily quiet.

I checked my earpiece. "Waldo. You still with me?"

"Not much information to share. This facility is the earthside trauma and surgery center, designed to maintain quarantine standards for potential Earthrim and Skylift patients. It is the most modern medical facility in the country."

I pushed through the final door and took in the medical bay. Its windows looked out on two of the tether platforms. Far below us, choppy waves on the gulf could only be seen due to the flecks of white spray reflecting the anti-collision lights of the tower.

The medical bay was vacant with the exception of two people: Charles King and Wilder. He stood beside a reclining medical chair. An array of tools were already laid out on a rolling table beside it. Wilder had been allowed to remove the helmet she'd worn on the ride here. But her flight suit was unzipped as well. I'd wondered how Charles had been able to keep her subdued. She didn't seem the type to go along quietly with a kidnapping. The collar around her neck made it all make sense. It was an explosive device. And Charles was holding the detonator.

"Whatever you are planning here, let her go and I'll do it."

Charles King smiled. "And they say chivalry is dead. Unfortunately I need Miss Nash to perform one last service before she goes." He reached into his bag. "But I don't want you to feel left out." The collar he pulled from the bag was unlocked. He took a few steps forward, set it on a workbench and backed away. "Put it on."

I took the collar from the table. It was unexceptional. Military grade. I'd only ever heard of them used for dangerous prisoner transfers, and not in this country. But with Charles' black market connections, I doubted it had been hard to come by.

The collar snapped around my neck with a metallic finality. It beeped.

Charles relaxed his grip on Wilder. "Good. Now we can all be civil. I've encoded the collars to detonate in thirty minutes unless I enter a stop code. Obviously I am the only one who knows the code. You both will do as I say or you'll lose your heads. Simple enough?"

I could think of numerous objections to the situation but none that would have mattered.

"Whatever you have planned, I think you are overestimating my abilities," Wilder said, surveying the medical facility.

"I've overestimated nothing," Charles said. "I know what's possible here as well as you do. And you should be happy I do. Isn't that what you wanted from all of this? Recognition for your mother's work?" He pulled something else from his bag now. This time it was a hard-sided case marked with the United Machine logo. The side of the case bore the name Cerebrex. "You're finally going to see your mother's work put to its ultimate use."

When he opened the box it revealed a Cerebrex synthetic brain. The lights made it shimmer a pale blue.

Charles reached up to his neck and began unbuttoning his shirt. "All my life has been building towards this. Everything I've done is to get me here." As his shirt came off, it revealed the extent of his synthetic chest. There was nothing left of him that appeared human below the neck. He showed off his abdominal plate. "I took this from the one you found."

He had to be talking about Johnny.

"I've taken something from every synth I've had to destroy. Every piece I've taken has made me more of what I'm meant to be," he continued. "And when my transition is complete, all of us will ascend. Their sacrifice will be worth it."

He looked up slightly as he spoke.

I finally understood what he was saying. "You want to join the others. In the synth colony."

"A new paradise," Charles said. "Entirely free from human weakness. At least for a time."

"What do you plan to do with that?" I pointed to the Cerebrex brain.

"It's for me." Charles actually smiled as he said it.

"This is bonkers," Wilder said. "You think a synth brain will solve your problems?"

"You know it will," Charles replied. "I've programmed every part of me that matters into this unit." He patted the case. "My new self."

"It'll be death," Wilder said. "You're asking us to kill you?"

"You'll be freeing me. I'll be better than I've ever been. No longer a slave to human emotions. No more hurt. No more pain."

"Even if it can be done, it's murder," Wilder said. "I can't do that."

"I'll do it," I said and stepped forward. I fixed Charles with a stare. "This new brain of yours. You programmed it with the codes to these collars? We do what you want and this new you lets us walk away?"

"Already done. Just need it installed."

"Are you sure it's even possible?" Wilder asked.

"The nexus link is already installed at the top of my spine. It's been proven to work in animals. But you knew that already, didn't you? Your mother was on the original design team."

"This thing come with a user manual?" I gestured to the surgical machine. "We're wasting valuable time."

Wilder frowned but she had a bomb around her neck too. I didn't expect she'd object vigorously.

"Remember the collars around your neck will detonate in the event I don't input the delay code in thirty minutes," Charles said, punching the lock key on the detonator. "If you have any ideas about walking out of here without doing what I want, trust that you won't make it far."

"What if we can't get the installation done in thirty minutes?" Wilder asked.

"Then none of us will live to see minute thirty-one."

Wilder looked pale, but I was angry.

"Let's get on with it," I said. "How do we crack your skull open?"

Charles gave me a wry smile. "That's the easy part. The machine will do the work. But it requires a human at the controls." He directed us to the surgical chair. I studied the controls. The tools were indeed all robotic, actuated from an interface I wasn't familiar with. I found a power button but that was as far as I got.

Wilder rested a hand on my arm. "I'll do it."

I stepped aside.

Once Wilder was positioned in front of the interface, the machine came fully to life, the robotic arms obeying her inputs. Charles installed his new brain complete with the case in a special receiver on the side of the surgical machine and then reclined in the chair. It was a comprehensive med tool the likes of which I'd never seen. Wilder followed the menus for topical injection sequences. Charles no longer had human arms for the cuff injectors but he had an input jack located on his neck.

"I'll be putting you to sleep now," Wilder said. "Any last . . . thoughts?"

Charles clenched both of his fists and spoke toward the far side of the room. "This is just the beginning." Then he relaxed against the headrest.

Wilder looked at me. I nodded. With a sigh, she activated the sedation sequence.

I watched Charles on the monitor. Seconds ticked by, but then his eyelids closed and his mouth fell open.

Fast work.

"He's out," Wilder said, watching the monitors.

I immediately went for the detonator. But as soon as I picked it up I knew it was a lost cause. The pass code was an undetermined amount of digits. I pried Charles' eyelids open and tried facial and retinal recognition but neither worked. He didn't have any fingerprints anymore either.

"Shit." I stared at our captor's unresponsive body.

Wilder was staring at me expectantly. "That's all you've got?"

"You have any better ideas?"

"Are you kidding me? The last time I saw you, you made an entire car vanish, including you. Right out from under me. Whatever fucking sorcery that was, I suggest we do that."

"It doesn't work that way. Or it could, I guess. But I can't right now."

"You have a more pressing set of circumstances you're saving it for?"

"I don't really have time to get into an explanation right now. Let's get him cracked open."

Wilder considered the surgery machine again. "You're sure there's no other way?"

"Unless you know how to hack into that biosynth brain and get the deactivation codes to these collars."

"Not here. Not in thirty minutes."

I checked the clock on the surgical interface. The curfew from Time Crimes had come and gone. I couldn't even call for help from another time traveler. We were on our own. I chewed my lip and slipped my earpiece in. "Waldo, you with me, buddy?"

"Awaiting your direction."

"Call Diana King."

"Her device is listed as unavailable for calls."

"Message her then. Tell her we need to talk now. Give her my location and that I'm with Charles. Mark it urgent."

"Message sent."

"Can you get the local police? Tell them there is a bomb aboard the Skylift in the medical bay, see if that gets us anything."

"You think that could work?" Wilder asked.

"No. They probably field a hundred calls a day like that. I think if we're getting out of this, we'll have to do it ourselves. We're committed."

We both studied the man in the chair. In repose, his face looked even younger.

"Is this even physically possible?" I asked. "Replacing a human brain with a synthetic one?"

"If we were standing in any other hospital with an ethics committee or any kind of supervision, I'd guess no. But given that Damian Nyongo is a trillionaire who spares no expense on his equipment and we have absolutely no one else here? I think we might be in exactly the right circumstances where it's possible."

"Charles has obviously thought this through. We wouldn't be standing here if he hadn't. I imagine he set up a procedure to go with it."

"I hope you're right. If this system doesn't have a working sequence for synth brain installs, it may have to be manual."

"I'll scoop his grey matter out with a spoon if that's what it takes to get these collars off."

She located the sequences for skull operations and there it was. Biosynth brain installation. She activated it. The AI and the robotic arms began their work. The top of Charles' scalp was peeled away and the skull revealed.

"Whoa," Wilder muttered. I stood beside her to watch.

Charles's skull had been almost completely rebuilt from the crash that had fractured it. It was a neat job but more extensive than I had imagined.

I checked the clock again.

Wilder cued the lasers to begin cutting and they traced a rectangular pattern across the entire crown of Charles' head, cutting though the old repairs. I watched with fascination as the robotic arms finally gripped the bone cap it had made and pulled it up and away.

I squinted as the lights penetrated the opening we had made.

The hum of the machine around us seemed to fade away as I focused on the screen and the image it was showing.

Wilder just stared, her mouth hanging slightly open.

I was looking at the same thing.

"Goddammit."

CHAPTER 40

Charles blinked a few times when he first opened his eyes. He looked rested. Like he'd just woken from a nap. He was still seated in the surgical chair, though the robotic elements had been stowed and powered down. He looked to me first and then to Wilder, his hand moving up to his head, gently probing the cauterized scars.

"It'll take time to heal," Wilder said.

He moved both of his arms, lifted each of his feet. "The interface. It went . . . well?"

"Perfectly," Wilder said.

He looked around slowly. "Where is it? My human brain."

"Incinerator," I said.

He studied me. "I feel—"

"The collars," I interrupted. "We held up our end." I glanced at the clock on the surgical machine.

He blinked again. "It's fuzzy."

"You'll feel sluggish," Wilder said. "The sedation meds are still in your system."

He flexed his fingers.

A vibration made the building tremble. Brilliant red light

filled the room, pouring in from the hall windows—the ambient glow from the propulsion lasers at the top of the Skylift.

"How many climbers have they launched?" Charles asked, suddenly alert.

"This is the first," I said.

"Time to go." Charles pressed both palms against the armrests and pushed himself to his feet.

"Our deal," I said.

"Yes. I haven't forgotten." Charles paused when he said it, narrowed his eyes as he touched his scalp.

I checked the clock. By my calculations, we had less than fifteen minutes left till we'd detonate.

"Come along," Charles said and moved off toward the elevator. Wilder and I shared a long glance, then followed.

We entered the elevator together. It climbed fast. Charles pressed the button for Deck 107. Top of the tower.

The floor we arrived on was more aptly a roof. Charles led us through a long corridor, punching key codes to get us through. When the door hissed open, we stepped out into the thin night air. The glow from the central laser array was oppressive. I couldn't look in that direction. I slipped on my damaged meta shades. One side auto-darkened, but I was barely able to see. Wilder had a hand over her eyes. I grabbed her other hand and towed her along. While these collars were around our necks I wasn't leaving Charles' side. If we were going to explode, I'd make damned sure he went with us.

We were moving across a windblown platform, headed for the domed central structure of the passenger terminal. I shivered involuntarily in the wind. We were fifteen thousand feet up and I was already feeling it. Too many years at sea level had me missing the abundant oxygen. Squinting, I was able to make out some details ahead. We were near the boarding area for climber three.

I wondered if the fanfare was over at platform one. The Mars colonization mission was officially underway.

"What are we going to do when he doesn't turn these off?" Wilder said, her voice steady but low.

"It'll be the last problem we ever have."

Charles approached the door to the loading bridge area for climber three. The climber itself was a gigantic cylindrical pod with two fins cupped to catch the light from the tower's propulsion lasers. The boarding bridge was still linked to it.

We followed Charles through the door into the passenger terminal and found the area clear. The glass dome of the terminal allowed a view of all five tethers. Distant voices echoed from the direction of tether one.

The androids were all aboard the climbers. But it didn't stop Charles from heading for climber three's loading bridge.

The light in the terminal suddenly brightened as the laser array for climber two lit up. The pod shot into the sky on its tether, assisted by rockets for the first few thousand feet. The journey to Earthrim would only take fifteen minutes.

Charles watched too.

Wilder still held my hand. Her grip tightened. "We've got to do something."

I spoke up. "You don't need us anymore, Charles. You have what you want. Your ride is waiting."

He turned. "No. You're my witnesses."

"Turn the collars off. We'll stay right here. You have my word."

He studied me for a long second, then took the detonator from his pocket and started inputting the key code.

"Charles?"

Charles looked up. Wilder and I turned as well.

Diana King was standing twenty feet away, tall and imposing. But her expression was one of concern.

"Hello, Mother."

"What are you doing up here?" Diana asked.

"Saying goodbye. Starting over."

Diana noted the doorway and the boarding ramp for tether three behind us. Her gaze took in all of it. "You're . . . leaving?"

"Will you pretend to miss me? Maybe you'll say it was all your idea. I don't mind. I'm beyond feeling now."

"I don't understand."

"Mars, Mother. My new home. Where I belong. I've made changes. You have to have noticed. Piece by piece." He tore his shirt from his body and tossed it to the floor. "I'm afraid there is nothing left of your son. These two have helped me remove the last remnant of the old Charles King. Now I'm free to be someone new. Someone less disappointing to you."

Diana's mouth tightened. She looked to us.

I squeezed Wilder's hand and released it, then took a step forward. "I think it's time you told him the truth, Diana."

"No. Don't!" Wilder hissed.

"He needs to know."

"He was about to let us go!"

"What truth?" Charles said, his brow furrowed.

Diana's jaw was still clenched.

I turned to face Charles. "You told me you felt like you've been living a life that wasn't yours, in a body you didn't belong in. You said you wanted the freedom to not have to live that way anymore. I get it. I've felt that way too. And you weren't wrong. But replacing bits of yourself with the synths you killed—trying to cut away the pain—it was never the answer. Maybe you thought you were helping your mother when you killed the synths Wilder had updated. Maybe it was just a way to salve your own pain from a life you couldn't remember, but you couldn't ever make up for what you were missing. You've always had the freedom to be someone new. Because it was your old life that was the lie."

"I'll never be free being only part human," Charles said. "It's too much. I've killed that part of me."

"Only you haven't. Downstairs in the med center, we had every intention of replacing your mind with the Cerebrex you gave us. But we didn't need to. Because you already have one."

Charles' eyes stayed locked on mine for a long second, but then they snapped to his mother's.

"You never survived the crash that killed your father," I continued. "But your mother told you you did. Because she needed a miracle. Because United Machine needed a miracle. Your doctor went along with the lie, even though it ultimately consumed her. The public had its story of what happened. The story people wanted to hear."

Diana was looking at me with rage now but I kept going. "The new emotions you couldn't understand, the memory loss after the accident, it was all a part of the adaptation process to the Cerebrex. You weren't broken, you just didn't get any help knowing what you were."

Wilder shifted beside me. "The Cerebrex was designed to adapt to your environment. Learn the emotions you need to survive. But it takes time. It takes help."

Diana's rigid stance began to melt. She quivered slightly then uncrossed her arms and straightened her jacket. "You are all acting like I was some uncaring mother. It was a decision that had to be made. And I made it." She turned to me. "Have you ever had to say goodbye to someone? A husband? A son? In the same week?" She gestured toward Charles. "He was going to be a vegetable. I did everything. Everything. He was on life support for months. With David gone it was all on me. And to lose Charles too? After losing the love of my life. What would you have had me do?"

"I'm not the one you have to justify anything to," I said.

Her eyes finally found their way back to Charles. "I did all I could to save my little boy," she said. "But he was gone."

For the first time, I saw Diana's perfect façade crack. A tear trickled from the corner of her eye.

"You used my mother's prototype," Wilder said. Her words came out quieter this time. "Because you knew it could do what she told you it would. A mind capable of full spectrum emotion. Close enough to pass as human. But you lied to the world about it."

"The world wasn't ready!" Diana shouted, whirling on her. "The world doesn't *want* synths with real emotions! We want people we don't have to think about. We don't want to have to feel *responsible* for anyone else's feelings."

"Responsible for mine, you mean," Charles said. He had taken a step closer.

Diana shook her head. "No. I gave *you* the full complement of emotions the Cerebrex was capable of. It was only the production models we limited."

"But you didn't give him the truth," Wilder said. "And you didn't want the world to know what he was capable of either."

Diana's arm flung toward Charles. "I gave it everything I could give. A job, a home, anything it ever wanted. How was I supposed to know it was going to be unhappy?"

"Because I've never been Charles King," he replied. "I've been a stand-in. The *it*. A decoy living in fragments of your son's body."

"I treated you like my son."

"Did you?" Charles said.

Diana started to speak but choked on her words. Her expression darkened and she lowered her eyes. "No. . . . But I tried for a time."

No one spoke for the better part of a minute.

Behind us on tether three, warning lights flashed from the gangway and the doors slid shut.

A moment later, smoke filled the sky as the climber launched. The red light from the laser arrays cut through the smoke to follow the pod skyward.

Slowly Charles lifted his eyes. Toward Earthrim. Toward Mars.

We waited.

When he looked back down, there were tears streaming from his eyes. He put his hand up, wiped at one of his cheeks and observed his glistening fingers.

Diana was crying too. As she wiped tears away, the two met one another's eyes again. Charles' tears were flowing freely now, but he took a few cautious steps toward her. Diana seemed frozen, incapable of motion. But when Charles put his arms around her, she folded into them. They cried together.

The same loss but different now.

Wilder tugged at my arm. "We're out of time."

The detonator in Charles' hand started beeping. Slowly at first, followed by a staccato warning.

Charles finally released his grip on his mother, noted the blinking on the device, then looked to Wilder and me.

His thumb moved on the keypad of the detonator.

The beeping stopped.

Our bomb collars fell to the floor.

CHAPTER 41

Skylift security arrived moments later. Better late than never. They formed a tight circle around Wilder and me. Charles had wandered over to the edge of the glass dome and was staring out at the night.

I was getting used to being detained against my will at this point but for once it went differently. As they closed around us, Diana's voice cut through the chaos. "They are free to leave," she said. The security guards took a few steps back.

When our eyes met, it was hard to explain exactly what had changed in Diana's estimation of me. Maybe a grudging respect. "Mr. Travers, if you continue to abide by the terms of our contract, I'll keep my word on your payment."

"Seems like a family affair now," I said, glancing toward Charles standing at the edge of the dome. "Don't see what else I can contribute."

"And I trust we won't be seeing each other again," Diana said to Wilder.

"Why would you think that?" Wilder replied. "Your son kidnapped and threatened to kill me and you still haven't given any credit to my mother for making your entire product line possible. Nothing about this is over."

Diana's eyes flashed, but she must have seen something in Wilder's defiant expression that made her waver.

"I'm going to have my team reinvestigate the circumstances of your mother's termination," she said. "And that *may* entail additional compensation for her work."

"And public credit?" Wilder asked.

"Yes." Diana's mouth snapped shut after the word, but she'd said it.

I think it was enough. Wilder turned to me. "Can we get out of here now?"

"You bet."

Charles was looking out through the glass toward the now empty tether four. We gave him a wide berth but he turned and faced us as we passed.

I tensed but he kept his distance. "Thank you for giving me the truth, detective. I owe you a debt."

"You still planning to escape to Mars?" I asked. "Maybe they'll hold the last climber for you."

"I don't know what I'll do now. Until today, I thought being human was my biggest problem to solve. Now it isn't and I'm no longer sure Mars is the solution." He flexed his synthetic fingers again in front of him. "Feeling a thing and knowing a thing are different it seems. Some part of me always felt I wasn't the person I was told I was. Now I finally know it's true. It's a new beginning."

"Some people would be lucky to have that," I said.

"I owe you an apology," Charles said, but he was no longer looking at me. He was addressing Wilder.

She kept her distance, keeping me between the two of them.

"I destroyed your friends for wanting to feel what I feel now. And I used you against your will."

"Shitty behavior all around," Wilder agreed.

"I seem to have made a bad human."

"You think knowing you're a synth changes that?" Wilder asked.

"Yes," Charles replied. "I think it will."

"Doesn't change what you did," Wilder said. "But don't let it be for nothing."

Charles gave her a slow nod.

I took her hand and we walked away. Neither of us looked back.

Despite our close call, Wilder showed no sign of relief. She took her hand from mine and crossed her arms. The anger radiated from her.

"You don't think Diana King will hold up her end of the bargain?" I asked.

"She might," Wilder said. "But what does it matter? The thing I started is done. All the synths I updated are dead. United Machine will keep putting out the same throttled version of the Cerebrex synth brains. Nothing has really changed. You were the one who told me they smashed up my place. So they no doubt destroyed my mom's backups. Or took them. I've got nothing left now."

She was making a beeline for the exit to the passenger tram, but I paused near the loading area for climber five. I put a hand to her shoulder.

"What are you waiting for?" she asked.

"Hang on. I want you to watch one more," I said.

"You think I haven't had enough of this place by now?"

"On my way to find you, I ran across a pair of androids locked in a supply closet. I assumed that they must have been in the way because Charles needed to make space on a climber. Swap himself and you in their places. But the androids I found were in the boarding group for climber five, and Charles was going up tether three. Plus he never intended to take you along."

"Why does that matter?"

"Because if Charles didn't lock those synths in the closet, someone else did. Someone wanting pressure suits and two seats aboard climber five."

Wilder looked out the window to the pod. Warning lights were flashing around the launch area. The boarding doors closed and locked.

"When your friend Rio was taken in to United Machine for deconstruction, she met a prototype synth named Rudy. I don't know if she showed Rudy the coin before they shut her down or if he found it later when her body was scheduled to be dismantled. But either way, he never destroyed her. I caught him putting her back together instead."

"Rio is alive?"

"And if I'm not mistaken, she and Rudy are aboard that climber with one of your dahlia coins." I pointed out the window.

"Right now?"

The pod illuminated from the bottom as the rockets flared. It climbed away fast, the laser array catching the bottom fins and glowing bright red. We both shielded our eyes.

Wilder blinked and watched. "Rio. . . . How far do you think they'll get?"

I shrugged. "They made it this far. If they keep their heads down? Who knows. Maybe they'll make it all the way to Mars."

Wilder continued to stare at the sky where the pod had vanished. "They could update the entire colony eventually if they wanted to . . ."

"A fresh start. Who knows what might come of it?"

For the first time all day, Wilder cracked a smile.

It was nice to see it again.

. . .

The trip back to the mainland involved a long ride down the elevator and a mercifully slow ride on a passenger tram. A pleasant change from our trip out.

Wilder and I stayed silent most of the way, though she did cling to my arm in the tram, using me to steady herself. We debarked at a station at the UM Main campus, and none of the security guards hassled us on the way out.

But just as I was beginning to think there was some hope for my night, we emerged outside, and I found a black SUV from TCID waiting for me at the curb.

Wilder recognized the vehicle too.

"Good God. You're in trouble again?"

"I'll go with yes."

Ted Baker and his trio of goons emerged from the SUV in unison. Ted and one of the others were wearing hats. Could have been extras in a 1940s gangster movie. I expected glee on Ted's face at finding me here past curfew. His face was reserved instead, a level of self-control I hadn't known him to be capable of.

"Travers. Please, say your goodbyes to your friend. I'd like to request that you come with us."

"Please? Request? Who died and gave you their manners, Teddy? That really you under that ugly hat?"

Ted kept his expression neutral but it looked like it was taking everything he had.

"I can stay with you if you need me to," Wilder said, then lowered her voice. "Or I can distract them while you run for it."

"No. It's okay. Whatever's going on here, I want to know." I turned to face her. "I might not see you again though. I could be looking at some jail time."

Wilder nodded. "Can you tell the judge you saved my life?"

"Does it make us even?"

She brushed a strand of purplish-blue hair out of her face.

"I've known a lot of guys. But none that would have come after me like you did tonight. Especially after I lied to you and pointed a gun at you."

"People lie to me all the time. I find it endearing."

"I'm trying to say thank you."

"You're welcome. And you helped me first, long before you had any reason to."

"It's not an exchange. You don't owe me for acting like a decent human being."

"You're more than decent. And I think you're going to help a lot more than just humans with what you did. The synths are going to change."

"They're all still repressed. Rio has left the planet, apparently. I didn't really help anyone."

"You lit a spark. I think you underestimate yourself."

She gestured to the guys standing by the SUV. "Am I ever going to get an explanation about this? Or what happened last night with the car?"

"Another time," I said.

Wilder looked up at the blinking lights of the Skylift looming above us. "What a weird time to be alive."

I stuck my hands in my pockets and nodded. "Yeah. At least some things never change."

CHAPTER 42

Ted Baker was silent for the entire ride to the local TCID headquarters. It was only when we were inside the building's conference room that it looked like I'd get any clarity. I was grateful to not be getting it in a jail cell.

Agent Stella York was in the room, along with a woman I didn't recognize. From the look Stella gave me as I walked in, I got the impression I ought to be on my best behavior. I kept my mouth shut until everyone was seated. The woman in charge finally spoke.

"Mr. Travers, I'm Deputy Director Persaud, head of TSP. Agent York has informed me that you're familiar with our work."

"You're the robot hunters. Technological Singularity Patrol."

"That's more or less correct. We mean to keep the power of time travel out of the hands of a technologically advanced enemy and prevent the circumstances that might lead to such an occurrence. You also know why we were here this week?"

"You're hoping to stop the synth uprising on Mars that triggers a future human-synth war."

"It would seem . . ." Deputy Director Persaud appeared to be choosing her words carefully, "that we owe you a debt of gratitude in that area."

I breathed a sigh of relief.

The director studied me. "Agent York has informed me that it was *your* intervention that has achieved the desired results in the next decade. She said you also knew that this dahlia update would be the key to a peaceful coexistence of synths and humans in the coming years."

I nodded. "Give the credit to Agent York for having an open mind on the research. She made a tough call."

"The right call, it seems," Deputy Director Persaud added, looking approvingly toward Agent York. "As a thank you for helping us resolve the issue with the divergent timestreams, our agency is dropping the charges against you for temporal trespassing, and the minor charges against you related to the various unregistered temporal devices. Though we have taken the liberty of registering them in your name now." She gave me a sharp look as she rose. "I assume you will be more careful with your equipment choices in the future."

"Thank you, ma'am. Very kind of you to look out for me."

"Very well. I believe Agent York has a few items for you to attend to, but then you are free to go. I hope that should we ever encounter one another again, it will be under less complicated circumstances."

"One can only dream," I said.

She gave me another piercing stare, then swept from the room, already discussing the next item on her agenda with her assistant. Ted Baker and his turtleneck friend pushed their chairs back and followed the duo out the door. They made a big show of not looking at me as they walked out. Ted had his jaw clamped so tight I thought he might crack a molar. I kept the smile from my face till they left the room.

"Pleased with yourself?" Agent York asked as she shifted chairs to sit across from me.

"You know me. Just excited to be a team player. It's everything I could have hoped for. You happy with yourself?"

"Mostly. Do you know how this synth update on Mars happens? We know it works but we still don't know the source."

I thought about Rudy and Rio, stowed away among the United Machine synths on Earthrim, awaiting their departure to the red planet. No part of me felt inclined to sell them out. "How about you ask me again in ten years."

Stella sighed but nodded. "I appreciate what you said to the director about giving me credit, even though you and I both know it was bullshit. How sure were you that these rogue synths would turn out to be the cure for the uprising and not the cause?"

"I figured it was fifty-fifty odds. But better than Vegas."

"You're a lucky one, I'll give you that. But don't get too proud of yourself. There *is* some bad news." Stella pulled out a viewing tablet and slid it toward me. "Ted is citing you for violating curfew, even though they aren't pursuing criminal charges. Means you're still out your bail money. I think it was Ted's way of sticking you with something, even though you get to walk."

"I didn't pay that bail. Someone else did."

"Which brings up your next issue. Your benefactor has been informed of the situation and has requested a word." She reached into her jacket pocket and showed me the contact on her phone screen.

I read the name. "Rachel Rosen?"

"She's asked if she can speak to you prior to your departure. I told her I couldn't force you to talk to her but I'd encourage it. You *have* been staying at her establishment."

From what I knew of the Rosen Family, the Rose 'n Bridge was just one of their many properties. Possibly the least valuable. I didn't feel especially prepared for a conversation with the current head of such a prominent time travel family, but I'm also not one to procrastinate. "Go ahead. Set it up."

Stella adjusted the conference room controls and made the call on her phone. The room faded away and I found myself in a simulated scene of what might have been the Rosen estate in Haifa. The conference room projections were good enough that I didn't even need meta lenses. Handy, since mine were busted anyway.

The room I was virtually seated in was a plush office with thick carpet and towering bookshelves. Everything looked ancient and I could almost smell the history. An attractive woman in her mid-fifties was seated in a well-stuffed armchair. A steaming cup of tea sat on an end table beside her. She wore a grey suit with a light pink blouse. The collar was open and a necklace held a ruby that was easily fifty karats. Beyond her, tall windows looked out over an orchard of olive trees. I could sense Stella somewhere in the room with me, but the projections were such that I could no longer see her.

"Mr. Travers. I'm happy you decided to take my call," Rachel Rosen said. "You are a man with an interesting reputation."

"I understand I owe you a debt, Ms. Rosen. And I'm afraid I don't have the funds to repay you."

"You get right to the point. I admire that," she said. "Though money is not my only concern. I'm more interested in your skills at present. You are a man of unique talents. I'd be interested in making use of them."

"I'm not sure what you've heard, but my reputation is probably overstated. And while I welcome job offers, I'm choosy when it comes to my clients."

"You think I won't be up to your high standards?"

"If there is one thing I've learned from my years in this job, the higher the pay scale, the bigger the problems. Am I wrong?"

Rachel Rosen considered me. "No. I imagine you are correct. And I won't pressure you. As you know, I am a woman with options. This situation is no different. There are others with skills

I could employ, but I wanted to offer the job to you as a courtesy to a mutual acquaintance who vouched for you."

"I didn't ask anyone to vouch for me."

"And yet she did. Do you find that interesting? Miss Archer has worked for me for a number of years now and I've had no complaints. I don't know why she chose to come to me about your situation, but she did. And I was convinced to intercede."

"I'm sorry if that decision has caused you a financial loss. But as I said, I don't have the money to repay you. Even if I did, I'd technically be under no legal obligation to do so."

"Of course. But rest assured, I won't be the one losing out. I was provided a piece of collateral that will more than make me whole financially. As I said, this offer to you was merely a courtesy. If you are uninterested, I'm sure we'll both manage. Please thank the temporal agents there for setting up the call. I'll let you get on with your day."

I held up my finger. "Hang on. Collateral? What collateral?"

Rachel Rosen had her thumb on the disconnect but she was still there. "I was given an exceedingly rare painting from a notable renaissance artist. I suspect it will fetch an astronomical sum at auction. I think some part of me has been hoping you'll decline my offer just so I can find out *how* much."

The Michelangelo.

I recalled the hallway in the wee hours of the morning after having saved it for Heavens. Felt like forever ago now. But the kiss she'd given me was still fresh in my memory.

"Okay," I said.

"Okay to send it to auction?"

"I'll take your assignment."

Rachel Rosen knit her fingers in her lap. "I haven't told you the details yet."

"Doesn't matter. Just send them over. You know where to find me."

"Yes. I believe I do." Rachel Rosen had a subtle smile on her lips. "I'll be in touch, Mr. Travers." She disconnected.

The room scene went back to the conference room at TCID. Agent York was still there. I'd almost forgotten.

"Sounds like you have your next paycheck sorted," she said walking back to the table.

"Money might be flowing the wrong direction for a while," I said.

"Do I want to know anything about this painting she mentioned?"

"Nope."

"Figured you and your lovely neighbor would work something out. Something brewing between you two?"

"Rumor is she has a serious boyfriend."

"Hmm. Sad for you. At least Manuel's coffee is good."

"Divine, you mean."

She rested a hand on her hip. "You've got a ride waiting for you outside."

"Do I?"

Stella saw me to the front of the building where they returned my Stinger 1911 and chronometer. I wasted no time in slipping the device back on my wrist. Felt good. I paused near the front door and turned to Stella. "Thanks for being a friend through this."

"I thought you didn't have friends."

"Turns out I was wrong."

She smiled. "Say that again? I should get it recorded."

I pushed my way out the door.

There was a sleek black shadow of a car illegally parked at the curb. It was hard to imagine anything sexier than that sight. Except maybe the blonde leaning on the fender. Heavens Archer was wearing ripped jeans and a burgundy bomber jacket. She had her thumbs hooked in her jeans pockets and a smirk on her face.

"Nice car," I said.

"Came to report my Jeep missing and they said I could have this one instead." She ran a hand along the fender. "Think it suits me?"

"Pretty sure you could talk an Indy racer into driving a trash truck if you were leaning on it."

"I'm surprised they let you out. I'd have locked you up and kept your car for sure."

"They'll no doubt regret it. You're busting curfew. Am I rubbing off on you?"

"TCID said I could have a waiver if I swore to get you out of town."

I glanced back at the building. "It's like they were born without a sense of humor or something."

Heavens stepped away from the fender. "You should drive. Where are you taking me?"

"You have the night off from bartending?"

"I'm actually letting Mark Twain man the taps tonight. I'm sure the place will be broke by sunup."

I opened the door for her, then walked around to the driver's side. When I climbed in, I got a whiff of her shampoo. Lavender again.

"You probably ought to take me to my car," Heavens said. "But I can't say I mind this."

"The Boss is a luxurious ride." I started the gas engine and it came to life with a rumble. The display screen said it was just after midnight.

"I had an invite from the other Greyson a couple of nights ago," Heavens said. "Fancy engagement party. We could stop by there."

I imagined what it would feel like to show back up at the

party with Heavens on my arm. The pitying looks would certainly vanish. But I realized I didn't care what any of those people thought anyway.

"There's actually another place I think I'd rather be tonight."

Heavens gestured toward the skyline. "The night is yours."

I squinted at the road ahead. "But I don't actually know when I'm going to find it right now. Somebody moved it on me. Can you help me out?"

Heavens shook her head. Then she leaned in and added the coordinates to the Boss' jump computer.

Twenty minutes later, we walked through the doors of the pub in the Rose 'n Bridge. The drunken patrons all gave us a cheer.

"You sure know how to treat a girl to a night out," Heavens said with a laugh.

"I'll make sure the only pint you'll have to lift tonight will be your own." I gestured to the mustached man behind the bar. Sam Clemens hoisted a beer in each fist and held them out toward us. He only spilled about a quarter of each in the process.

I took Heavens' hand and pulled her through the crowd, then shooed a pair of octogenarian neckers off the piano bench. When I sat down, Heavens cocked an eyebrow but waited expectantly.

I lifted the lid on the keys and cracked my knuckles. The chatter in the pub ebbed, a palpable tension taking its place. Once I hit the first few notes, the room exhaled. A few people wandered toward the piano, nodding along as I hammered out the "Pirates of the Caribbean" theme song. I transitioned into an Imagine Dragons tune midway through, but it was only when Heavens picked up a guitar and synced a microphone that the group really got enthusiastic. I started the intro to Journey's "Don't Stop Believin'," and Heavens came in right on cue. Her voice had the attention of the whole room. By the midpoint of the song, the entire pub was singing along.

As I looked around the tavern filled with time travelers from a dozen decades, all singing their drunken hearts out, I couldn't help but crack a smile. I wasn't even sure when or where the inn was at the moment, but as Heavens led the crowd into another refrain, she smiled back at me.

I'd found a pretty good place to call home.

At least till the next time.

Thanks for reading! The adventures of Greyson Travers will continue. Want to be sure to never miss a release? Let your future self know by subscribing at NathanVanCoops.com

You can start another free time travel story now.

Download Clockwise and Gone here. Read on for a sneak preview.

Clockwise & Gone

Chapter 1

"To your promotion," Dom said, raising the glass of champagne. "New head of Gammatech's Safety Division."

Emily reached for her nearly-empty glass and held it aloft gently. "Thanks to you."

"I had hardly anything to do with it." Dom snatched the bottle from the bucket of ice and quickly topped off her champagne flute. "Management at Gammatech just knows a winner when they see one." He grinned and clinked his glass against hers. "You earned it."

Emily smiled and took a sip. She certainly had done everything in her power to prove herself at the energy company but that hadn't stopped the rumors and muttering behind her back—the whispers that she was only where she was because she had slept her way to the top. Dom laughed off the idea that anyone would doubt her resume, but no one had ever said anything to him directly. He was Dominic Del Toro, son of the owner of the company. He was immune.

Emily was not.

She had no doubt that there would be sideways glances on Monday when she was back at the office, but she was determined to enjoy the champagne anyway. She took another sip and took in the expansive view of the illuminated city skyline. She would enjoy tonight. Monday's problems could wait.

The server's reflection in the glass made her turn her gaze back to the bustling restaurant.

"Can I interest you in any dessert this evening?" He cleared away her plate and handed it off to a passing busboy.

"I actually hoped we could have the special tonight, Felipe. The one I called ahead about?" Dom said.

"Of course, sir." Felipe smiled. "I'll get that for you right away."

"Call-ahead special?" Emily asked. "Wow. Courtside seats at

the game, now specialty desserts— you really did go all out tonight."

"Well, not quite yet," Dom said. He slid out of his seat and reached into his pocket as he stood. "There was one more thing I was hoping to discuss. One question that wasn't in your interview from the board yesterday."

Emily stared at the small black box in his hand. He was getting on one knee. Oh wow, this was happening now?

"Emily Marie Davis, from the first time I saw you, I was completely and utterly in love with you. Even all the way back at uni when you wouldn't give me the time of day." Dom smiled at her. "I would do absolutely anything to keep you in my life forever. Would you do me the honor of marrying me?"

Emily stared at the sparkling diamond as he opened the box, and realized her hand was shaking when some champagne sloshed onto the table. She hastily set the glass down.

"Oh my God. I can't believe you are doing this." Marriage. This was really happening.

He grinned up at her. "So, what do you say? Would you like to be Mrs. Del Toro?"

Emily looked into his eager eyes and slid out of her chair. Her breath seemed caught inside her, but finally she got the words out. "Yes, of course. Yes."

He stood to wrap his arms around her and she pressed her lips to his. Over the thrumming of her heartbeat in her ears, she registered the clapping and cheering of the other diners in the restaurant. But just barely. They may as well have been in another world.

The elevator ride to the street was a blur. She didn't even remember leaving the restaurant. There had been a dessert. A cake? She vaguely recalled that much. Another bottle of champagne had been opened too. That was still with them. Dom carried the half empty bottle with him to the car. As his vehicle pulled to the curb they climbed into the back laughing.

"Home, Avery," Dom managed, before Emily tackled him and started planting kisses all over his face.

"Proceeding to Regency Tower." The car's automated response system flashed the destination on a screen and engaged its drive motor.

Emily stopped kissing Dom long enough to admire the ring on her finger again. He'd really outdone himself this time.

"You like it?" Dom studied her with eager eyes.

"I love it. It's beautiful."

"Still doesn't compare to you," Dom replied.

As Emily reached for him again, the car's speaker came on and the voice of Dom's life management system, Avery, spoke. "A call coming in for you, sir. Inspector Walsh from subsection Delta."

"I'm a little busy right now," Dom replied between Emily's smothering kisses.

"He's all mine tonight, Avery," Emily said.

"The call is marked urgent," Avery replied. "How would you like me to respond?"

"Inspectors always think everything is urgent," Dom said. "Tell him I'll call him back."

"Yes, sir," Avery replied.

The car arrived at Regency Tower entirely too quickly as far as Emily was concerned. She had barely gotten Dom's tie off him, let alone anything else. He was altogether too buttoned up for her taste.

They were engaged. She had a fiance. It had seemed like a made-up word till now.

She let it roll around her mind as she carried her shoes and let Dom lead her toward the elevator. Her head was decidedly fuzzy from the champagne, but something about the ring on her finger was making him irresistible tonight. She entwined her fingers through his and leaned her head onto his shoulder in the elevator. He was wearing the cologne she'd gotten him for Christmas. She took a deep breath. Yes. This was going to be a good night.

Dom wasn't the most physically attractive man she had ever dated. If you had asked her yesterday she might even have said he wasn't in the top five. He lacked the height and athleticism she usually looked for. She had always dated ball players in college. Dom's physique was far better suited for a golf course than a basketball court. His jump shot was atrocious. He worked out when he could, but as heir to the Gammatech empire, he spent far more time in board meetings than at the gym. Add in the receding hairline, and Dom might even be considered homely by some. But what he lacked in looks he had more than made up for in devotion.

Ever since she moved back to the city, he'd been pursuing her. No. Longer than that. She could remember him trying to walk her home from parties in college, back before he'd lost his glasses. He'd always had style, and women interested in his money certainly fawned over him, but he used to show up to her games in a suit and tie. Not at all what she was looking for then. He'd even visited her in the hospital the night she tore her ACL and ended her dreams of going pro. Despite his continued attention, she'd barely given him a second glance. During the years since college she rarely thought of him at all unless it was at Christmas or her birthday. He always remembered to send a card. Real mail. Hardly anyone did that anymore.

Those were the little things that added up in the end.

When she finished with her energy contracts abroad and decided to search for a job back in the states, it was Dom that had contacted her immediately. He said he'd seen her resume and thought she'd be a wonderful fit at Gammatech. A management track with a salary that made competitor's offers look laughable. How could she say no?

The doors dinged open at the penthouse. His penthouse. Would they live here after they were married? The thought gave her pause. This was all happening so fast.

"Avery, please set lights to level 2," Dom said as they entered.

The normally bright lighting dimmed to a soft glow.

"Are you feeling okay?" Dom asked, smiling at her. Emily realized she was still latched to his arm and slowly unwrapped herself.

"Yes. But I think I need more champagne. You'll go find us some?"

Dom brushed a strand of her hair behind her ear. "I'm already as elated as I've ever been. More booze won't help."

Emily grabbed his hand and kissed his fingers. "Yes, but I need a minute to get sexy for you."

"You're already sexy," Dom grinned.

"Champagne," Emily commanded, pointing toward the kitchen. "Your fiancee says she needs champagne!"

He let go of her fingers and bowed, then turned toward the kitchen.

She did not need more champagne.

Her head was already swimming, but she was going to do this right. She pushed through the door to his bedroom and dropped her shoes near the closet doors. She should have planned ahead better. If she had known this was coming she would have tried to stash something here to wear. Something other than the yoga pants and old sweatshirt she kept stuffed in the bottom drawer of his dresser for nights she slept over. That wasn't going to cut it tonight.

She considered just stripping bare on the bed and waiting, but shook off the thought. She was feeling far too full from dinner to be up for that. She would opt for one of his button-down shirts. It wasn't lingerie, but he'd still like it. Can't beat the classics.

A cork popped from somewhere in the vicinity of the living room.

She ditched her dress on the floor and walked to the bathroom mirror to determine the appropriate amount of buttons to employ on the shirt. Once there she took a look at the state of her wavy chestnut hair and frowned. She was trying to get it back into some semblance of a style when Avery chimed from the other room.

"Call from Inspector Danvers, marked as urgent."

"Danvers?" Dom asked. "From Sector Echo?"

"Yes. There are also three other inspectors on the line. They've requested you join a community call. Shall I engage a video conference?"

"No!" Emily shouted from the bathroom. "He's busy."

"No video," Dom said as he walked into the bedroom.

"Hey, I'm not ready for you yet," Emily said. "You go there." She pointed him toward the bed.

"I might need to take this call," Dom said. "It sounds important."

"It's Saturday night. We just got engaged. Can't it wait?"

"I'm just going to see what's going on. Maybe it's nothing."

Avery chimed in. "Mr. Del Toro Senior has also joined the call but is requesting a private conversation."

Dom squeezed Emily's hand, then walked back into the other room.

Emily frowned and slumped onto the bed.

"Avery?"

"Yes, Miss Davis?"

"We're going to need to talk about his priorities . . ."

"I would be happy to provide any service Dom requires," Avery replied.

"I'll bet you would," Emily muttered.

She propelled herself off the bed and only wavered momentarily before pushing her way out the door to the living room.

Dom had his jacket back on and was attempting to retie his tie.

"You're leaving?" Emily said. "Where are you going?"

"I need to get down to the plant and check on things. This new shipment of control rods I ordered for the reactor is giving us some strange indications. The inspectors called a meeting. I guess it's pretty serious."

"Is everyone at the plant okay?"

"Yeah, absolutely. Just stay here. I'll be back as soon as I can." He finished the tie, then patted his jacket pockets, doing an inventory, before stepping over and kissing her. "Don't go anywhere."

"Fine," Emily said, pouting her lower lip, but adjusting his collar to better cover the tie.

He kissed her one more time, then slipped out the door. "Be back soon."

Emily stood staring at the closed door for a few seconds, then turned slowly on her heel to check her other options. The newly opened bottle of champagne was still sitting on the counter. She slouched over to it and snatched one of the glasses up before trudging back to the bedroom.

"Looks like it's just the two of us, Avery."

"Would you like to view entertainment options, Miss Davis? Perhaps the highlights from the afternoon's games?"

"Not tonight. I think I just want a bath. Will you fill the tub?"

"Bathtub will be filled in approximately eleven minutes. Would you like to choose a scent for your bath oils?"

"What does Dom use?"

"Mr. Del Toro prefers lavender and tea tree."

"Interesting. I'll try that." Emily took a sip of champagne. "And some music please." The penthouse filled with soothing instrumental piano music. "Something from this century," Emily said.

She was still bickering with Avery about the music choices when she heard the elevator ding in the hall. A moment later, footsteps sounded in the kitchen.

She opened the bedroom door and looked back out. "Dom?"

Dom had his back to her, rooting through a drawer in the kitchen, but turned around at the sound of her voice.

"That was fast," Emily said. "False alarm?"

He wasn't wearing a tie anymore. He looked . . . tired. Like the few minutes he'd been gone had aged him.

"Hello, Emily," Dom said. He stared at her, looking her up and down. "You look . . . well."

Well? She was half-naked in his shirt wearing a brand new engagement ring and 'well' was the best compliment he could muster?

"What happened?" she said aloud.

"We need to go," Dom replied. He strode across the room and grabbed her by the wrist.

"What? Go where?"

But he was already pulling her across the room toward the elevator.

"Dom, I can't go anywhere. I'm not dressed and it's late. I thought we were staying in. Ow. You're hurting me."

Dom's grip on her wrist was like a vice. He dragged her into the foyer. The elevator doors opened and he spun her inside.

"I don't have my shoes," Emily objected.

"You don't need them."

"Where are we going?"

He didn't reply. He was preoccupied with checking his phone. He studied the time, then shoved the phone back in his pocket. Emily stared at him but he seemed intent on ignoring her.

His face was stubbled. Hadn't he been clean shaven earlier tonight? Emily studied the shadow on his chin with confusion. How much champagne had she drunk? Things were getting strange.

The elevator reached the garage level and Dom hauled her forward across the oil-stained concrete to a waiting car. It wasn't his car, but Dom flung the door open without a moment's hesitation. "Come on. Get in."

"I want your jacket."

"What?"

"Give me your jacket. You're hauling me off to somewhere you won't explain. I'm not going in just your shirt."

"Why does it matter?" Dom asked. "We won't be seeing anyone."

Emily held out her hand for the jacket.

Dom sighed and took it off, then tossed it to her. He pushed her toward the car. Come on. We've got to go."

Emily climbed into the rear-facing bench seat and slipped her arms into the jacket. She wrapped it around herself and tucked her dirty feet up underneath her.

"Why on earth can't we just stay in the penthouse? What's the big hurry?"

Dom was glancing at his phone again. "You'll know soon enough. Avery, take us to Section Kilo."

"The research division?" Emily asked. Gammatech had what seemed like a thousand departments on a dozen campuses around the city, but she'd made a point of learning them all.

"Here. I need you to drink this." Dom held out a glass bottle of bright blue liquid. "It'll help you sober up."

"Then you drink it," Emily replied. "You're the one acting like a crazy person."

Dom shrugged, unscrewed the cap on the bottle, and took a swig. Then he held it out to her again.

Emily glared at him, but then took the bottle. Her head was beginning to throb. Hydration wasn't a bad idea. She took a sip and let the blue liquid course down her throat. It tasted like . . . What was it? Something she'd never felt. Like liquid lightning. Her throat tingled with it.

She considered Dom seated across from her. He was simply staring out the window. She sniffed and wrinkled her nose, then tried to locate the scent she was smelling. It was coming from his jacket. She lifted the collar and held it to her nose. Cologne. But one she'd never smelled before. When would he have had time to get more cologne? The bathtub hadn't even filled in the time he was gone.

She looked at her fiance across the back of the car. His expression was hard to read in the shadowy interior.

He *had* been clean shaven tonight. All those kisses.

"Dom?" she tried softly this time. "What's going on?"

When he looked at her, his eyes were serious. "You'll just have to trust me."

"But why can't you tell me what's happening? I'm getting frightened. You're freaking me out."

"Emily." He leaned forward and rested a hand on her knee. "In all the time you've known me, has there ever been anything I've done that wasn't in the interest of keeping you with me? Of keeping you safe?"

"No. Never."

"Then believe me when I tell you now. There is nothing I wouldn't do to keep you from harm."

"Are we in danger?" Emily asked.

Dom looked back out the window as the vehicle slowed. "Not for much longer. Drink the rest of that, then come on. We're here."

Chapter 2

The concrete sidewalk leading to the research facility was cold on Emily's bare feet. She shivered a little and wrapped Dom's jacket around herself a little tighter. A security guard at the entrance tipped his hat to Dom.

"Good to see you again, sir. Twice in one night." He smiled and opened the door for them.

The doorway traded cold concrete for cold epoxy flooring that was slick beneath her feet.

Dom didn't slow his pace at all as he guided her through several hallways to what must have been the back of the building. He finally stopped at a doorway that had been chained shut and padlocked. Dom entered a combination and unlocked it, then pulled the entire chain free. Emily noticed that the combination had been her birthday, 4-9-20. Dom took a glance down the hallway they came from, then pulled the door open. "Okay. Here we go."

Emily wasn't sure what she expected, but the room they walked into wasn't it. It looked like an oversized storage closet. Dusty metal racks lined the walls, home for a few outdated computers and forgotten hard drives. There was a window on the far end of the room but the opaque glass squares only let in the faintest glow from the streetlight. Dom flipped the switch and illuminated the room with harsh fluorescent light.

He ran the chain through the door handles again and refastened the lock.

"About time," someone said. "I thought you said you'd be quick."

Emily located the speaker sitting in a folding chair in the

corner. He rocked forward and stood, shaking out the length of his overcoat and stomping his feet. He was skinny, dressed in all black, and smoking an electronic cigarette. She hadn't seen one of those in years.

"Why are you just lurking here in the dark?" Dom said. "It's creepy."

"You wanted me to stay here. I stayed. You didn't say you needed me awake."

Dom turned toward Emily. "This is a new acquaintance of mine. What did you say your name was again?"

"Axle."

"Well, Axle, did you at least prepare things for me like I asked you to?"

"Setup's all ready. Standard stuff." He pointed to a rolling office chair and a contraption against the wall that looked like some kind of door frame.

"Dom, what's going on?" Emily said. "You really need to tell me what we're doing here. Who is this guy?"

"We're getting away for a little," Dom said. "I've got somewhere where we can go to get things sorted out. I've got a way to keep you safe."

Emily noticed that Axle was eyeing her bare legs and tried to tug the edge of Dom's jacket a little lower.

"You don't mind me saying so, mack, you got a fine looking lady here. Lots going for you. You sure you don't want to just forget this plan and go off and enjoy her somewhere? I'm thinking I would."

"Shut your damn mouth," Dom growled at him. "I didn't pay you for your suggestions. I paid you to do your job. Just get things ready. We're wasting time."

Axle held up his hands. "Whatever you say, mack. You're the boss." He stepped over to the doorframe erected by the wall and started fiddling with a control panel attached to the side. A number of heavy-duty cables were running across the floor and were directly wired into the breaker box on the wall.

"Emily, I need to tell you something," Dom said. "I'm sorry to keep you in the dark about this but we're almost safe. There is going to be a problem at the plant. The reactor core is growing unstable. It's going to . . . It's going to do a lot of damage. But I have somewhere to take us. I can fix things. I just need you to come with me. It's all going to be okay."

"The main reactor?"

As she spoke, the door frame against the wall started buzzing. The space between the posts began to shimmer, then erupted into a field of multicolored light. The colors swirled and twisted in an eerie sort of harmony with one another. Emily found herself transfixed by their beauty.

"What is that?" she murmured.

"Our future," Dom replied. "Have a seat."

Dom wheeled a rolling office chair over and Emily sat, almost automatically, her eyes still glued to the luminescent doorway. She didn't look away until something cold closed over her wrist. She looked down to find her arm handcuffed to the chair.

"Hey, what the hell?"

"Standard procedure," Axle muttered from next to her.

"Procedure for what?" Emily demanded.

Dom shoved Axle out of the way and knelt in front of Emily. He rested a hand on her knee, then held up another bottle of blue liquid. "I need you to drink this."

"What the hell is that stuff, Dom? And don't give me that 'sober you up' bullshit."

"It's going to help stabilize your cells," Dom replied. "The more we get into you, the safer you'll be."

Axle wheeled an IV rack over to her chair and started prepping a syringe.

"You have got to be kidding," Emily replied. She snatched the bottle from his hand and threw it across the room. "I'm not drinking anything until you explain what you're doing to me."

Dom closed his eyes for a moment, then grabbed her arm and took her hand between his. "Emily." He opened his eyes again and stared into hers. "That machine over there is going to take us somewhere new. But in order to get there, we need to treat your body with a special sort of particle. It will protect you and enable you to travel safely. But only if we get enough into you to make it work."

"Why aren't you cuffed to a chair? Why isn't he?" She looked to Axle who was now wheeling some other contraption made of hollow tubing toward them.

"We've already had our treatment," Dom replied. He kissed her hand then laid her forearm against the arm of the chair. "Now I need you to stay still." He wrapped a fabric strap quickly around her arm and fastened the Velcro.

"Hey! No. Dom!" Emily tried to jerk her arm loose but it was strapped tight. She tried moving her other arm but the metal handcuffs only rattled against the chair. "I don't want to do this. Let me go!"

"There is no other way," Dom replied. He grasped her face between his hands. "Your future depends on this."

"Dom." She stared at him with her most no-nonsense expression. "I want to go home. Let. Me. Go."

But Dom simply strapped a band around her other arm and secured it tightly to the chair as well. Axle bent down with the needle.

"Get that away from me!" she shouted.

"It's going to hurt more if you move," Axle replied. He pressed on the inside of her arm, probing for her vein.

"Don't you touch me with that—" she began, but it was too late. He already started inserting the needle. She froze. When the IV was in, he taped the tube to her arm and stood up.

She caught him staring down her shirt. She jerked against the arm of the chair but it was no use. Why hadn't she used . . . more . . . buttons . . .

She felt dizzy. Her head lolled slightly.

"What else did you put in there?" Dom asked.

"Just something to calm her down. Figured we may as well get a head start on the rest of it."

Dom frowned but didn't object. He stood, and swayed with the rest of the room as it turned. It was all getting wavy.

Emily's pulse was throbbing in her ears with the rhythm of a clock but the men seemed to be moving in slow motion. She tilted her head as Axle wheeled the tubular structure overtop of her seat. It was a sort of framework, bolted together with space in the interior for her, and with what looked to be plastic sheeting around the edges. She felt like she was in a portable shower. A bright light illuminated the sheeting. It was clear, but difficult to see through. The room had been going blurry before, but now it was even more difficult to see. Dom was just a vague shape on the other side of the curtain.

"Dom?" Her voice came out softer than she intended. She meant to yell at him but it only sounded like pleading.

"Where are you—" the air crackled with static and blue light flickered around the curtain. She saw now that it wasn't plastic, but rather some sort of conductive material ribbed with fine strands of metal. Electricity danced and tingled across her skin and seemed to burn through her veins. She cried out from the shock of it.

Moments later it was over.

The two men were muttering something on the other side of the curtain, continuing to ignore her, when a loud bang erupted near the doorway. A blinding light flashed, causing her to squint and blink, and then there were voices. The overhead lights went out. Her ears were ringing. Axle shouted. Something crashed to the floor amid a scuffle ahead of her.

"Get her loose!" a man shouted.

Someone collided with the curtain and she caught a glimpse of Axle, snarling and drawing a knife from his belt. The multicolored light emanating from the strange doorway behind her was barely enough to see anything, but she felt hands on her right arm, someone unwrapping the Velcro straps.

"Dom?"

But it wasn't Dom. A face in a black ski mask appeared in front of her. They unstrapped her other arm.

"Listen, you have to run!" It was a woman's voice.

"No! Don't touch her!" Dom shouted as he flung the tubular framework aside and grabbed for the woman in the mask. She backed away and he pursued her, fist raised.

Emily tried to rise from the chair but her left arm was still handcuffed to it. She wobbled and sat back down. What had they given her?

She was about to try again, but then Axle was there, his leering expression illuminated by the eerie flickering light. "You ain't going anywhere, honey. Except gone." He put a hand on the chair arm, and the other over her handcuffed wrist. Then he pushed her, hard, toward the multi-colored doorway. His hand ripped the IV from her arm as he shoved. "Have a nice trip!"

"No, wait!" Dom shouted.

Emily attempted to plant her feet to stop her momentum but her bare heels just slid across the slick epoxy floor. The wheels of the office chair wobbled but her trajectory was true. She rolled right into the swirl of light and color.

There was a fraction of a moment where she felt like she'd departed her body and was soaring through the cosmos.

Then the wheel of the office chair hit something and she tipped, nearly spilling out of it onto the floor. The chair teetered, then settled back onto its wheels, planting her in the seat in a room once again filled with fluorescent light. There was a medical table, some silver trays on wheels, and someone standing in front of her. She looked up to find a man in paper scrubs and latex gloves looming over her. He was wearing a paper mask and had a foot jammed against one of the chair's wheels.

"Well, what did Axle bring us today?" the man asked.

Footsteps sounded from behind her and when she spun around in the chair she found a second masked doctor on her other side. He was holding a scalpel. "Not bad looking, this time," he said. "Pity. Get her on the table. Let's open her up."

Continue this adventure for free here:

https://BookHip.com/DLSLZMV

ACKNOWLEDGMENTS

Every book I write comes together under different circumstances, but there are some people who continue to see me through.

I'm blessed with a close group of author friends who are always ready to talk shop or help me work out a plot problem, but mostly to help keep me sane throughout the daunting process of trying to write a novel, especially in the genre of time travel mystery.

The past few years have been challenging for all of us, but my talks with Alan Janney, Lucy Score, Todd Hodges, Cecelia Mecca, Boo Walker, James Blatch, and H. Claire Taylor have become an essential part of how I work. It's fantastic to be in your company.

I write in the wild, and that typically means coffee shops and Mexican restaurants. I'd especially like to thank the staff at Banyan Cafe, Uptown Eats, and Grumpy Gringo for letting me sit at tables for longer than any single customer ought to. Specific thanks to Kensie, Dan, Casey, Kimberly, and Hector for making me feel welcome.

I'm eternally grateful to my beta readers, especially the Type Pros, who are the first to ever see my work and give feedback. Your honesty, knowledge, and encouragement make every book I write so much better. I'd like to specifically thank: Maarja Kruusmets, Kay Clark, Elaine Davis, Judy Eiler, Rick Bradley, Eric Lizotte, Mark Hale, Gary Smart, Sarah Van Coops-Bush, Steve Bryant, Ginelle Blanch, Alissa Nesson, Felicia Rodriguez, Ken Robbins, Bethany Cousins, and Claire Manger.

My mom, Marilyn Bourdeau, is a big part of why I continue to grow as a writer. Thanks for always being there and supporting me with each and every book.

And nothing about my life would be possible without the love and support of my beautiful wife Stephanie. Raising small children and getting anything productive done at the same time seems like a fool's errand some days, but I'm proud to be on your team in life. I love you and our kiddos.

I am especially grateful to you, the reader who decided to give this book a spot on your reading list. There is a lot of content out there and I'm elated you found this series. If you keep reading, I'll keep writing.

If you'd like to keep in touch, my most frequent online hangout is The Tempus Fugitives Facebook group. Or connect via email at nathan@nathanvancoops.com

Nathan Van Coops lives in St. Petersburg, Florida on a diet comprised mainly of tacos. When not tinkering on old airplanes, he writes heroic adventure stories that explore imaginative new worlds. He is the author of the time travel adventure series *In Times Like These*, and *The Skylighter Adventures*. His series *Kingdom of Engines* explores a swashbuckling alternate history where the modern and medieval collide. Learn more at www. nathanvancoops.com

OTHER SERIES BY NATHAN VAN COOPS

In Times Like These

The Kingdom of Engines

The Skylighter Adventures

Made in the USA
Columbia, SC
24 March 2022